LETTERS TO A LOVER

Crime and Passion, Book 2

Mary Lancaster

© Copyright 2021 by Mary Lancaster
Text by Mary Lancaster
Cover by Wicked Smart Designs

Dragonblade Publishing, Inc. is an imprint of Kathryn Le Veque Novels, Inc.
P.O. Box 7968
La Verne CA 91750
ceo@dragonbladepublishing.com

Produced in the United States of America

First Edition April 2021
Print Edition

Reproduction of any kind except where it pertains to short quotes in relation to advertising or promotion is strictly prohibited.

All Rights Reserved.

The characters and events portrayed in this book are fictitious. Any similarity to real persons, living or dead, is purely coincidental and not intended by the author.

ARE YOU SIGNED UP FOR DRAGONBLADE'S BLOG?

You'll get the latest news and information on exclusive giveaways, exclusive excerpts, coming releases, sales, free books, cover reveals and more.

Check out our complete list of authors, too!

No spam, no junk. That's a promise!

Sign Up Here

www.dragonbladepublishing.com

Dearest Reader;

Thank you for your support of a small press. At Dragonblade Publishing, we strive to bring you the highest quality Historical Romance from the some of the best authors in the business. Without your support, there is no 'us', so we sincerely hope you adore these stories and find some new favorite authors along the way.

Happy Reading!

CEO, Dragonblade Publishing

Additional Dragonblade books by Author Mary Lancaster

Crime & Passion Series
Mysterious Lover
Letters to a Lover

The Husband Dilemma Series
How to Fool a Duke

Season of Scandal Series
Pursued by the Rake
Abandoned to the Prodigal
Married to the Rogue
Unmasked by her Lover

Imperial Season Series
Vienna Waltz
Vienna Woods
Vienna Dawn

Blackhaven Brides Series
The Wicked Baron
The Wicked Lady
The Wicked Rebel
The Wicked Husband
The Wicked Marquis
The Wicked Governess
The Wicked Spy
The Wicked Gypsy
The Wicked Wife
Wicked Christmas (A Novella)

The Wicked Waif
The Wicked Heir
The Wicked Captain
The Wicked Sister

Unmarriageable Series
The Deserted Heart
The Sinister Heart
The Vulgar Heart
The Broken Heart
The Weary Heart
The Secret Heart
Christmas Heart

The Lyon's Den Connected World
Fed to the Lyon

Also from Mary Lancaster
Madeleine

CHAPTER ONE

ONLY ONE GUEST remained in Lady Trench's drawing room. Since it was the handsome Mr. Gunning, tongues would inevitably wag.

"We are alone," he observed softly.

"Don't allow me to detain you from more interesting pursuits," Lady Trench drawled.

His eyes glowed in a familiar manner. "You know I have none."

"Then you must acquire some immediately. Lest you become dull." She smiled. "More tea, Mr. Gunning?"

He leapt from his chair and all but threw himself onto the brocade sofa beside her. "We are alone," he repeated. "Where is the need for this sudden return to formality? Will you not call me George again?"

She stared at him, hiding her sudden unease. She could not remember being on such friendly terms with this stranger. Was it happening again?

"No," she replied flatly.

He tried to take her hand from her lap. She moved it casually out of reach, pretending to pat her perfectly pinned hair into place.

"My sweet Azalea—" he began.

"I would rather you did not make free with my name," she interrupted.

"That isn't what you said before."

Oh, God, please let it not be happening again... "I think perhaps you should go."

"You are expecting your husband?" he asked quickly.

She stared at him. "No. I simply find your conversation tedious. I did warn you."

The color of annoyance seeped into his face. "Dash it, Azalea, must you blow hot and cold so constantly? I've had enough."

He lunged.

Azalea stood. "So have I. Good afternoon, Mr. Gunning."

Azalea had been adept at dealing with over-amorous gentlemen since she was in her teens. But it seemed that at the ripe old age of twenty-eight, she had finally misjudged her opponent. He did indeed rise to his feet, but only to seize her in his arms.

Outraged, she grabbed the teapot from the tray, but blood was singing in her ears, and panic stole her breath. Had she invited him here? Something terrible surely must have happened, was about to happen...

As she froze, rigid, his open mouth latched to her throat, greedy, wet...disgusting.

She gasped, raised the teapot, and upended it over his head. At the same time, she stepped smartly back out of his suddenly loosened arms. The lid had dropped first, bouncing off his head onto the Turkish carpet and releasing a deluge of cold tea behind it.

He grunted with the shock and stood still, shoulders hunched, staring at her open-mouthed as tea dripped down his hair and neck and coat. A scattering of dark leaves had spattered over his shirt.

Calmly, Azalea lowered the pot, although she kept hold of it, for fury quickly replaced his astonishment, and the set of his mouth turned ugly.

He took a pace toward her. "Why, you little..."

"Dear me," observed another, very different voice.

Azalea's gaze flew to the doorway.

Eric Danvers, Viscount Trench, strolled into the room, filling it with his presence. He had always been a handsome man, tall and fair, with deep-set blue eyes and a well-defined mouth inclined to smile.

At the sight of her husband, the last of her panic fell away, drowned in a sea of very different emotion. She didn't know if it was fear or gratitude or simple annoyance, but it was threatening to erupt as laughter.

Gunning whipped around to face the man he had, presumably, been hoping to cuckold.

Eric glanced from him to his wife. "Has there been an accident, my love?"

"Why, yes," Azalea managed. "Mr. Gunning has become covered in tea."

Behind the vague concern, her husband's hooded, sleepy eyes betrayed the kind of conspiratorial laughter she had always found irresistible. She looked hastily away.

"What appalling luck," he said mildly.

Her breath caught. "Indeed."

"Allow me to ring for the footman to—er—dry you off," Trench offered, reaching for the bell pull.

"There is no need," Gunning said shortly. "Forgive my hasty departure. My lady, your servant." He bowed jerkily. "My lord."

"You are very damp," Trench observed as Gunning strode past him to the door. "Be careful you don't catch a chill."

Azalea shivered, for a distinct threat lurked in the amiable words. She hoped Gunning heard it, too. As his footsteps retreated to the staircase, Eric walked away from her. For a moment, Azalea thought with considerable pique that he was simply going to leave the room, until he closed the double doors.

Her heart gave a funny little twist.

Eric turned to face her. "You do enjoy flirting with disaster, do you not, Azalea?"

She tilted her chin as he walked deliberately back toward her. "It certainly seems to stalk me." God help her; she had almost forgotten the butterflies, the pleasurable little jumps of the heart caused by his increasingly rare presence.

He came to halt on the carpet, right beside the tea stain and stood gazing down at her.

"Tell me," he murmured, "how did Gunning become—er... *covered in tea?*"

"I poured it over him," she replied candidly.

"For fun?"

"No, though I did quite enjoy it." She held his gaze. "I misjudged him and my ability to deal with his advances. He is a vulgar fool, and I am ashamed not to have seen it." Catching a certain flash in his eyes, hope sprang up once more. "Are you angry?"

"No," he replied. "Merely surprised you did not actually hit him with the teapot."

"I thought about it," she confessed. "But it's my favorite teapot. And truly, he is not worth that. Although," she added in the interests of honesty, "I am glad you arrived when you did, or I might have been obliged to break it over his head."

"That would have been a pity." Eric bent and picked up the lid. As he took the pot from her, their fingers brushed. He laid both parts on the tray. "You need not worry about him anymore."

She curled her lip. "I don't worry about him now."

He continued to regard her, his expression impassive although she didn't think he was. "How was it, do you think, that he came to believe his advances might he acceptable to you?"

"Because he's a coxcomb who thinks he's irresistible? How should I know?"

"You are not a fool, Azalea," he said dryly. "I imagine you might have an inkling."

"He seems to think I encouraged him," she blurted. "But I assure you, I did not. To be frank, I barely noticed the man." Hidden in her skirts, she crossed her fingers.

An instant longer, he searched her eyes, his own unreadable. Then he walked away to the cabinet and poured two glasses of brandy, one of which he presented to her. She took it in some surprise and sat on the sofa.

To her secret delight, he chose to sit beside her, his arm resting along the sofa back. He sipped his brandy thoughtfully. "Perhaps you and I are giving the wrong impression. We are so much apart that a certain type of man might imagine you are fair game."

She stared at him. "What am I? A pheasant?"

"A wife involved in an admiring social whirl that is mostly separate from her husband's. If you do not hate the idea, perhaps we should show both—er...whirls a more united appearance."

She regarded him cautiously over the rim of her glass. "You mean...spend more time together?"

"We are married. The idea should not be too shocking."

"Why should you imagine I am shocked?" In fact, she was delighted, but they had been here before. "If you have no better plans, we could cancel our engagements and dine together tonight. To counter any talk about us, of course."

His lips twitched. "Of course. But I believe I don't need a reason to dine alone with my wife."

"Of course not," she managed. There was a glow in his eyes that suddenly made her as nervous as a bride.

His hand covered hers in her lap, his fingers clasped and held. Her heart thudded, for she had missed his touch, his attention...that *particular* spark in his deceptively sleepy eyes. His thumb caressed her wrist.

"We could do better together, Zalea," he said softly.

She clung to his hand. "I would like to."

His head dipped, almost as if he would kiss her, and those butterflies in her stomach took flight in anticipation. How long since he had kissed her? *Really* kissed her? Too long...

But he paused, the faintest smile flickering on his lips. He raised her hand and kissed her fingers instead. "Then I look forward to dinner." He clinked the bottom of his glass off hers, drained it, and stood.

Disappointed though she was, she watched his graceful stroll from the room with the kind of hope that had eluded her for months, even years. Had Gunning done her a favor after all, induced her husband to look at her again as a desirable woman? As the wife he had once loved so passionately?

Perhaps he still does love me. Perhaps.

LADY AZALEA NIVEN, eldest daughter of the Duke of Kelburn, had never wanted for suitors. Added to the advantages of her birth and wealth and the considerable political influence of her father, she had been endowed with great beauty and personal charm. Or so everyone told her.

Certainly, Azalea had taken to Society like a duck to water. She had laughed and chatted, danced, and flirted her way through her first two London Seasons with thorough enjoyment. Lauded by all, she knew that she was London's darling. Sometimes she felt a fraud. Sometimes she was sure the adulation was faked. Either way, she enjoyed the game, a bright, enchanting fairytale that ended, as it was supposed to, with marriage to the handsome prince.

Of course, her prince was actually a viscount, and she met him just as the fawning of other suitors was beginning to pall. But after the first evening she had encountered the teasing, mercurial Lord Trench, the rest of the world had paled into nothing. He had courted and won her with a great deal of fun and no resistance.

They had married and traveled across Europe in a haze of love and lovemaking. For Azalea, young and innocent, had never dreamed of the physical joys of married life until Eric had taught her, with patient tenderness and clear delight. Azalea had adored his passion from the beginning and indulged him so often that it was not surprising she was already expecting their first child when they came home to Trenchard, his country estate.

It had given them little time for adjustment, but Eric had proved a considerate husband and a loving father to their firstborn son, Michael. Their life had been perfect.

So where had their idyll gone wrong?

Azalea pondered the mystery yet again as Morris, her maid, helped her dress for dinner. Things had never been the same, she acknowledged, after little Lizzie's birth. She loved both her children and her husband, and yet some blackness had seemed to fall over her, making her lethargic and snappish, so unlike herself that it frightened her.

Eventually, in desperation, she had begged Eric to take her to London again for the Season, and there, she had forced herself to laugh and play her old part until, gradually, it became real again. She was Azalea once more, adored and just a little fast. Eric had been wonderful then, too, giving her all the space and freedoms of a married lady and never criticizing. And yet...and yet they had grown apart.

She had only realized it one day when she had arrived late to a ball she hadn't even known he was attending and found him waltzing with the beautiful Mrs. Mayfield. There had been no real reason for Azalea's jealousy—why go to a ball and not dance? But the green-eyed monster had forced her into her own flirtation. She had left early for another party, escorted by a man she could no longer remember.

And when she and Eric had met again, he did not even seem to have noticed.

Silly, foolish incidents, minor in themselves. But amounting to something close to estrangement. And pain. And, on Azalea's part, a determination to win back her husband.

At last, they had an evening alone together. And now, perhaps, they would talk again, as they had used to.

So, it was with rising excitement that she watched Morris dress her hair. She chose her jewels with as much care as if she were going to the largest ball of the year. She knew by Morris's smile that she looked well, and so she smiled back and rustled off to say good night to the children.

Morris would probably have been aghast at the risk to her artistry as two ebullient children hurled themselves at her from across the room. Elsie, the nursery maid, merely smiled.

Laughing, Azalea knelt to receive her offspring. Michael landed like a cannonball against her, while Lizzie flew into her lap and climbed. Azalea forgot her determination to look her best and simply hugged them, asking and answering a babble of questions all at once.

Only after several moments did another movement in the room catch her eye, a very un-Elsie movement. A man was rising from a large heap of toy building bricks like a monster from the deep, while the disturbed bricks spilled around him.

The children howled with delight at the sight of this monster in elegant evening dress, who complained, "You forgot about me."

"Only for a moment," Michael assured him, grinning. "I knew you were in there."

"You did not," Lizzie argued.

It was not the first time Azalea had unexpectedly come across her husband in the nursery, but it was a rare enough occurrence to throw her off balance. Of course, she knew he saw his children frequently, but the times of their visits and outings had not often coincided.

"Let your mother stand up," Eric suggested, and at once, the children dropped off her. Eric was there to help her rise. "How fortunate Elsie cleaned them up before you arrived. Jammy fingers would have done little for that ravishing gown."

"I cleaned my own jammy fingers," Michael said with dignity,

LETTERS TO A LOVER

which at least enabled Azalea to hide her unexpected blush.

For once, both parents were there to read bedtime stories and tuck them in, which may have made Elsie's job of settling them to sleep slightly harder, but Azalea knew they were happy as she and Eric pretended to creep from the room.

It was interesting to watch him change from clowning father to elegant gentleman. He did nothing so obvious as adjusting his coat or smoothing his hair, but his posture altered, his shoulders straightened, and his expression lost the boyish playfulness that had been such a revelation when Michael was tiny.

There were many facets to her husband, and she loved them all. The surge of emotion brought a lump to her throat.

"Dinner is ready to be served, my lady," Given, the butler, informed her with a bow as they reached the landing. "Shall I have it sent up immediately?"

"Are you ready to dine, my lord?" she asked her husband.

"Famished," he replied promptly, offering her his arm.

CHAPTER TWO

I T FELT QUITE strange to enter the dining room on her husband's arm. She could not remember the last time they had dined alone together, and to this unfamiliarity was added a tangle of desperation, for this was her chance to win Eric back. Perhaps there would never be another.

She had ordered their places set at one end of the grand table, Eric at the head and she on his right-hand side. He held her chair for her to sit, a mundane courtesy that seemed to assume much greater importance as his arm brushed against her hair.

"So how come you have no other plans for this evening?" she asked lightly as the servants brought in the soup.

"I did," he admitted. "I changed them."

"Not on my account, I hope?"

He met her gaze. "Do you?"

She smiled. "No." She saw the answering gleam in his eye before she demurely lowered her gaze to her soup and picked up her spoon. After all, there were servants in the room. But her heart lifted because it was still possible to flirt with Eric, and she remembered the fun of it.

It was Eric who dismissed the servants when the main courses were brought in. "We'll serve ourselves."

"I do not miss company for dinner," Azalea remarked.

"Does that surprise you?" He helped her to asparagus and potatoes scattered with mint.

"No." She met his gaze. "I have always enjoyed *your* company."

"And I yours, a fact we seem to have lost sight of."

"Not lost. Just...mislaid. We should do this more often."

"I hope we do. At the risk of sounding like Augusta, a slightly quieter pace of life might be...beneficial."

"You could never sound like Augusta," she said, dismissing her sister-in-law, "but in what ways would it be beneficial?"

It was an opening to flirt, but again, he took her by surprise. "To your health, for one thing."

She blinked. "My health? But I am perfectly well."

"Are you?"

She had forgotten how penetrating that blue gaze could be. What had he seen? "Do I look so haggard?" she asked lightly.

"No, you are lovelier than ever." He laid down his knife and fork and curled his long, sensitive fingers around the stem of his wine glass. "After Lizzie was born...you had a year of darkness and lethargy. Followed by three more of constant activity that has recently become... hectic."

"I am not," she said firmly, "hectic."

"Whatever you say, Zalea, but something is wrong."

She tried and failed to drag her gaze free, to laugh off his insight with a joke. She could not think of one.

"Won't you tell me?" he asked gently.

That lump was back in her throat. His voice was compelling, tempting, and God knew she wanted the relief of sharing this anxiety. But his eyes, the eyes she longed to see once more clouded in passion, were too *kind*. She did not want kindness from him. She wanted love.

"Tell you what?" she asked, just a little huskily.

His lips stretched into a rueful smile. He raised his glass and drank. "We used to be better friends, you and I. We solved our problems together."

Abruptly, she reached out, clasping her hand over his on the glass.

"I miss that," she whispered. "I miss…the way we were. I miss you."

"Do you? Or do you say so to stop me asking questions?"

She withdrew her hand as though burned, but he caught it in his own and held it.

"I am not a fool, Azalea. We have let this drift too long to change in one evening's conversation. But surely we must begin with honesty?"

"I have never been dishonest. Have you?"

He shook his head. "Do you love someone else?"

Her lips parted in shock. "*Love some…* Of course not!"

Something changed in his eyes, a spurt of relief even he could not hide. He had really been afraid.

Torn between outrage, guilt, and triumph, she withdrew her hand. "Somehow, I thought you would know that."

But he had himself in hand once more. "A man needs reassurance every so often," he drawled and took another sip of wine.

"And a woman does not?"

"I am sure Her Grace, your mother, explained you must never appear to notice when I stray."

"*You* explained to me once that you never would."

"I never did. Which is one reason I find it curious that the unspeakable Gunning imagined it was acceptable to try and seduce you in my house."

"Or in anyone else's! Perhaps my instincts have grown blunted. I shall take more care that careless politeness is not misconstrued."

Amusement crept into his hooded eyes. "No, you won't. You'd rather upend a few more teapots."

She would have laughed, except she remembered that moment of panic when she had suddenly been in his power. It had felt like every woman's fear of male violence, and yet there had been such a confusion of images flashing through her mind that it was almost memory.

A frown had dragged down Eric's handsome brow. "Did he hurt you, Azalea?"

"No." She shivered. "No, but I am glad you entered when you did." Another picture swam across her mind, of Gunning, gasping and dripping under the deluge of cold tea, his pristine white shirt speckled with leaves. A gurgle of laughter escaped her. "Though he did look awfully funny."

Eric grinned. "Awfully."

"Do you think we should go home, Eric?" she said impulsively.

"Home? To Trenchard?"

"We have not been there since Christmas. Though I know you have matters to attend to in town."

"Nothing that cannot be rearranged." His smile was warm. Clearly, he liked the idea, which made her even more hopeful.

"I have a sudden longing for peace," she confided.

"Perhaps we could both benefit from that."

She was still smiling at him as the footmen entered discreetly to clear the table and bring desert. "It has been on my mind that we should engage a new governess," Azalea said, finding a more neutral topic of conversation while the servants were present. "Miss Hollister has been gone for more than two months. Oh, and did you know Lizzie has begun to read? Michael has been teaching her letters!"

The subject of the children continued when they were left alone, exchanging amusing stories tinged with pride. It had been a long time since they had discussed more than general necessities regarding the children, such as their health or education. But now they recalled the daily fun of family life, and Azalea's hope grew warmer as did her physical awareness of her husband.

When she rose to leave him to his wine, as was the formal custom, he merely swiped up the decanter and followed her to the drawing room. The lamps had been lit, making the room welcoming and cozy.

Emboldened by the wine and her desires, Azalea sat at the piano and played and sang for him, as she once had. He lounged beside her, supposedly to turn the music that she didn't use, and he didn't touch. Instead, his gaze burned into her face, and she remembered the tenderness of his touch, the excitement of his kiss.

They moved to the sofa, discussing the music of Beethoven and Berlioz, forked briefly into politics and family, and by then, it no longer mattered, for whatever they talked about it, it was with humor and fun, and she remembered all over again how much she liked him. How could she have let them grow so far apart? How could he?

She could see no trace of boredom in him. On the contrary, his eyes were warm as they dwelled on her. He refilled her glass, and they talked on, of everything and nothing. As a companionable silence fell between them at last, she thought of Gunning, of the things she could not remember.

"Eric?"

"Azalea."

"I…" *I have blanks spaces in my memory. I can't remember whether or not I invited Gunning or if I encouraged him. Or anyone else.* Appalled by the damage her admission could do to this frail closeness they had achieved, she gave a shaky little laugh. "I have had a very pleasant evening."

"So have I." His hand, draped behind her along the back of the sofa, dipped to caress her cheek. "Shall we do it again?"

"Yes, please."

"But you are tired. And I must be up early tomorrow." He took her empty glass and placed it with his on the table before rising to his feet and holding out his hand. "Shall I escort you to your chamber?"

"If you would be so good," she said with mock formality, although behind the joking, her heart was beating a wild tattoo.

Would he stay with her tonight?

They climbed the stairs together, and when he walked past his own door without hesitation, her insides seemed to turn to molten liquid.

At her door, he halted and took her hand from his arm, raising it to his lips. His mouth burned her skin. She clung to his fingers, lifting her face to his.

His breath hitched. In the shadow of the dim, solitary landing light, his eyes seemed to blaze. He leaned down and found her lips.

Her stomach dived. Every nerve in her responded to the sweet, tender kiss. He cupped her cheek, and her arms slipped around his neck. When their bodies touched, his arms swept around her, and she drowned in bliss.

"Stay with me," she whispered against his lips.

He smiled against hers. "Not yet."

She drew back, staring into his hot, clouded eyes. Oh yes, he wanted her. "Not yet?"

"I'm courting you," he said. "Anticipation is all. Goodnight, my lady."

And he actually released her and walked away.

Indignation warred with amusement, especially when she noticed his faint, uncomfortable limp. "Sweet dreams, my lord," she drawled.

He turned at his door and cast her a fleeting smile. "Not sweet enough," he said ruefully, and she laughed as she opened her door and went in.

Closing the door, she leaned against it, listening to the pounding of her own heart. Disappointment lingered, along with frustrated desire. But, almost with surprise, she realized that for the first time in *years*, she was so happy she couldn't help smiling.

THAT HAPPINESS WAS still with her when she woke the next morning. Even better, she could hear Eric's voice in the outer room. She had always loved his voice, low and deep, usually with just a hint of sardonic humor...except in the throes of passion when it turned arousingly husky.

She wanted to jump out of bed and run to him, but Morris's voice, answering him that her ladyship was still asleep, held her back.

They had spent one evening together, enjoyed one sweet, exciting kiss. He had been right last night. After all these months, *years* growing apart, they were merely courting, learning each other all over again.

She smiled into the pillow. She looked forward to it. Oh, but she did...

The voices fell silent. She could not help feeling disappointed when the outer door closed, and only Morris's footsteps entered the bedroom.

"Good morning, my lady. I've brought your coffee."

Azalea sat up, yawning. "Did I hear his lordship's voice?"

"Indeed, my lady. He came to tell you he was going out but will join you for luncheon if you are free. He wouldn't let me wake you to find out."

Azalea took a reviving mouthful of hot coffee and sighed. "I cannot remember my engagements for the day. My diary will be in the sitting room. Perhaps you would bring it along with breakfast."

"Of course, my lady."

Until her breakfast arrived, Azalea spent the time much as she had the morning after she had first met Eric—going over every word exchanged, every look, every accidental touch of the previous evening. Now, at least, she could laugh at herself, but she did it anyway.

Breakfast arrived on its familiar tray, which Morris carried in and placed over her knees. A pencil and her diary lay on top of a pile of letters.

With fresh coffee and toast, she inspected her schedule for the day. She was delighted to find she had no engagements until the evening, apart from a vague plan to join her mother, the duchess, for tea before a visit to the Great Exhibition in Hyde Park. Perhaps Eric would enjoy a visit to the Crystal Palace. He had been, of course, but there was far too much to take in with just one viewing.

She would take the children to the park this morning, she decided. And begin a more serious search for a governess to replace Miss Hollister.

Wiping crumbs from her fingers onto the napkin, she began to open the day's post, which usually consisted primarily of invitations to parties and respectfully begging letters from charities. Today, there were also a couple of letters from friends and one from her sister Athena in Yorkshire. She read those first, smiling over amusing anecdotes. Then she set about those addressed in hands she did not recognize and set each aside in piles to be answered later.

The last letter was in a firm, masculine hand and written on expensive paper. She had hopes it was a note of apology from Mr. Gunning, but when she opened it, she saw at once that the sender had forgotten to sign it.

Nor was it headed with an address of any kind. It began merely, *My lady…*

Frowning, she scanned the very odd epistle and then, in some outrage, read it more carefully.

My lady,

Allow me to come directly to the point, which is that I am in possession of certain letters written by you, which do not speak to your advantage. Indeed, apart from the distinctive signature, they are of a subject matter and type of vulgar, florid language that would play better in a bawdy house. I venture to guess that your ladyship's distinguished family would find it impossible to save you from the scandalous consequences of such folly, should these letters become public, or, indeed, come into the possession of his lordship, your noble husband.

However, I beg you do not despair, for there is a simple solution to prevent such calamities. The sum of five hundred pounds, left in your ladyship's box at the Theatre Royal in Haymarket on Wednesday evening, will ensure your privacy. Place the money in a packet under the seat at the farthest left of the box.

For your sake, I hope your ladyship will not disappoint me.

The letter fell from her nerveless fingers.

"Not bad news, I hope, my lady?" Morris said anxiously.

"Mmm? Oh, no, nothing like that." She forced a yawn. "I just seem to be tired..." Hastily, she folded the letter, pushed the tray away, and rose from her bed, clutching all the morning's letters in one hand. She padded into her sitting room and shut them all away in the desk.

I should burn such arrant, threatening rubbish. Or pass it on to the police.

But she knew she wouldn't for one very good reason.

Although she could not imagine writing any such letters, she could not swear that she hadn't. The same way she could not swear she had not encouraged Gunning to hope for a liaison, or....

Panic surged through her, much as it had yesterday. Her heart pounded so hard she could barely breathe. She struggled desperately to see, to understand the blurry images that sped past her mind. Something was missing from her memory. Many things surely were missing.

She needed a doctor.

But more than anything, she would not allow that vile letter to disrupt her promising new closeness with Eric.

So, she determined, as she went about the mundane business of choosing her morning gown, washing, and dressing, she had to get the letters back.

She could pay the five hundred pounds, but she doubted such a sum would deliver the letters to her. It would be but the beginning of a cycle of blackmail and shame, spoiling whatever hope she had to regain Eric's love.

Surely we must begin with honesty? he had said to her last night.

I have never been dishonest...

Was there a worse way to begin their new courtship? But if she laid all this before him, now, revealed that she might have written such letters to another man...?

Dear God, how could she?

"I couldn't have," she whispered aloud, then stared guiltily around the room.

Fortunately, Morris had gone, leaving her to gaze at her troubled reflection in the mirror.

But if I did, how on earth do I go about getting them back? Or even finding out who sent them?

Frowning, she rose and walked out of the room to the nursery, which was where, in the midst of the children's chatter and laughter, that she realized who might just be able to help her.

Griz.

CHAPTER THREE

L ADY GRIZELDA TIZSA was Azalea's youngest, most recently married sister. In fact, she had only returned from her wedding trip a fortnight since.

After playing with the children in the park for a little, an activity that did much to restore her confidence, Azalea took them by the hand and walked round to the Tizsas' home off Half Moon Street.

This was a charming house reached by a lane and a stone path. It was small by the standards they had grown up with, but then Griz had not married into wealth. Her husband was a heroic but penniless refugee from the recent conflict in Hungary, where he had been on the losing—revolutionary—side. Exactly how Griz had persuaded His Grace, their father, to agree to the match, Azalea had never found out. Though she was aware their brother Horace had thrown some kind of government post Mr. Tizsa's way.

As she climbed the path to the front door, the children ran ahead of her, eager to see Aunt Griz. Music drifted to Azalea's ears, a quartet, perhaps. Was Griz entertaining? Certainly, it was an odd thing to do so early in the day, but if it was so, Azalea's chances of a private word with her sister were somewhat reduced.

The front door was opened by a familiar maid who smiled and curtseyed as she threw the door wide. "My lady! And the little master and mistress, looking very grown-up."

"Good morning, Emmie." The girl had once been her mother's

maid but had clearly followed Griz to her new abode. "I gather my sister is at home. Is it a bad time to disturb her?"

"Oh, no, my lady, I shouldn't think so. It's just one of her musical mornings. They usually all go home about this time." Emmie took her shawl and bonnet and the children's coats and pointed to a closed door across the asymmetrical hall. "They're just in there in the music room, but if you'd rather wait upstairs in the drawing room...?"

"No, thanks. Michael, wait..." Impelled by curiosity, she took the excited children's hands and walked across to the music room, where she released Michael's hand in order to open the door.

The pianoforte had been a wedding gift from her parents, but a young, bespectacled man was playing it. Griz was playing the harp. An unknown young lady was swaying over a violin, and another young man was playing the clarinet.

Azalea, quite a connoisseur of music, paused to listen. Clearly, they were nearing the end of the piece, one she did not recognize, but they were really rather good. Griz had always been musical, of course, although she had hated to perform her accomplishment in public. She had no qualms here. No one even noticed Azalea or the children until the piece finished with a flourish and the musicians all grinned at each other with satisfaction.

Azalea clapped, and the children joined in, causing all the other heads to jerk around in surprise.

"Zalea!" Griz sprang up for her stool, beaming as she opened her arms to the children. "Mikey! Lizzie!"

"Auntie Griz!"

Laughing, Griz hugged them and turned to embrace Azalea. Marriage had been good for Griz. Her affection was more natural and open than for several years. And she looked well, glowing with contentment.

Briefly, Azalea wondered if she had looked like that eight years ago when she had returned from her honeymoon. Before life had become so complicated. Griz introduced her friends, who seemed both awed and embarrassed as they hastily packed away their instruments and music and effaced themselves. Griz followed them into the hall, making plans for another meeting.

Then she turned to Azalea. "We can go to the drawing room, if you like? Tea? Luncheon?"

"I'm having luncheon with Eric, but tea would be lovely. And I daresay the children would enjoy raiding your kitchen—if your cook is good-natured?"

"Oh yes. Emmie, will you take them down and send up some tea? And scones?"

While Emmie obliged, Griz led the way up to the bright drawing room. "Her Grace insists it is a parlor, not a drawing room," Griz observed. "Just because it is smaller than all her massive rooms."

"I don't see that it matters what you call it," Azalea observed. "I think it is a charming room." Her gaze was caught by a framed pencil drawing above a side table. "Why, it's you! Did Dragan do it?"

Griz blushed endearingly. "It flatters me. And shows his talent. Otherwise, I could not bear to confront my own face so often!"

"It is a beautiful face," Azalea insisted. "And he has caught you exactly." He had, too, the upward tilt of her chin, the curve of her mobile mouth, and the observant yet humorous glint in her fearless eyes.

"Now *you* are flattering me," Griz said wryly. "Why?"

"Don't be silly. Why would I trouble? Oh, do you have that odd boy in *your* kitchen now? Or did you leave him in Their Graces'?"

Griz had inflicted a street urchin upon her parents' kitchen, one of her charitable projects, no doubt.

"Young Nick? Oh, no, he's at the Sussex estate now. He loves horses and other animals, and he's going to school, too."

Azalea sat in one of the armchairs while another servant brought in a tray of tea and scones.

"How is Dragan?" Azalea asked. "Is he home?"

"No." Griz wrinkled her nose. "He has gone to some office in Whitehall—not Horace's—every day for a fortnight now. He found a flaw in some accounts, so they asked him to look at more, but I think he is bored."

"I suppose it is money," Azalea said with sympathy. "But what of his medical career?"

"He is studying for the examinations."

"He sounds a very busy man. Don't let him be too busy." Before her sister could respond to that, Azalea hurried on. "What of you, Griz? Are you happily settled?"

"Oh, yes." Grizelda's lips twitched. "Though I wouldn't mind a little more excitement." As the door closed behind the maid, she said, "I had Dragan to myself for six weeks and now..." The expression in her eyes changed. "Is something wrong, Azalea?"

"Oh, no! I—" Azalea broke off, staring helplessly at Griz. "What am I saying? Of course, there is something wrong, and I came especially to ask for your help. Yet every instinct prompts me to hide it. Griz, I need your confidence more than anything."

"Well, of course, you have that," Griz said, pushing a cup of tea across the small table to her. "And I only have two house servants who have no time to listen at doors. What is wrong?"

Where to start? As the most immediate problem. Azalea drew the anonymous letter from her bag and passed it over the cups to Griz. Having done so, she wanted to look away, ashamed, but her gaze remained fixed on her sister's face, searching for signs of disgust.

Grizelda's eyes widened, then her lips curled, and she threw the letter down. "What a vile thing to send anyone! Where did it come from? Who received it?"

"I did. This morning."

Grizelda's jaw dropped. "*You?*"

"Yes, I. What can I do, Griz?"

"Ignore it. Burn it or give it to the police. What does Eric say?"

Azalea stared at her. "Why would I let Eric see such a thing?"

"Well, if you don't, you're playing right into this blackmailer's hands. Like me, Eric will know it is nasty lies. Why would—"

"How can he know that?" Azalea interrupted intensely, "when *I* do not?"

Griz closed her mouth and swallowed. "You are telling me you actually *wrote* such letters? I thought you loved Eric."

Azalea closed her eyes. She hadn't expected it to be so hard to be judged by her little sister. "I did," she whispered. "I do." With determination, she snapped her eyes open again and met Grizelda's curious stare. "But my trouble is, things have happened that I don't remember. People I apparently met, conversations I apparently had, events that apparently occurred, and I do not recall them. There are blank spaces, Griz. In those, who knows what I did? If I were sure they were lies, I would do exactly as you suggest. I would not even need to trouble you."

Grizelda's eyes were stricken. "Oh, Zalea, you need to see a doctor."

"I know. And I will. Foolishly, I have been putting it off because I didn't want to admit it was happening. I thought it was mere nerves and would go away. But now it is threatening everything, and I—" She drew in a shaky breath. "I *will* see a doctor. But whatever he can do for me is worth nothing if Eric is given proof of my faithlessness."

Griz swallowed. "Do you really believe you were unfaithful?"

"In my right mind, I would never be. But the mind can be tricky, Griz. After Lizzie was born, I was so low I felt quite mad. And Eric…"

"Eric?" Griz prompted.

"Eric has been growing away from me," she said with difficulty. "It troubled me. I have even tried to make him jealous. What if I went too far? What if those letters are the result?"

Griz nodded slowly. "I see your dilemma."

"I want to get the letters back, find out who sent them, and *then* I shall tell Eric everything. If I have not truly been unfaithful." She pressed the back of her hand to her lips. "If I have, I do not know what I will do."

Griz shoved aside her cup and reached for Azalea's hand, squeezing it. "I cannot believe you have been unfaithful, and you should not either. It is not in your nature. Should we not make Eric part of our inquiries?"

Azalea shook her head. "Yesterday, I had…another such incident. Some man I had apparently encouraged to come to the house for more than tea. I barely knew him. Eric walked in on us as I emptied the teapot over this fool, and he not only understood but… We talked, Griz. Just for a few hours, I felt us growing closer again, as it used to be. And now *this!*" She waved her hand at the letter in revulsion.

Griz was gazing at her. "I didn't know. I always thought your life so perfect."

"Nothing is perfect," Azalea said tiredly. "If it were, we would stop trying to make it better. Maybe that's what I did."

"No," Griz said finally. "That isn't you either. Very well, we shan't tell Eric yet, but what *are* we going to do?"

Azalea drank her tea. It was strange, peculiarly painful confiding in Griz, but her hand and her heart felt steadier. "I want the letters back without giving myself over to a lifetime of blackmail. So, I imagine the first step is to find out who sent *that.*" She pointed at the offending note.

Grizelda's eyes began to sparkle. "Well, we can trick him—or her. You obey, leave money in the theatre box, while I secretly watch who picks it up."

"Can it be as simple as that?" Azalea marveled. "But who would stop him if it was a strong man?"

"Dragan."

Azalea regarded her doubtfully. "You would tell Dragan?"

"You chose me to help you because of Nancy Barrow, didn't you?"

Nancy Barrow had been their mother's maid until she had been murdered in a back lane near Covent Garden. Griz had found the body, and the killer, too, in the end.

Azalea inclined her head. "You worried at it, against everyone's advice and disapproval, and you found her murderer, uncomfortable as it was."

"Yes, but I did not do it alone. Dragan and I worked together."

At least Dragan did not live in Eric's pocket. And besides, she could not let Griz put herself in danger.

Danger. "It might be dangerous for Dragan to confront this person," she warned.

"Perhaps that is a decision we should make when we see who it is." Griz picked up the letter and read it through again, frowning. "The writer is educated," she observed. "He knows who you are and who your family is. That you and Eric maintain a box at the Theatre Royal."

"You think it is a *friend?*"

Griz flicked one contemptuous finger against the letter. "An acquaintance, perhaps. But equally, these things are not hard to discover. You are all over the society pages of all the newspapers, and Their Graces are not unknown in the world." She raised her eyes to Azalea's. "Does five hundred pounds seem a lot of money to you?"

"It could change a poor man's life."

"But not that of a man of *your* world. Who would also know it is a mere drop in the ocean of Lord Trench's wealth."

"I thought of that," Azalea admitted. "Which is why I think it could be the first of many demands which will only get higher."

"You are probably right," Griz said with distaste. "But...it could also be less to do with the money than with hurting you. Who have you offended? Besides the man you tipped the teapot over—which, I have to say, was very well done of you."

"Thank you," Azalea said, touched. "He did look quite ridiculous. Eric did not quite manage to keep a straight face."

"And the very next day, you receive this."

Sudden, unexpected hope caught at Azalea's breath. "You mean this could just be Gunning's spite? That there are no letters to reclaim?"

"It's possible. I certainly cannot imagine you writing such letters as he describes."

Azalea sat back, frowning. "Then how could he imagine I would believe such nonsense?"

"Have you told *anyone* else about your memory lapses? Your maid? Mama?"

Azalea shuddered. "God, no."

"At any rate, we cannot rely on there being no letters. We must find out who wrote this, what he has, and what he wants. Then we can find a way to bring him down."

Azalea regarded her with fascination. "You believe we can?"

"There is always a way," Griz assured her. "We just have to find it." She frowned, thoughtfully for some time, then took a deep breath. "This is what I think we should do. Follow the instructions, only do not give him five hundred. Give him one hundred, along with a note that to receive any more, he must return the letters."

Azalea felt the blood drain from her face. "But what if he publishes them? Or gives them to Eric?"

"Why would he do that? It might give him satisfaction, but it would mean he gets a mere hundred pounds for his valuable letters when he must know they are worth thousands to you."

"You just said he might only be trying to hurt me! In which case, publicizing them is the quickest way!"

"Yes, but if his aim were *immediate* hurt, and he had the letters, he would already have sent them to Eric or the newspapers. He must want to string this out, to hurt you for longer. Or milk you for longer.

Either way, we need to know who he is and what his next move will be."

Azalea nodded slowly but said, "By the same reasoning, if he has them, he would not give me the letters for a mere hundred pounds."

"No, but he might give you proof that they exist. A page, or even a scrap of incriminating writing. If such things don't exist, he cannot send you proof, and the chances are you'll hear no more of him. If you receive proof, then at least we'll know where we stand."

"So, you will come to the theatre tomorrow evening and watch?"

"You must watch, too," Griz warned. "Everyone who enters your box, especially those who sit near where you have left the money."

"And if no one has taken it by the time we leave and the theatre closes?"

"Dragan and I will still watch."

"Griz, you are mad," Azalea said with a laugh that caught in her throat.

Griz only grinned at her. Then, as the smile died, she said, "But you must see a doctor, Zalea. Now. Not after we have dealt with this. Go now, this afternoon, or write and summon him."

"As soon as I have a moment," Azalea promised. This very situation proved she could hide from the problem no longer. But she would not sacrifice her luncheon with Eric.

"Let me know," Griz said as the children erupted into the room, refueled and ready to let off steam. Fending them off, Azalea did not miss the anxiety in her sister's eyes and felt both gratitude and guilt.

CHAPTER FOUR

ERIC DANVERS, FIFTH Viscount Trench, having conducted his necessary business successfully and in good time, strolled into one of his lesser clubs off Pall Mall. He chose it deliberately over White's or his preferred Reform Club because he remembered seeing Gunning there one evening.

Trench had no intention of allowing yesterday's incident to assume any importance in Gunning's imagination. But nor was he prepared to overlook it. He imagined his parting shot—that Gunning should be careful not to catch a cold from the incident—had been understood, but he meant to leave no room for doubt. He would not have Azalea upset.

Fortune favored him. No sooner had he settled into his armchair with a newspaper and a steaming cup of strong, black coffee than his quarry walked in.

Gunning was scowling in company with another man who, Trench recalled with difficulty, was called Roberts.

Roberts smiled respectfully at Trench and inclined his head, murmuring, "My lord."

Gunning turned his head in vague annoyance and, seeing Trench, colored to the roots of his hair.

Trench lowered his newspaper. "Good morning, gentlemen. Won't you join me?"

Flustered and clearly flattered, Roberts immediately swerved into the second chair in Trench's group of three. Gunning hesitated, but Trench did not even glance at him, merely summoned the waiter back.

"Tea, here, if you please," he said blandly and glanced at Roberts. "And for you, sir?"

"Coffee," came the quick reply.

"Excellent choice," Trench murmured, smiling at Gunning.

Anger deepened the flush in Gunning's face. "Actually, I would prefer coffee, too," he threw at the waiter who was already bowing and backing away.

"Tired of tea?" Trench mocked. "I do hope so. It can do terrible things to a man."

"Don't you like the brew, my lord?" Roberts asked, as though sensing a joke he was eager to understand.

"Oh, I daresay it has its uses," Trench mused. "The ladies prefer it to something rougher, don't they?"

"But you do not, sir?" Gunning flung at him, somewhat foolishly deciding to play him at his own game.

Trench smiled. "Whatever comes to hand. But tea stains so, don't you find?"

Gunning stared at him. Oh, yes, he understood the threat plainly enough. Trench drained his coffee and rose.

"Alas, I must leave you to the beverage of your choice. Good day, gentlemen."

Roberts jumped up in surprise while Gunning scowled. Trench sauntered away, but by the time he reached the door, Gunning caught up with him.

"A moment, my lord," he said stiffly.

Trench paused, holding the door half-open. "Just one."

"If you have something to say to me," Gunning said with dignity, "be so good as to say it plainly."

"I thought I already had." Trench smiled, though he made sure his eyes were icy cold. "But if you will have it plainer yet, it is this. If you anger my wife again, if you upset her, or even cause her as much as one moment of irritation, I will annihilate you."

Still smiling, he threw the door wide, forcing Gunning to jump back, and strolled out. He felt like dusting off his hands as he left the club and turned his feet toward home and luncheon with his wife.

⋙⋘

AS TRENCH ENTERED his townhouse in Mount Street, his heart beat rather faster than was warranted by a brisk walk.

"Any luncheon, Mrs. G?" he asked the housekeeper carelessly as he passed her in the entrance hall.

"It will be served in five minutes, my lord. Her ladyship is in the morning room."

Trench was careful not to bat an eyelid, although his relief was ridiculously profound over such a trivial matter. In truth, he would not have been entirely surprised to discover his wife's apologies awaiting him with the news that she had been obliged to attend a previous engagement.

"Inform her I'll join her directly, if you please."

It was the work of moments to reach his rooms, which he had begun to hate because Azalea was never in them, and wash hands and face. Lowering the towel, he gazed at his reflection in the glass. His naked, anguished face gazed back at him.

He was setting too much store by this midday meeting. The troubles of years could not be mended in a day. But still, an unexpected beginning had been made yesterday. He had not expected it to grow out of the discovery of a man importuning his wife, and indeed, his initial desire was to tear the man limb from limb.

But she had already poured the contents of the teapot over him, which had given him a moment's time to realize that violent reaction would have seemed to accuse her, to assume her guilt. He was walking on eggshells with this familiar wife of eight years, like a new suitor uncertain of his welcome.

But she had welcomed him last night. Her kiss, sweet and eager, had told him so, even before her husky invitation. He had lashed himself for not giving in to that temptation, for part of him—the arrogant, over-confident part—had been sure that in one night of passion, he could enslave her once more.

His lips curved into a rueful, self-deprecating smile. There had been other nights since Lizzie's birth. Infrequently, it was true, but they had happened. He had given her pleasure and received his own, and yet it had not been...enough. It had been as if they were both holding something back. In his case, at least part of it was imposing gentleness and care on a desire that had grown fierce with suppression. In hers, he had been very afraid it was mere lack of interest. She would submit to her lord, her husband, but that was not enough. It had never been enough.

And now, she was no longer that young, naïve girl melting with wonder in his arms. She had a life that barely included him.

As I have one that barely includes her.

Swinging away from the glass, he picked up his coat and put it back on. He ran the comb through his hair without looking, removing all vulnerability from his expression and replacing it with his usual sleepy amiability that came quite naturally, now. But he had to force his eager feet to stroll, not run as he made his way to the morning room.

She sat at her desk, writing in a beam of summer sunshine. Her beauty caught at his breath. It hurt him, though he couldn't work out where. And yet, the very sight of her lifted his heart and made him smile.

Sensing his presence in the open doorway, she glanced up and smiled. She put the pen back in its stand. "Ah, there you are. I believe luncheon is served in the dining room."

She rose, crossing the room with graceful tread as she spoke, and he offered her his arm with exaggerated formality. She took it in the same, humorous manner, and as they walked along the passage to the dining room, he wondered if she even guessed the effect on him of her mundane, simple touch on his sleeve.

A light luncheon was laid out on the table. Azalea dismissed the hovering footman and said she would ring when they wanted anything else. As he had done last night, Trench held her chair, and as she sat, he caught a whiff of her familiar perfume, a delicate rose with a hint of spice, elegant, elusive, and sensual as the woman who wore it.

He could not resist leaning nearer to inhale the scent of her skin beneath. No other woman in the world had ever smelled as delicious as Azalea. Or possessed such a tempting, slender neck. He let his knuckles brush against her nape and could not help delighting in the swift catch of her breath. He just hoped it was pleasure and not tension.

Straightening, he released the chair altogether and sat in his own. Azalea ladled soup into their bowls, and he murmured his thanks.

"So, what have you done with your morning?" he asked lightly.

"Oh, I have been *terribly* busy," she replied. "I took the children to the park, and I wrote to the agency to send me three excellently qualified governesses to interview, as soon as may be possible. And in between, I called on Griz."

"And how is she?"

Azalea smiled. "Happy. Busy. When we arrived, she and a group of friends were playing music I would not disdain at one of my soirees. She was always accomplished. What a pity she would not play the usual debutante games."

"If she had, she would, no doubt, have been well married before Tizsa even thought of coming to England."

"That is true," Azalea agreed. "I am so glad she held out for true love."

He could not help his quick glance at her face. Was that it? That she had married too young to know her own heart? He had grown adept at hiding such pain, so he was able to smile as he held her suddenly stricken gaze.

"I did not mean—" she began.

"Of course you did not," he agreed blandly. "That would have been rude."

She bit her lip and elected to change the subject. "What did you do this morning? Something much more important, I'm sure."

"I boldly saw off a challenge to my authority in the new housing venture."

"In Belgravia?"

"And St. Giles. Fenner wants to cut costs in building and increase prices."

"Were the others behind him?"

"A few. Until I explained graphically the consequences of poor building and the subsequent loss of reputation and revenue. It seemed to carry more weight than other consequences such as misery and death."

"I am glad you are there," she said stoutly.

"Most wifely. Thank you. I, then, made arrangements that will enable us to leave for Trenchard tomorrow."

Her gaze flew to his. "Tomorrow?" she repeated in clear dismay.

"I was under the impression you wished to go."

"Oh, I do," she assured him. "Only, I have agreed to go to the theatre with Griz tomorrow evening. There is a comedy she particularly wishes to see. You should come, too."

"Should I?" He spoke blandly, but he searched her eyes very carefully, for, in eight years of marriage, he had learned enough about her to know when she was hiding something.

"Please. Dragan will be there, also."

"Anyone else I should know about?" Only when he asked did he realize it made him sound like a suspicious husband. Which, in fact, he suddenly was.

"Such as whom?" she asked.

He set down his spoon and poured a little wine into each glass. Picking up one of them, he sat back in his chair and regarded her. He might as well say it, he decided, since they had begun clearing the air.

"I hope, Azalea, that I have never given you the idea that I would ever become that creature of scorn, the complaisant husband."

She stared at him, raising one haughty eyebrow. "Is he more scorned than the jealous variety? I do not recall marrying either, who would need, in any case, an adulterous wife to function correctly." She offered him new-made bread and an herb-scented salad. "If you are making arrangements to go to Trenchard, next week would suit me better. It would give me time to prepare and, hopefully, even appoint a governess before we depart."

The spontaneity of youth had vanished, it seemed, into the responsibility of parenthood. It was understandable, and yet he missed it.

"Then we are both content," he said and sipped his wine.

"Are we, Eric?" she asked suddenly. "Are you not at least a little *less* content with me?"

For an articulate man, it was odd to find his tongue fixed to the roof of his mouth. This was his moment for poetry and tenderness. A thousand words, foolish, passionate, and loving, jostled to get out. And stuck.

"No," he managed at last. "I am only less content without you."

Her lips parted as though she would at least admit, *And I without you.* But instead, she closed her mouth again and seized his hand. "Then let us go next week to Trenchard."

Oh yes, something was definitely wrong in Azalea's world. But he knew her well enough to understand that he could not demand or trick it out of her. He turned her hand, tracing one of the lines across her palm with his thumb.

"By all means. And what is this play Griz is so desperate to see?"

"I don't even remember," Azalea replied with a quick laugh. "I am just glad to spend time with her."

She rose to ring the bell, so if he betrayed the sudden fierce and childish desire to be the one she wanted to be with, she did not see it. The servants entered to clear away the leavings and place a lemon tart and a jug of vanilla cream before Azalea. A board of cheese and fruit was set down in front of Trench.

"What are your plans for this afternoon?" he asked casually.

She was cutting the tart and did not look up. "Oh, the usual round of calls and charity meetings. Donations to attend to. What about you?"

"I find myself at leisure," he replied, not entirely truthfully. There were a few matters he really needed to set in motion, but they could go hang, at least until tomorrow, if only she suggested it.

"You could take the children out," she suggested brightly. "Perhaps to call on your mother. She is always complaining she doesn't see them often enough."

"That is only until she does see them," Trench said, hiding his disappointment. He cut a wedge of cheese. "Perhaps it is time to remind her how badly we bring them up."

"How badly *I* bring them up," Azalea corrected, spooning cream over her tart. "You are merely their father, saddled with an incompetent wife."

Trench bit into a plum. "I prefer my wives incompetent."

"I prefer my husbands to be masters of the back-handed compliment. Or is that no compliment? In any case, I thank you for the preference."

"You're welcome."

In this way, they bantered through to the end of the meal, which was amusing enough, although it avoided the matters pressing on his heart.

When she stood at last to go and change for her afternoon outings, he imagined a certain reluctance that both warmed and worried him. He stood with her, deliberately blocking her way, and took her hand.

She watched it, lying still, white and soft against his.

He said, "You would tell me, would you not if anything were amiss? Large or small, I am happy to help."

He felt the slight pressure of her fingers, although it may have been involuntary for her eyes sought only escape. Her smile was faintly nervous as she said, "Of course I would!" And yet, as she slipped past him, her eyes shone. It might have been relief or unshed tears.

AZALEA COULD NOT explain it to herself. Having admitted her memory lapses to Griz, she should have explained them to her husband, too. But they were so wrapped up in her mind with something shameful, something that might truly be an impediment to their reconciliation, that she could not force out the words. Had he not just said he would never be a complaisant husband?

It was one of the many things she would find the words for when they went to Trenchard. When the blackmail business and, hopefully, the memory problem was dealt with, or at least diagnosed.

And this afternoon, she hoped to have that dealt with. She had already summoned the family physician and had every expectation that he would be punctual. Such were the advantages of her birth and position in life. She had chosen the time when Eric was nearly always out, though he could be unpredictable. To her relief, she saw from her sitting room window when the town coach arrived at the front door, and he bundled the children into it. It seemed he was taking her advice.

As it drew away, she noticed a young woman who had pressed

herself into the railings around Trench House, as though trying to appear invisible. She was young, wearing a cheap little hat, and she seemed very unsure of herself. She moved toward the area steps, then changed her mind and hurried away. Perhaps she had been considering asking about work and taken fright.

Azalea sighed. There was nothing to do but wait, pacing, for Dr. Gibson's arrival. Perversely, she now wanted the comfort of Eric's presence, to assure her all was well and that whatever was wrong with her would be fixed. And part of her knew only too well that she did not deserve that comfort, that she had made her bed of solitude and must lie in it.

Returning to the window, she saw another carriage had stopped outside. Her heart lurched. A knock on the door made her jump.

Morris appeared. "Dr. Gibson is here, my lady."

"Show him in, if you please," she said calmly.

⇒⇒⇒⇐⇐⇐

"I SEE NO cause for alarm, my lady," Dr. Gibson said comfortably. He was a stocky yet imposing man who oozed a soothing aura of confidence. "You report only minor headaches of a quite normal frequency, and in all other ways, you are a fit and healthy young woman."

"Then why have I forgotten things?" Azalea demanded.

He smiled. "We all forget things, my lady. And if your lapses are a little larger, it is due to your sensitive nerves. Such as you exhibited after the birth of your daughter."

"I did not forget things after Lizzie was born," she pointed out.

"No, but they are both symptoms of the same nervous condition. You are merely highly strung, like an over-sensitive pianoforte."

"Then what can I do?" she asked helplessly. "I cannot have chunks of my life disappearing. It could be dangerous for my whole family."

"Oh, I doubt that," he soothed, standing up. "If you are worried, I would prescribe you a drop or two of laudanum to calm your nerves when you are overwrought, but you should not rely on it."

"I do not want laudanum." Indeed, she could imagine nothing worse for an already unreliable memory. "Is there nothing else that would help me?"

"Rest," he said, rising and closing his bag. In his mind, she could see he had already moved on to his next patient. "Remove yourself if you can from situations which stress you."

"My husband and I were talking of retreating to the country for a while."

Dr. Gibson beamed. "The very thing. A month or two in the country, with plenty of fresh air and gentle exercise and nothing to worry you. Town can be too busy, entertainments too overwhelming for ladies of sensitive nerves. I thoroughly recommend peace and quiet, and you will soon be right as rain."

"Thank you, Doctor." Somewhere, she could not believe it was quite as simple as that, but she was certainly happy to try. And there was undeniable relief in his clear belief that nothing serious was amiss. She rang the bell. "Morris, show the doctor out if you please, and then come back."

As the doctor left, she walked to her desk and sat down to scribble a quick note to Griz, telling her of the doctor's diagnosis. When Morris returned, she bade her have a footman deliver the note by hand and rushed to prepare for the calls she had told her husband she would be making.

Tomorrow morning, she thought, would be the best time to go to the bank and withdraw the money for her blackmailer.

CHAPTER FIVE

O NE HUNDRED POUNDS in cash was not an unusual amount for a lady of Azalea's wealth and position to withdraw. It may have been unusual to do it herself, but Eric had never kept a close eye on her spending, and she doubted he would pay any attention to this, if he even noticed.

All the same, she felt guilty as her smart carriage brought her home. The banknotes in her reticule seemed unduly heavy.

Her well-trained servants handed her out of the carriage and bowed as she hurried into the house.

"Lady Trench is in the drawing room, my lady," Given, the butler, told her.

"Lady Trench?" she repeated in annoyance. Eric's mother was the last person in the world she wished to see right now—or at any time, really. "Is his lordship with her?"

"No, my lady. His lordship is not at home."

Then why the devil did you admit her? She did not ask aloud, for she already knew the answer. Several of the servants here, including Given, had been here for many years, and the dowager viscountess, as their former mistress, still held rather more sway over them than Azalea liked.

"I trust her ladyship has something to entertain her in our absence?" she said coldly.

"Her ladyship was content with a cup of tea."

"So shall I. Have a fresh pot sent up, if you please."

With her heart sinking further, she contemplated going straight to her rooms to leave the money and perhaps even change her dress. It would waste more of Lady Trench's time, and with luck, she would leave as soon as Azalea appeared. Or even before.

However, the woman was Eric's mother and was owed more respect than that. Forcing herself, she climbed only to the first-floor landing and turned her steps toward the drawing room.

The dowager viscountess was seated in an armchair, dressed in her usual, severe black and grey ensemble, a cup and saucer on the table beside her, an open magazine on her lap.

"Lady Trench," Azalea greeted her with a curtsey, for the older woman had never encouraged greater warmth. "I'm so sorry I wasn't here to receive you."

"Obviously, you have more important matters to attend to."

Unease clawed at her. "Did I forget an arrangement?"

Lady Trench looked down her nose, a difficult feat when she was sitting and Azalea standing. "I have no idea of your *arrangements*." Her emphasis made them sound shameful.

"Well, I am glad to see you," Azalea lied brightly, taking a seat on the sofa and laying her reticule beside her. "How are you?"

"Well. I am always well." Her tone scorned those who chose not to be. Her gaze flickered over the reticule as though she could see the guilty money inside it. "I gather my son did not return with you?"

"No, ma'am. I'm not perfectly sure where he is. Did you want to see him particularly?"

Lady Trench glared at her. "I saw him yesterday, as you should know."

She did know, though only because the children had told her. "Ah, here is tea. A fresh cup, Lady Trench?"

"I have had one. That is sufficient."

When the maid had deposited the tea tray, Azalea dismissed her with a murmur of thanks and poured herself a cup which she drank almost convulsively. Her mother-in-law always had this effect on her. Criticism, either implied or blatant, seemed to drip from the dowager's every word to her, especially when Eric was not present.

"Perhaps you would like to see the children?" Azalea suggested with sudden inspiration.

"I saw *them* yesterday, too. You, I gather, were busy elsewhere."

I was seeing a doctor about a serious health problem. But of course, she didn't say that, either. "Sadly, I was," she murmured instead. "I hope the children were on their best behavior."

"I hope it was not their best! Wild to a fault. They need discipline."

They are not wild, they are spirited and happy. "I am in the process of finding a replacement governess."

"Governess! The boy needs to be at school."

He's only just seven years old, and he most certainly does not need to be away from us at school. "Perhaps. Is there news with you, Lady Trench?" From experience, she knew her ploy to change the subject was unlikely to succeed, except to redirect the criticism to herself.

But quite unexpectedly, the dowager said, "I spoke to Lady Royston today. We met by accident in the park."

Lady Royston's was one of the names that made Azalea uncomfortable these days, but she was so pleased by the change in conversation that she said pleasantly, "How agreeable. Is her ladyship well?"

"Going on about servants, mostly. It's my belief she doesn't pay them enough. She told me you were taken ill at her ball the other week."

Was I? Oh, God, I don't remember that either. "Oh, it was nothing," she said hastily. "Too warm and stuffy, I expect."

"And Eric was not with you," she said sternly.

No, he was escorting you to a dull dinner with your poisonous old friends. "Alas, no."

"He doesn't know anything about it. Denied you were ill."

"I'm not."

"You should have stayed at home."

With an illness I didn't yet have? "I expect I should."

"Then there was no reason for your indisposition?" Lady Trench said sharply.

"None that I can think of," Azalea replied, almost touched by the dowager's concern. "I assure you I am perfectly well."

Lady Trench looked disappointed. "Then you are not expecting an interesting event?"

"Interesting event?" Azalea frowned, receiving a fulminating look from her mother-in-law, who was clearly irritated by her obtuseness. "Ah, that sort of interesting event. No, I am not expecting a baby."

"I should have known. Your nursery should be twice as full by now." Lady Trench stood, causing Azalea to lay down her cup hastily and stand with her. "I shall take my leave. Give my love to Eric if you see him."

Old bat.

⋙⋘

"WHAT DO YOU think?" Azalea asked anxiously.

Griz, who had come early to Mount Street to make last-minute plans, and was closeted with Azalea in her sitting room, leaned over her shoulder and read aloud,

"*Sir,*

"*Since you appear to be in grave need, I offer the enclosed donation. However, though your epistle is clearly intended as blackmail, I am at a loss to understand who you are or to what you refer. Please, therefore, send me these strange letters at your earliest convenience that I might judge for myself. I assure you there can be no further transaction between us until this is done.*"

"Will it do?" Azalea asked. "I did not sign it."

"Oh, no, quite right. I think this is perfect. Just in case we do not catch the blackmailer in the act. How will you carry it to the theatre?"

"Hidden in my shawl." She drew the money from her desk, placed the note on top, and began to wrap the whole tightly in paper which she sealed. "Did you speak to Dragan?"

"Yes. He approves our plan and will help." She seemed to hesitate, watching Azalea, then she said abruptly, "I am glad you saw Dr. Gibson. But I think you should get a second opinion."

"Well, if he is right, worrying myself to skin and bone over my health isn't going to help."

"Speak to Dragan, at least. I know he is not quite a physician, but he has a lot of practical and unusual experience. He would at least be better able to advise you whether or not to seek another consultation."

Azalea stared at her. "I cannot speak to Dragan about... Oh, Griz, you have not told him that, have you?"

"How else could I explain about the blackmail letter and why you had to take it seriously?"

Azalea rubbed at her forehead, digging her fingers into her temples. "This is a nightmare. Where is Dragan?"

"On his way, I think. He has finished with the accounting tasks and is catching up on studying, but he will definitely be here in time for dinner."

⤜⤜⤜⤜

IN FACT, DRAGAN Tizsa was at that moment closeted in Trench's study, listening to suspicions about recent housing investments.

"These people worry me," Trench said frankly. "In my own association, I can keep my eye on their actions, but I know they have fingers in several building and renovation projects, and if they are implementing those sorts of sloppy jerry-building practices, people will be defrauded and even die."

"It would certainly make a nonsense of your Prince Albert's designs for decent housing for the poor," Tizsa observed in his pleasantly foreign accent. The perfection of his English and the quickness of his mind had been the first things to impress Trench about him, although it was true, he was also one of the most handsome men he had ever encountered.

Trench, who was fond of Griz, had at first thought him a most unlikely and possibly dangerous suitor, but like Azalea and everyone else, he had been proved wrong. He was different, as Griz was different, but his principles, while unconventional, were strong and compassionate.

"I believe so," Trench said, "and since I have His Highness's backing in these projects…"

"I see." Tizsa glanced back from the row of books he had been contemplating. "Do you want me to poke around?"

Trench's lips twitched. "*Investigate discreetly* was the term I was about to use, but I suppose poke around covers it, too. I would like a detailed report, something I could show to my colleagues, but the bill should come to me."

Tizsa frowned. "There will be no bill. You are family, and I am happy to help if I can."

"I know, but the matter is not about family but business. I will pay, and be damned to your pride."

A reluctant smile curved Tizsa's lips. He took out his ever-present notebook, which seemed to be full of close writing and pencil sketches. "Lord Verry and Arthur Fenner," he said, scribbling.

Taking that for assent, Trench added, "Besides, there *is* a family matter I would like to discuss with you. Have you seen much of Azalea since your return to London?"

"No, I think I only met her once in Park Lane when we were all there."

"Will you talk to her?" Trench said abruptly because the question was difficult. "Tell me your opinion."

"Of what?" Tizsa asked.

"Her health. Something is wrong, something elusive. Even my mother has noticed, and she rarely pays attention to such matters. I need to know if it is physical."

"I'm sure you have a trusted physician."

"I want to know if I need to persuade her to go." Trench met the younger man's gaze. "There are reasons I do not wish to play the heavy-handed husband."

Tizsa looked away, then back to his face. "I can approach her if she lets me. But you should know that I will respect her confidentiality if she wishes me to."

"That is perfectly fine."

"You should also know that Griz asked me more or less the same thing."

Fear clawed at Trench, sharp and shocking. "Then I do have reason to worry."

"Not necessarily. Where is she now?"

"Upstairs with Griz."

Tizsa's eyes brightened. "Griz is here already?"

Trench smiled ruefully to himself, reminded of the first, uncomplicatedly blissful months of his own marriage. At least, they seemed uncomplicated, looking back. "Let's go and have a glass of brandy before they join us," he suggested.

⫸⫷

AZALEA SPENT THE evening on tenterhooks. It was in her nature to cover this in conversation and laughter, but she felt brittle, over-excited. If Eric noticed, he must have assumed she was eager to see the play.

Which she barely watched.

Having smuggled her packet of money into the theatre in her shawl, as soon as she reached their box, she threw herself into the chair at the far left, and while Griz spoke to Eric at the front, she dropped the packet over the side of her chair and casually kicked it under the seat.

Dragan watched her. She didn't know if his expression was amused or admiring. Either way, she rose, cast her shawl over the back to prevent any visitors from moving the chair, and rustled forward to join the others at the front of the box.

While she chattered and the stage came alive, she felt peculiarly detached. She paid little attention to the plays but spent her time watching the audience.

Early on, she spotted Gunning, in a box in the row above, with Lord Darchett and Mr. Fenner, one of Eric's business associates. She looked hastily away. Lord and Lady Royston and their two grown-up children waved and bowed from a few boxes along. Sir George and Lady Naseby did likewise. Lewis Hammond, another old friend, leaned close to a pretty, young debutante.

She could not help wondering if any of these strangers, friends, or acquaintances were her blackmailer. If—*please, God, no*—she had been intimate with any of the gentlemen who bowed to her from the other boxes or simply ogled her from the pit. She wondered the same of their visitors during the intervals.

When their box was busy, one visitor, Mr. Edgerton, sat on the chair on the left-hand side, but he did not move it nor appear to notice the package beneath, which was still there when he left. Azalea exchanged glances with Griz.

"Are you quite well?" Eric murmured in her ear as she returned her ostensible attention to the stage. He had stood to bow the visiting ladies out and now bent toward her, his breath tickling her ear.

"Of course," she replied in surprise. "Why should you ask?"

The backs of his fingers brushed her nape, sliding to the pulse at the base of her neck and away. Her breath caught in pleasurable shock.

"You seem…fevered," he replied.

There were several answers to that, most of which she could not say in front of their companions. Or, indeed, while this blackmail vileness hung over her.

"No," she managed, without wit. "I am fine."

He moved away, taking his place beside Griz, who laughed her way through the final act of the pedestrian comedy with apparent delight.

And now was the moment she had been so desperately awaiting, when they should be able to unmask the blackmailer.

"Shall we join the throng?" Eric suggested, and she rose obediently, snatching up her shawl from the chair on the far left.

At the door, she glanced back, and sure enough, the shadow of the package still lurked beneath the chair.

By the plan she and Griz had agreed, Azalea would walk away with Eric for the benefit of the blackmailer, while Griz and Dragan would fall behind and watch. Azalea took Eric's arm, and they joined the other departing guest in the slow procession along the corridor. Griz nodded once when their eyes met, and then she seemed to stumble to a halt. Dragan stopped with her.

Azalea's fingers curled involuntarily, digging into Eric's sleeve.

He patted her hand. "I know, it's a bore," he murmured. "I hope the play was worth it."

"So do I," she said fervently. But that was in the hands of Griz and Dragan.

GRIZ HAD PRETENDED to turn her ankle while Dragan protected her from the crowd as they both glanced back to the door of the Trench box. Unless Azalea's blackmailer was a member of the theatre staff, now was the likeliest moment for him—or her—to collect his money. It would be easier to slip in and out while the corridor was busy.

So Dragan kept his attention on her while she surreptitiously watched the box doorway. And she was rewarded with the sight of a top-hatted head ducking inside the box. Triumph soared.

"Now!" she uttered, and at once, Dragan spun around and darted back to the box. Although people tutted and looked disapproving, his size, or perhaps his considerable presence, meant that they got out of his way, while Griz battled against the tide of departures to toil after him. He bolted inside alone, but she felt no fear for him, for he could take care of himself. She was just fiercely glad they were about to solve the most immediate of Azalea's troubles.

She slid into the box, at last, to find Dragan the only occupant. He lifted up the far-left chair to reveal the packet was gone.

Griz stared, then slowly raised her gaze to Dragan's. "How the *devil* did he do that?"

⤜⤛⤚

THE SHORT JOURNEY back to Mount Street was torture for Azalea. Although Griz and Dragan joined them just before the carriage appeared, she could hardly ask questions in front of Eric or even watch them unduly to gauge their mood. Instead, she watched the lights of the other carriages go past the window and talked of she knew not what.

"You are coming in with us?" she said suddenly to Griz.

"Well, only if you're not off to some other party," Griz replied.

"I am not." But for the first time ever, she wished Eric was.

He only smiled sleepily and murmured that they were most welcome. But his gaze was on her, amiable as ever. She was not fooled. Those heavy-lidded, blue eyes hid a perception and sharp intelligence that only an idiot would underestimate.

"Did I tell you we are going to Trenchard next week?" She spoke to Griz, but the words were for Eric, to distract and remind. *Trust me, please trust me, just one more hour...*

It was only as Dragan followed Eric into the Mount Street drawing room that Azalea was able to drag her sister upstairs to her sitting room under the pretense of refreshing themselves.

"You may go, Morris," she dismissed her maid, waiting impatiently for the door to close behind her before she swung upon Griz. "Well? What happened?"

"We lost him," Griz said flatly. "I'm sorry, Zalea. He took the money and got away."

The disappointment was as intense as an ache, but while she'd hoped, she hadn't really expected things to be quite so easy. She sat down abruptly at the dressing table, turning to face Griz, who sat in the nearby armchair, polishing her spectacles.

"But it was a man?" Azalea said urgently.

"He wore a top hat when he ducked into the box."

"Then he is a gentleman!"

Griz shrugged. "Or a man of wealth enough to mingle with that crowd. Neither Dragan nor I saw him come out again, though he must have. Perhaps there are secret doors between the boxes. I shall go there tomorrow and ask."

Azalea was briefly distracted by her willingness to do something quite so odd. "Really?"

Griz cast her a quick smile. "Really."

Azalea sighed. "I knew it would not be so easy. What shall I do?"

"Watch for another letter. He's bound to send one, as we talked about yesterday. Which will give us another chance."

"He's clearly cleverer than we imagined," Azalea remarked. "Or at least wilier."

"Well, we shall just have to be wilier, too. Come," she added, rising to her feet, "we had better not lurk up here, or Eric will ask you awkward questions."

In fact, now that the excitement of the evening had passed in something of an anti-climax and was thrust to the back of her mind, Azalea found she *could* enjoy herself. Griz and Dragan were good company, lively and funny, and there was a great deal of infectious laughter.

Azalea was genuinely sorry to wave them off. On top of which, being alone with her husband was an exquisite form of torture in the present circumstances.

"I suppose we should go to bed," he murmured as the front door closed behind their guests.

A delicious weakness threatened her limbs. "I suppose we should." She turned toward the stairs. "You may lock up, Given," she added to the hovering butler at the foot of the staircase.

Her heart thudded as they walked upstairs in silence and, just as two nights ago, turned toward their bedchambers. He was close enough to touch, to feel his heat. To remember the intense, bodily joys he could give her.

"You did mind going to the play, then?" she asked, just a shade desperately.

"On the contrary. It was a delightful evening." His fingers brushed against hers—impossible to know how deliberately.

"It is good to see Griz so happy," she pursued. "She seems to have lost a lot of prickles since her marriage."

Again, he walked past his own door toward hers, and she couldn't breathe.

"She has found her soul mate," Eric said.

The sadness in his voice nearly destroyed her. How could she say the words forming in her mind, her heart, when she was hiding things from him, when she could have betrayed him?

Abruptly, as tears started to her eyes, she seized his big hand, dragged it to her lips, and then fled into her room, closing the door behind her. Again, she leaned against the door, but this time she did not smile in hope. She wept.

It seemed worse somehow to know he hovered on the other side of the door for almost a whole minute. And then he walked away. She heard his footsteps fade along to the end of the passage and then downstairs. It seemed he did not wish to go to bed after all, not without her.

CHAPTER SIX

A ZALEA SPENT THE first part of the following morning interviewing governesses with impeccable references. In each case, she had the children brought in and watched their interactions. The first governess, Miss Smithson, fawned and gushed over them, which made them back off. The second, Miss Farrow, was distant and polite, her manner severe. The third, Miss Alsop, was younger, a little unsure, but asked what games they liked to play.

To each, Azalea said, "Thank you. I will make my decision by this afternoon and inform the agency." And when the three were gone, she asked the children who they preferred—while fairly sure they would choose the inexperienced but play-loving Miss Alsop.

But not for the first time, they surprised her.

After exchanging glances with his little sister, Michael said, "Miss Farrow."

"The older lady?" Azalea said cautiously, just to be sure.

Lizzie nodded.

"Why?"

"She seemed more interesting," Michael said.

"And she makes her mouth prim like this," Lizzie added, imitating the governess's severe expression. "But her eyes smile."

"Do they?" Azalea said curiously. But actually, now that she thought of it, Lizzie was right. Miss Farrow's eyes *had* laughed, just not for the benefit of the other adult in the room. She spoke and secretly smiled to the children.

"Can we go shopping with Elsie now?" Michael asked.

"If she says so, yes. Shall I ask Miss Farrow to be your governess, then?"

Michael nodded and herded his sister out the door.

Children saw things more clearly, sometimes, Azalea reflected, without all the other concerns adults had—like references, experiences, and physical energy, and how long a governess might stay in their employment.

And how pleasant she might be at dinner. The gushing Miss Smithson would be annoying. Miss Alsop would be pleasant and obliging, and since, like the others, she had excellent references from her previous employer, Azalea would have been happy to engage her.

But now she thought of it, she realized Miss Farrow would fit perfectly with their family. In her forties, she was both independent and sensible, knowledgeable and experienced. She was neither disrespectful nor awed by Azalea. She would not fall apart when confronted by Eric or even His Grace.

And the children liked her.

With a sense of relief, she sat down at her desk and wrote a short note to the agency, requesting the services of Miss Farrow, starting a week today, on Thursday the thirteenth of June.

Leaving the room, she handed the letter to Henry the footman. "Please deliver this immediately. Oh, and Henry, is his lordship at home?"

"No, my lady."

"Any post or messages?" she asked casually, for there had been no communication from her blackmailer with the morning's first post.

"No, my lady."

Well, she could not, *would* not sit at home all day, waiting and worrying. She would invite herself to luncheon with Griz to discuss matters.

She was happy to find both Griz and Dragan at home in their cozy drawing room. They sat at either side of the tea-table, each busily writing in a companionable silence that Azalea found rather sweet. Dragan had his own study, but he chose to work, apparently, in the company of his wife.

"What a hive of industry," Azalea remarked. "I hesitate to interrupt."

Dragan rose to his feet at once, but Griz only glanced up. "Ah, Zalea, just who we needed. We are trying to narrow down our culprit."

"How?"

As she approached, Dragan placed another chair for her, and she saw the long list of numbers and names between them.

"How did you even come up with those? Are they my entire London acquaintance?"

"No, they're the people who lease the theatre boxes closest to yours," Griz informed her. "I persuaded the clerk to let me copy it. Now we're eliminating the empty boxes that we noticed and noting the extra guests we recognized—which is where you could help."

Azalea closed her mouth. "I would never have thought of any of that. And did you discover, *is* there a door between boxes?"

Grizelda's eyes gleamed. "No, there isn't, but we discovered how he escaped us. I should have thought of it, but it never even entered my head. I spoke to one of the ushers in the pit who saw a man climb out of your box and clamber around into the next. The usher was terrified he would fall to his death, but he was apparently quite nimble. Once he was safe, the usher shouted up at him, but he got no reply. He charged out to report the incident to his superior, so he doesn't know when the climber left the new box. Dragan and I could have walked right past him."

"Goodness," Azalea said, gazing at her sister as some strange new species. Then she frowned. "But if he escaped in such a dangerous way, he must have known we were watching him."

"Or just suspected it," Dragan put in. "He might have noticed Dragan and me, hovering further along the passage, but in the crowd, I don't think it is likely. I think our man was just being careful."

"Did your usher recognize him?" Azalea asked without much hope. She was sure if they knew who it was, they would have told her at the outset.

"No," Griz said. "And the only description he could give was that he was probably a gentleman, for he wore a silk hat and what appeared to be black evening clothes. He had his back to the usher most of the time he was in view and somehow kept the hat on his head while he was climbing."

"Bizarre," Azalea remarked.

"Not really," Dragan said. "He left the usher with the impression of a young gentleman on a silly wager."

Azalea sighed. "Which probably means he is nothing of the kind."

"Probably."

"Look at the names, Zalea," Griz encouraged. "Some of them came into the box at the intervals. Who else do you know? And is there any reason any of them could either have a grudge against you—or Eric—or know anything at all to your discredit?"

"Even a misunderstanding," Dragan added, "that might have amused you and yet left him with the wrong impression?"

She frowned at him. "Do I do that?"

"You can be careless of appearances," Dragan replied, undaunted.

"Secure in the knowledge I will be forgiven such transgressions because of my father's position and the indulgence of my husband? What a spoiled creature I am."

"Beauty is nearly always spoiled," Griz said briskly. "Be grateful. Now, look at the names."

Azalea knew most of the men listed and had acknowledged them in some way last night. Another couple of the names she recognized as associates of Eric's. She recalled a few other guests she had noticed in the same boxes.

"But I can't imagine any of them behaving in such a way or writing that letter," she finished. "I cannot believe it is someone I already know." *Can't I? Was Gunning not someone I already knew? Did I not misjudge him?*

Discontented, she pushed herself back from the table. "It needn't have been any of them, anyway. Someone could have come from anywhere in the theatre without waiting for the play to end first. The only man I know to have a grudge against me is Gunning, who was in Lord Darchett's box last night, though fortunately, he came nowhere near us. I told you about him, Griz. I poured tea on him."

"I'll look into him," Dragan said. "Do you know where he lives? We would just need to compare his handwriting with your letter."

Azalea's eyes widened. "Then you think it *might* be him?"

Dragan's smile was crooked. "No. But at this stage, just eliminating somebody is a step forward."

"I could be bled dry in hundred-pound installments before we discover this rat of a man."

"Nonsense," Griz said bracingly. "Are you staying for luncheon, Azalea?"

"If I may."

Griz bustled off, and Dragan pushed back his chair. He seemed lost in thought while she continued down the list of names once more, trying to dredge up some memory that might help. So she was taken by surprise when he said, "Griz is worried about you. So is Trench."

Her gaze flew involuntarily to his. "Eric? Why is he worried about me?"

"I think he senses your…anxiety and fears it has a physical cause."

"Grizelda told you," she said flatly. "About my memory…gaps."

"But you did not tell Lord Trench."

"Did you?" she countered.

"It is not my memory to discuss."

"Meaning you think *I* should? Did Griz also tell you that I saw a doctor yesterday who says it is merely my nerves and I need rest? If we can solve this wretched blackmail problem, I mean to go to Trenchard next week and rest extremely well."

"Good," Dragan said. He seemed to struggle for a few moments with what to say next. "I have heard doctors say that before. It is merely nerves. Particularly to women, though men can suffer similarly. In my experience, there is no *merely* in nervous conditions."

"Meaning what?" she asked with a touch of aggression.

"Meaning…did Dr. Gibson talk to you about the cause?"

Azalea shrugged. "Gadding about town and burning the candle at both ends."

"Did he *ask* you? Or is that what he told you?"

"He implied it," she admitted. "And it's true I live something of a hectic life in town. Perhaps it is catching up with me now I am older."

He blinked. "Twenty-eight?"

"You think he is wrong," Azalea said uneasily.

"No, as far as it goes, I think he is probably right. I presume he discussed injuries and headaches with you, examined you physically?"

"Yes, he said I was fit and well. I have had no injuries—that I can recall—and suffer no pains. He assures me everyone is forgetful." She smiled with difficulty. "So, you see, I am merely a hysterical woman."

"There is that word merely again. There is usually a reason behind hysteria, too. Would it surprise you to know, for example, that I, too, have a nervous condition? It turns me into a helpless, shivering wreck. In my case, the reason is easily found. It happens when I hear sudden, loud noises that make the earth shake, and I am reminded of a particularly nasty battle."

She frowned. "You think something happened to me that caused my blank memories?"

"I think it is possible. Look, I am not yet a qualified physician.

Worse, I am your sister's husband. But I would like to know how you became aware of the gaps, where they start and finish. You don't have to talk to me," he added quickly, perhaps seeing the dread in her eyes. "Talk to Griz if it is easier. Or another physician. I can recommend one more understanding than most toward women."

She searched his dark, intense eyes. "Do you think it might relate to this blackmail business?"

"I think it's possible, considering you can remember nothing referred to in the letter."

"If the things in the letter are true, I'm not sure I want to remember."

"That," Dragan said quietly, "could be your problem in a nutshell."

"I don't remember because I don't want to?"

"Perhaps."

She dragged her gaze free. Griz came in and paused, looking from one to the other.

"Griz can stay if you wish or go," Dragan said. "Either way, what you say goes no further. Think about it."

He rose, but Azalea reached up and caught at his sleeve. "No. I don't need to think. I would like your help. And Grizelda's."

"Well, luncheon will be half an hour," Griz said practically.

"It doesn't have to be now," Dragan assured her.

"Why wait?" Azalea countered.

"Then come and sit somewhere more comfortable."

When Griz and Azalea had arranged themselves on the sofa, and Dragan in an armchair, with his notebook on his knee, he asked, "When did you first realize there was a definite blank in your memory, rather than just something like a forgotten appointment, which popped back as soon as you were reminded?"

"A little over a week ago," she replied promptly. "We were at a dinner party, and a woman—Mrs. Carston—came up and greeted me like an old acquaintance. A lot of people *pretend* acquaintance with me for their own ambitions, but I don't usually meet them at friends' houses. So I merely smiled, hoping I hadn't forgotten her face. I certainly didn't want to be rude. But she must have noticed my blank expression, for she began to look embarrassed. *We met at Lady Royston's*, she said. *But it was such a crush. I'm not surprised you don't recall everyone.* And she moved on, leaving me feeling I had been unnecessarily rude to a perfectly pleasant woman."

"Have you remembered her since?" Dragan asked.

"No. Not only that, I don't remember going to any event at Lady Royston's. I checked my correspondence, though, and the invitation to her ball was marked as accepted. I had even written it in my engagement diary."

"Perhaps you did not go in the end."

"No, I was there, for I asked Morris. My maid," she explained to Dragan. "I didn't want to admit I couldn't remember it, so I asked her what I wore to it, and she told me. I even asked Eric if he had been there. He said no, I had gone alone while he escorted his mother somewhere else that evening." She drew in a breath. "Lord and Lady Royston are friends of Their G.races. I know their house. I have been there before, several times over the years. But I have no recollection of a ball this Season. I don't remember dressing for it, traveling there, or coming home again. That was the first blank."

"And when did this ball take place?" Dragan asked, his pencil poised.

"Friday, the twenty-third of May."

He wrote that down. "And this is Thursday, so almost two weeks ago, now. Can you remember what else you did that day?"

"I have pieced it together." From a mixture of her diary entries and subtle questioning of her staff and family. "Her Grace called because she had a letter from you, Griz, and she wanted me to read it, though you were already home ahead of it. The children were paraded before her, and Michael offended her by racing around the room and knocking over a table when my back was turned. But after that, I don't seem to remember anything."

"And after the ball? Do you remember going to bed?"

Azalea shook her head. She gazed at her hands in her lap, fighting with her habit of glossing over things she didn't wish to think about, let alone discuss with other people. But if Dragan was to help her with this or with the blackmail, then she had to tell.

"But I think I remember waking the following day," she said in a rush. "At least I think it was that day. I felt…odd. And my wrist felt bruised. And when I tried to remember why, I felt dizzy. Panicked. So I didn't think about it until that meeting with Mrs. Carston a few days later."

"Which wrist?" Dragan asked.

Azalea dragged her gaze away from her sister's shocked expression and held up her right hand.

"May I see it?" He sat forward on the edge of his chair, reaching out, and she showed him the wrist. He held her hand, bending it gently at the wrist, turning it, pressing his fingers lightly into the skin.

"There was no damage," she said hastily. "Not even an actual bruise. It just felt as if I had knocked it on something."

"How big an area was sore? This size?" He placed his fingertip against it, then replaced it with his thumb. "Or this?"

"Finger-sized maybe." She was relieved when he released her hand, which she placed back in her lap. "It faded quickly."

"Did you notice any other injuries, any other pains?" he asked neutrally.

"No," she said firmly. "I know what you are imagining, and there were no signs of it. Whatever happened or did not happen, I was not *forced*."

He inclined his head without obvious embarrassment or relief. His steady, unjudging attention made it much easier than she had imagined to talk.

"Moving on, when was your next memory gap?" he asked.

"I'm not sure. But a couple of days after I became aware of the Lady Royston gap, I was at the Exhibition in Hyde Park. I had taken the children, and afterward, outside the exhibition, we ran into a group of men I knew. Well, I knew some of them. Timothy Worth was among them, and Gordon. Brother-in-law Gordon," she added for Dragan's benefit. "Rosemary's husband. And young Lord Darchett. But one man I didn't know. He hovered at the back, avoiding my gaze, as though embarrassed to come across me. I had no idea who he was, but everyone seemed to think we were acquainted, for no one introduced him to me. I exchanged a few pleasantries with Gordon and left them in order to help Elsie with the children, who naturally wanted to run all over the place.

"But the man I didn't know followed me, as though he wanted to speak. And then, Lord Darchett, of all unlikely people, almost jumped out of nowhere in front of me. The unknown man melted away. And Darchett said to me in a low, urgent voice, *I hope that we may both count on your discretion. Talking of it benefits neither of us. Talking of what?* I asked him, being completely baffled. He smiled as though I'd said something clever, bowed, and ran back to the others. I still have no idea what Darchett was talking about or who the other man was."

"Did you ask Gordon or Timothy?" Griz asked. "About the stranger?"

Azalea shook her head. "Coming after the Mrs. Carston incident, it alarmed me too much. I decided it was unimportant, a mere forgetfulness. Until the day before yesterday when Gunning called and seemed to imply some closeness between us that I certainly don't recall either."

"What happened?" Dragan asked.

Azalea waved one impatient hand. "He called during my at home, but when everyone else departed, he lingered. I let him."

"Annoying Lady Monkton again?" Dragan guessed.

One of the first times Azalea had met Dragan, she had, in front of her disapproving sister-in-law, Augusta, Lady Monkton, invited him into the house without even knowing if Eric was at home. She had suspected not, and she had been right. And quite honest with Dragan about her motive.

She smiled ruefully. "Something like that. But when he started talking...improperly, I told him to leave. He made a clumsy lunge, grabbing me as if I were some poor creature he had paid for. So I emptied the teapot over him."

His lips twitched in response. "You are indeed my wife's sister. How did you feel when you poured the tea over him?"

"Satisfied, I think, although Gunning was angry, and I was glad when Eric walked in. Whether or not I misled him, he is not a pleasant man."

"That is an understatement," Griz muttered.

"Before that," Azalea said with a little more difficulty, "I had begun to panic. I am used to side-stepping the over-amorous. But when he grabbed at me, I froze. The world seemed to rush on me. I couldn't breathe. It was...horrific."

"Why?" Dragan asked, holding her gaze. "Was he so frightening?"

She frowned with the effort of remembrance. "I don't...*he* wasn't frightening, but something was. I remember being afraid I would faint..."

"And when you say the world was rushing on you, what do you mean?"

She blinked, forcing herself back into the memory. "Images flashing through my mind, but they were blurred, incomprehensible, too quick."

"Do you think they might be the memories you've forgotten? Which you were then trying to grasp, perhaps, as something similar happened?"

"Maybe," Azalea said doubtfully. "But if so, I still don't see why I can remember Gunning's would-be assault quite clearly but not anything at all about any other passage between us. If it happened, which I doubt. All I could really *think* when Gunning seized me was that I couldn't remember whatever intimacy he was talking about. Or Mrs. Carston or the man at the Exhibition, or whatever Lord Darchett was talking about."

A knock at the door made all three of them jerk around to face it. But it was only Emmie announcing that luncheon was served in the dining room.

Obediently, they all moved across the hall, and Griz closed the door.

"So," Azalea said as they sat down, "am I mad, Doctor? Will I ever remember?"

"You seem perfectly sane to me," Dragan replied.

"He's gullible," Griz said with a quick grin at Azalea.

"Honestly," Dragan continued, ignoring his wife, "I don't know whether you will remember everything. But we'll do our best to fill in the gaps for you."

"How?" Azalea demanded.

"By finding out what happened at Lady Royston's," Griz said. "Who this strange man at the Exhibition was, and looking at him and Gunning a little more closely. And Darchett, come to that."

Azalea regarded her unhappily. "You mean why I might have written inappropriate letters to any of them?"

"Or how they might have stolen them," Dragan pointed out.

"Or made them up in vengeance of some kind," Griz said. "We don't even know if they exist."

That would be best of all, Azalea thought. A nasty joke which cost her a hundred pounds and a couple of sleepless nights and then vanished, leaving her to enjoy the rest of her life with her husband and children.

CHAPTER SEVEN

A ZALEA WAS BOTH relieved and miserable to separate from her husband for the evening, especially since he strolled into her bedchamber with an alternative suggestion.

She was preparing for Mrs. Halland's ball at the time and sat before the glass in her shift and stays, while Morris artfully dressed her hair high on her head with diamond combs.

"An important evening, I perceive," he said from the doorway, making her jump and blush like a new bride. He strolled into the room, his attention apparently on the gorgeous blue ballgown spread out on the bed beside the numerous flounced petticoats it required.

"The Halland ball," she said, watching him in the glass. He was in evening dress, looking particularly handsome. "Do you intend to go?"

He turned to meet her gaze in the mirror. "I am happy to escort you there, but I believe I declined the invitation, being previously promised to a much duller affair."

"You could send your dull people a note of regret and come to Mrs. Halland's anyway," she suggested. "She would not mind."

"I could," he agreed, and her heart beat faster at the possibility. "But my perfidy would surely be discovered. I have a better idea."

"You want me to send my regrets to Mrs. Halland and help relieve the dullness of *your* evening?"

"Though a tempting proposition for me, I could not inflict an evening of such boredom upon you. My proposition is quite different.

You may go," he added to Morris. "I will help her ladyship with her remaining toilette."

Morris bridled, opening her mouth to object, only somehow, when she met Eric's gaze, she only mumbled, "Yes, my lord," and curtseyed before leaving the room in a sweep of silent disapproval.

"What is your better idea?" Azalea asked nervously, rising from her chair and walking to the bed to pick up the first petticoat. She stepped into it, deliberately not looking at him. Although quite capable of tying it herself, she was very aware of his movement toward her.

His fingers brushed hers away, unhurriedly tying the tapes. "That we dine together and simply stay at home."

Even through the fabric between them, the brush of his fingers seemed to burn her skin. He was too close, too intimate to ignore, and God knew she didn't want to. Her breath caught as he reached beyond her for the next petticoat.

"And let both our hosts down?" she managed, stepping into the garment, which he drew up over the other.

"Why not?" The petticoats were bunched between his body and hers as he tied it in place. "The tyranny of the Season is not absolute. We are entitled to look to our pleasure occasionally rather than the gratification of our hosts."

Instead of reaching for the third petticoat, his hands closed around her waist, drawing her back against him. For an instant, she remained stiff, too conscious of the blackmail and the hidden memories that stood between them. Then his recently shaved cheek touched hers, and she inhaled his familiar, masculine scent. She closed her eyes and leaned back, allowing herself the moment of sweetness, of longing. But it could only be a moment.

Impulsively, she turned up her face to speak. "Eric—" But his mouth covered hers, and she was lost.

Eric's kisses had always devastated her, from that first stolen embrace outside the ballroom of Kelburn House to bolder, much more intimate moments when they were engaged.

Oh God, how I love him... Her hand crept to his cheek, while his arms drew her closer against him. She resented the wretched thickness of her petticoats that she could not feel the glorious hardness she was sure grew behind her. But then his hand swept down over her stomach, and she gasped, her mouth opening wide to receive him.

"Is that a yes?" he whispered against her lips.

Oh, why can it not be?

Because if I have betrayed him...

She forced a laugh, whisking herself from his hold. "Sadly, I promised Mrs. Halland today in person. But if you wish to avoid your dull dinner, I shall happily spread the word that you are indisposed."

She was almost surprised when he tied the third petticoat, too. She might even have imagined the coolness following the heat of that kiss.

"I have never asked you to lie for me," he said. "I won't start now. Is this a new gown?" He dropped it over her head as efficiently as any maid. It reminded her of their early days together, the new addictive wonder of love and lust.

"Yes, it is," she managed. "It is such a vibrant shade, and I could not resist. Is it not charming?"

"Delightful." His deft fingers on the fastenings did not linger.

She wanted to cry. "Then I shall wear it again," she said lightly. "When we finally do enjoy our dinner alone."

His hands fell away. "I look forward to it," he said and strolled away without a backward glance.

THE BALL WAS a glittering, over-crowded affair, just as it should have been. Azalea's face felt numb with smiling. Her whole being seemed to scream with boredom because she wanted to be with her husband, whether here or at his dull dinner or alone in their own home.

She returned home at two in the morning, exhausted and disappointed, grateful only that she had encountered no more memory lapses or over-amorous admirers. And, she reminded herself, there had been no reply from her blackmailer. Which hopefully meant he had retreated back under his stone.

The house in Mount Street was cold and silent, unwelcoming with barely any lamps or candles lit.

She paused with her foot on the first step. "Good night, Given."

As the man bowed and retreated toward the servants' quarters, she found the courage to turn and look toward the silver tray that sat on the side table. Post was left there until it was delivered personally to her or Eric. A letter lay there, small and unthreatening, and yet to Azalea, it took on the significance of a loaded gun pointed straight at her heart.

She wished she hadn't looked.

But since she had, she darted back down, snatched up the letter, and knew at once it was the same hateful handwriting as the blackmail letter. She fled with it tucked into the folds of her gown.

She crept past Eric's rooms, but she did not even know if he had come home. There was no light seeping under his door. Part of her longed to rush in there to see, to wake him, cry in his arms, and pour out the truth, laying it all at his feet.

But how could she tell a beloved husband who wanted to "court" her again that she may have been unfaithful in thought and deed? Would he even believe in her loss of memory? Did the unlikely story not sound more of an excuse for transgressions that she was afraid were about to find her out?

Entering her rooms, she immediately heard Morris bustling toward her from the bedchamber. She dropped the letter casually on the table.

"Sorry to keep you up," she said civilly to the maid. "Just unfasten the gown and stays. I can manage the rest."

Morris obeyed. "Anything else, my lady? A warm drink, perhaps?"

"No, thank you. Go to bed, Morris, and sleep well. I shan't be up early in the morning."

"Very well, my lady." Morris curtseyed and left, hanging the ballgown on her way out.

Immediately, Azalea strode back into the sitting room, snatched up the letter, and returned to the bedchamber, closing the door behind her. She extinguished all the lamps save the one beside her bed and pulled the bed curtains most of the way around before climbing into bed and holding the reviled letter in front of her.

She could not put it off any longer. With her heart hammering and her stomach twisting, she broke the seal and unfolded the epistle. A scrap of paper fell onto the bed. Temporarily ignoring the enclosure, she scanned the message from her blackmailer.

My lady,

I admire your courage, if not your good sense, though I cannot advise any further deviation from my instructions. As a token of my good-will, and to prove the truth of my previous communication, I enclose a fragment of one letter in your own hand.

I now require the sum of one thousand pounds before anything further is returned to you. The thousand, in this case, will include the four hundred you already owe me. Since you will be in the vicinity of Grosvenor Square tomorrow evening, I shall make it easy for you. Go alone into the Grosvenor Square garden at precisely ten o'clock. Place the money on the bench on the south side of the square and return to your party.

Unless you do EXACTLY as I instruct, your letters will be with every newspaper in London by midnight.

The letter fell from her shaking fingers, which then grabbed the fragment of paper that had come with it. Clearly torn from a larger document, it was covered in writing. With horror, she saw that it was indeed her own hand. Worst of all were the appalling words dancing before her eyes.

I long for us to be together. I miss the tenderness of your touch, the joy of your embrace. I long for the sweet pleasure of a whole night in your arms. I do not care for the world's

The words ran out mid-sentence. She crumpled the fragment in her fist, closing her eyes in shame. She would give every penny she had to keep Eric from the humiliation of reading this and whatever other drivel she had written.

➤➤➤◄◄◄

"DEAR GOD," SHE said to Dragan the following day. "No wonder I have blocked my memory!"

She had seen him emerging from Eric's library and immediately hauled him off to her own morning room. She all but threw the crumpled fragment into his lap. It showed the depths of her shame that she did not even try to hide the wording from him.

"You must have suppressed a sizeable chunk," he said neutrally, handing the fragment back to her. "To have had a passionate affair and written love letters."

She sank onto the nearest chair, trying not to bury her head in her hands. "Perhaps I truly am mad."

"I doubt it," he said with a casualness that was peculiarly soothing. "If the letter is related to your memory lapses at all, it's possible you were forced to write the words, precisely for purposes of blackmail, in some traumatic incident that your memory refuses to acknowledge."

"It's refusing to acknowledge a great deal," she said bitterly. "Lady Royston's ball, Gunning, the man at the Exhibition, this letter…"

"You could have met them *all* at Lady Royston's," he pointed out. "In which case, it would still be one incident, one event with lots of people."

"I suppose that makes sense," she said dubiously. "As much as any of it does. Except I fail to see how I could have had an illicit relationship and written love letters all in one night."

"If you were not yourself, you could have imagined yourself falling madly in love in that one evening."

She shuddered.

Dragan stirred. "Griz has gone to call on Rosemary and on Annabelle Worth to see what she can discover from them or their husbands."

She frowned, realizing for the first time the oddity of him calling without Griz. "Why are you here in any case? Did you come to see me?"

"I hoped to see you," he corrected. "But I came primarily to call on Lord Trench. I have an investigation to carry out for him."

"You do? It's not connected with me, is it?"

He smiled reassuringly. "Of course not. It is a business matter. Did this fragment come with a note?"

"Yes," she admitted. "In the same hand as the first letter. He wants a thousand pounds this time. It's a bargain, apparently, because he will kindly include the remainder of the five hundred in that sum." She met his gaze. "I've decided I'm going to pay. I cannot risk Eric reading it, or, worse, everyone else reading it and humiliating him."

"You could always tell him," Dragan said mildly. "It's the only way to deprive the blackmailer of his power over you."

"I know. And I know the chances are he will only go on to demand more. But once I have staved off the immediate threat, lulled him, if you like, we can surely go on investigating him, find out the truth about him and the wretched letters I don't even recall writing."

"Is it not possible," he said slowly, "that the letter was one you wrote to your husband? When you were first married, perhaps? Or even before?"

She smiled sadly. "Our was something of a whirlwind courtship and conducted very much in person with no need of letters. We were never apart when we were first married, either. I had no need to write to him, and I don't believe I ever did. In fact, we have always lived in the same house, and whatever the emotional distance between us, we always travel together, to Trenchard or to house parties.

"Besides, though I have crumpled it now, the fragment seemed too new to be seven or eight years old. The paper was too clean and smooth, the ink too clear."

"And you are sure it is your handwriting? It is not someone forging it?"

She looked at it again. "I don't know. I never thought of that. It *looks* like my hand."

"Will you trust me with it? Along with other documents in your hand to compare it to?"

"Yes, of course," she said eagerly, latching on to the hope. She sprang up, going to her morning room desk and digging up a letter she had begun to her sister Athena, along with a couple of household inventories. "Would any of these do?"

"Perfect," he said, taking all of them and the fragment. He folded them and hid them away in the inside pocket of his coat. "How are you to deliver this next installment of money?"

"In the Grosvenor Square garden tomorrow evening. He seemed to know I would be at a party nearby."

"Did he, by God?" Dragan murmured.

She gazed up at him anxiously. "But you and Griz, you must not come, Dragan. The instruction is to come alone, and I don't want him to see you. I have already decided what I will do."

"What?" he asked, scowling.

"Exactly as he asks. I will leave the money and return to the party. Only then, I will find a way to watch from the window where he cannot see me. I hope I will recognize him, or at least be able to describe him."

"What if I watch from the window instead?" Dragan said quickly. "I am good and quick at sketching likenesses. And if nothing else, I will be able to see that you are safe."

"Are you invited to Lady Braithwaite's soiree?" Azalea asked doubtfully.

"No, but perhaps you could let me in as you go out."

Azalea thought about that. She would feel undeniably safer with Dragan watching close by, but... "What if he sees what we are about? He might already have seen you watching at the theatre. No, it has to be me, doing exactly as he demands. We are already agreed he is not going to hurt his milch cow. Besides, the more I think about it, the more I think I must know this person. He knows too much about *me*. I believe I will recognize him, and so there will be no need of your artistic skills."

"A man who climbs from one theatre box to another, at risk of life and limb, is not easily going to allow himself to be recognized. Besides, will you not be watching from the wrong side of Grosvenor Square to see much?"

"He has to approach from somewhere. And surely he will be watching the house for my exit, to be sure I am playing by his rules. Please, Dragan, it has to be this way, just while you and Griz find him and the letters. I could not bear—" She broke off, turning away from him. "It's not just Eric's hurt and humiliation I'm trying to avoid. Our last chance of rediscovering happiness hangs on this."

For a moment, Dragan was silent. There wasn't much he could say. She just wanted him—and Griz through him—to be aware of the stakes.

"I did not realize you felt things to be at such a pass," he said at last. "I cannot begin to guess the workings of your marriage. But whatever happens now is *not* your last chance. There is always another."

She swung on him, almost in anger. "How can you know that?"

His lips quirked. "I am not unobservant. You will let us know what happens?"

"Of course," she said to his retreating back.

CHAPTER EIGHT

L ORD TRENCH STAYED away from his wife that day. Having dined early at his club, he returned home to discover his wife on the stairs, dressed to go out.

Something very like panic flickered in her eyes before she smiled and said, "Lady Braithwaite's soiree. What entertainment do you have planned?"

He almost groaned. "Why, the same."

It would be a simple matter to send her ahead and go alone when he was ready. Pride urged him to do just that, for he was damned if he would play the jealous husband at this stage in the game. But it was pride that had led to their growing estrangement, and more than anything, he wanted to end that. Whatever the pain, he still had to try.

"If you can wait five minutes, I will escort you," he offered.

Her eyes were unreadable, although she smiled and agreed to wait for him.

He cursed silently as he changed into evening clothes. He hated being churned up like this. He preferred to be in control, to follow a plan that did not always swerve and change.

In truth, he had grown tired of waiting for his wife to come back to him and resolved to pursue her before she drifted so far off that reunion would be impossible. His initial volley had bestowed both hope and excitement to a life that had grown meaningless without her warmth.

But since that evening alone together, something had changed. There had been no repeat of the cozy dinner, the flirtation, the passionate kisses... Well, apart from when he had kissed her before last night's ball and despite her involuntary response, her delicious melting against him, she had still left him without any noticeable regret. In fact, it had seemed she was trying to be rid of him. That had not only taken him by surprise, it had *hurt*.

Trench did not consider himself to be a suspicious man, and even though they had grown increasingly apart, he had never doubted Azalea's fidelity. He had ignored his mother's and Augusta Monkton's warnings about his wife's behavior and any rumors which had, in any case, quickly died. He had believed in Azalea because he knew her and because he loved her through the good times and the bad.

But now... Gunning, he dismissed as an opportunist well-sent about his business. But something in Azalea had changed. She was hiding something. He prayed it was not illness. But she seemed torn, he feared, between her old affection for him and some other emotion. Some other love...

Used to keeping his feelings in check, Trench was unprepared for the jealousy, the anger, the sheer pain tearing him apart, ever since this possibility had entered his head last night. Hence his deliberate avoidance of his wife. But here he was, like the proverbial moth to the flame.

For once, as he straightened and glanced in the mirror, he had to compose his turbulent expression into the lazy, slightly sardonic one that was most familiar, but it took him so long that his valet began to shift nervously from foot to foot.

"Is everything satisfactory, my lord."

"Infinitely, Ford," Trench said, turning away with a faint smile and walking to the door. "Infinitely."

Azalea awaited him in the entrance hall, seated on one of the ornamental chairs. By the soft lamplight, her wide skirts spread out, she looked like a fairy-tale princess. Her creamy shoulders rose delicately from the low bodice, enticing, arousing. His whole body hummed with the desire to touch, to kiss.

But she gazed into the distance, lost in thought that clearly didn't make her happy. Her mouth drooped slightly at the corner, lending her breathtaking beauty an air of tragedy.

The pain in Trench's heart sharpened to a vicious point, though he continued to descend the stairs without pause.

Her head jerked toward him. The sad abstraction vanished into a spontaneous smile of pleasure, and she sprang to her feet. "There you are! And they say women linger over their toilette."

"I had to make the effort to live up to my wife's beauty," he spoke lightly, covering the delight, the fresh hope her smile had given him. He picked up her shawl from the chair beside her and draped it over her shoulders, careful not to let his fingers brush the smooth, taut skin.

She took his arm to descend the front steps, and he handed her into the waiting carriage before climbing after her and dropping onto the seat beside her. The step was folded up, the door closed, and the horses set in motion.

It was not far to Grosvenor Square. There would be no time for serious discussion. But he wanted to keep that sadness he had witnessed at bay, to make her laugh, to flirt with her. But before he could begin, she broke into a speech of her own.

"I saw Dragan on his way out this morning. He said he was investigating something for you."

"Well, it's useful to be able to keep such things in the family."

She glanced at him with a shade of unease. "What things?"

"Just business. Building to be precise. A couple of my associates seem inclined toward dubious practices. I want to be sure they have neither broken the law in the past nor intend to flout our agreements in current projects."

Was it his imagination that her expression seemed to lighten?

"Well, I'm sure Dragan will ferret out the truth. Though you do know, he will involve Griz, as likely as not."

"You mean Griz will involve herself."

Azalea laughed. "I'm still not sure whether they are good or bad for each other."

"It is certainly too late to part them."

"I tried once," Azalea said unexpectedly. "When I first met him, I thought a man with such dazzling looks would never look at her as I saw her look at him. And if he did, I did not think he would be faithful."

"And now?"

She shrugged. "I underestimated both of them. Who are your shady partners? Why did you get involved with them in the first place?"

For the rest of the short journey, he told her about Verry and Fenner and their efforts to thwart the original vision of the buildings. She listened, even interrupted with the odd question, and he realized, almost with shock, that he had never discussed his many business ventures with her. He had grown into the habit of thinking such matters could be of no interest to her. But Azalea had never been an empty-headed socialite. If her beauty had first attracted him into her orbit, her humor, character, and unexpected knowledge had kept him there. She was cultured, educated, accomplished, and capable of both deep feeling and deep thought.

Had he really forgotten all that? The distance between them was not just Azalea's doing. He had taken her for granted, the beautiful wife who would, in time, remember that she adored him. He had been supportive in her melancholy after Lizzie's birth and patient since. But that was not enough. Perhaps his reticence had grown out of care, but there was no longer any need of such kid gloves. He had stopped sharing his life, so how could he expect her to share hers?

The revelation gave him pause, making him silent as he handed her down at the Braithwaites' elegant townhouse and escorted her inside.

They had missed the first crush of guests, which meant everyone saw them arrive together in Lady Braithwaite's salon. Every man must envy him, his lovely wife. Could he blame men like Gunning for trying to take her from his careless hold? His neglectful hold?

Yes! he answered himself savagely. *And I do.* But their opportunities were over. And he would find a way to extinguish that sadness in her, to win her back from whatever or whoever was distracting her from him.

After they were greeted by their host and hostess, he strolled beside Azalea, greeting acquaintances, pausing to talk to friends. Inevitably, they became separated over time, but he refused to watch and glower, suspicious of every man who approached her.

Which did not mean he could not look occasionally. Or that he was not secretly thrilled when, as he leaned against a salon doorway, listening to a rather fine pianist within, she stood beside him and leaned closer to whisper, "He's one of Grizelda's musicians."

He bent down to murmur back, "He's very good." He smelled her skin, the perfume of her hair. But they were in public. He had to straighten, stand aside to let others into the room, and when he saw her next, she was sitting in a chair close to the pianoforte, beside Sir Jeremy Naseby, whose attention was clearly divided between the music and Azalea.

Azalea was listening intently, but the set of her shoulders told him she was aware of observation. Sir Jeremy's? Was she waiting for Trench to leave so that she could speak to him?

Appalled by his baseless jealousy, he gazed at the pianist instead, and when the piece was finished, he quietly left in the enthusiastic applause.

Several minutes later, she entered the same room. The center of a group of admirers as usual, she absorbed their admiration and flattery with her usual careless humor, never allowing it to be serious. Oddly, one of the first things he had learned about her all those years ago was that she didn't actually believe in men's admiration or the depths of her beauty. She put her popularity down to her wealth, her father, fashion, and, occasionally, old friendship.

From the corner of his eye, while conversing with other people, he saw her gracefully extract herself from this group and move on to others. He glimpsed Sir Jeremy Naseby, presenting her with a glass of wine and had to squash the silly surge of jealousy when she smiled at him in thanks.

Sir Jeremy only bowed and strolled away. Which relieved Trench, but only for a moment, for Naseby walked out of the door into the passage beyond, and an instant later, Azalea, without her wine, followed him.

Had the glass of wine been a signal? Prearranged for them to meet somewhere more secluded?

The green-eyed monster resurged with fresh fury. Somehow, he managed to keep his usual cool smile as he excused himself and left by the same door. To his left, at the end of the passage, Naseby was disappearing into the room being used as a temporary gentlemen's cloakroom. There was no sign of Azalea.

Or was there? To his right, a shadow flitted down the staircase.

Frowning, he followed the shadow, rounding the curve of the staircase in time to see his wife's distinctive golden skirts vanish through the front door.

Since it was too late for arrivals and too early yet for departures, there were no servants in the entrance hall. They were all busy upstairs, keeping guests supplied with wine and tasty morsels of food to soak it up.

Had Azalea planned it this way? There was no time to be relieved that she had not gone to meet Naseby. Quite aside from his raging jealousy, it was not safe for her to be out alone in the dark. And if she wasn't alone…

Blood was rushing through his head, singing a warning in his ears. Without conscious volition, he found himself outside the front door. He left it, as Azalea had, not quite closed. So, she meant to come back as discreetly as she had left.

She was flitting across the road and entering through the gate to the garden in the middle of the square.

She only wants some air, some peace. Why am I behaving like a suspicious husband, deranged by jealousy? Is there a quicker way to ruin our relationship?

No. But neither could he leave her out here alone, at the mercy of any passing villain. He walked quickly around the square and entered by a different gate, keeping his eye on the almost ghostly figure of his wife gliding across the garden.

Her head turned every so often, glancing all around her. If she glimpsed him in the light of the streetlamps, she gave no sign of it, just kept moving rapidly until she veered toward a wooden bench.

Trench paused by the nearest tree. He did not mean to disturb her moment of peace, merely ensure her safety until she returned to the party. And next week, they would go home to the country and *talk*.

Arriving at the bench, she glanced around her once more, perhaps to be sure it was safe. Then she took something from under her shawl and dropped it on the bench.

An alfresco supper? Trench wondered, amused in spite of himself. She did enjoy her food. But she did not sit down and eat, merely turned on her heel and bolted back across the square, even faster than before.

Startled, Trench did not at once move. *What the devil…?*

But someone else was entering the square from the south side. A man in a dark coat and silk hat. Trench tensed, but the man did not pursue Azalea. Instead, he walked straight toward the bench.

Not a snack. A fat letter. Containing, perhaps, some token of love.

Something snapped in Trench's brain. Fire ignited behind his eyes.

An agony of fury and loss exploded. *You shall have nothing of her! She is mine!*

He erupted from his tree like a cannonball, covering the distance to the bench before the unknown man had even picked up the packet so clearly left for him.

The man's head jerked around. He seemed frozen by surprise, which gave Trench all the time he needed to swing back his fist and strike. His knuckles connected with soft wool over hard bone, which gave him a fierce satisfaction. His opponent staggered backward, and Trench lunged forward to finish the job.

Despite the pleasant summer evening, the man wore a thick scarf over his nose and mouth, leaving little visible between that and the silk hat, which had fallen forward over his brow.

"Eric, no!" cried the familiar voice of his wife.

He spun around to see her running back toward him, which distracted him just enough. His opponent snatched up his packet from the bench and fled. Trench started after him, but Azalea, even impeded as she was by the heaviness of her skirts, threw herself at him, catching his arm.

"Leave him!" she almost sobbed. "Oh, please, Eric, leave him! You'll spoil everything!"

Stricken, he stopped and faced her while his world crumbled and fell around him. "Do you love him so much?" he whispered.

She stared up at him, her eyes wide and turbulent. His one and only love.

And then she stamped her foot. "You *imbecile*, Eric!"

SHE HAD NEVER seen Eric like this before. She had never even imagined the violence of what he had just done, of the desperation in his eyes.

The only time she ever saw her urbane husband lose his cool exterior was in the throes of passion. Odd that she should remember that now when another, strangely exciting layer of his personality was revealed. A surge of heat hit her stomach, wild and entirely inappropriate.

"Imbecile?" he repeated.

"Imbecile! If you believe that vile creature to be my lover."

At the last word, his arm jerked under her grip as though to strike again, and she hung on tighter. He tore it free but only to throw it around her waist, hauling her hard against him. His face swooped, and his mouth seized hers, fierce and passionate.

Astonishment held her still. By the time her mind realized he was kissing her as she'd longed to be kissed, her whole body was on fire, her insides melting into sweet, heavy desire.

And then it was over. He seemed to tear himself free of her instinctively grasping hands before tugging her fingers through his arm and striding off across the square.

"We're going home," he said grimly. "And you are going to tell me everything."

Azalea stumbled as she tried to keep up. She said pleadingly, "Eric, it isn't…"

"Not now," he interrupted.

Despite the sudden outburst of passion, he was rigid with anger as she had never seen him. At least, such fury had never been directed at her. She realized she was shaking and didn't know if it was the cold reaction to what had just happened or fear of her husband. Of the final estrangement she had been trying to avoid and which seemed likely to be her lot now anyway.

Griz and Dragan had been right. She should have told him everything from the beginning.

With a start, she realized they were reentering the Braithwaites' house through the front door that she had not fully closed. A scurrying footman in the hall halted in surprise to see them, though fortunately, he appeared to recognize them.

"Her ladyship needed a breath of fresh air," Eric said, once more the urbane man-about-town. "She is feeling faint. Wait here, my dear," he added, handing her into the nearest chair. "While I make our apologies to our hostess." He set off toward the stairs, requiring the footman to send a maid to Azalea.

"There is no need," Azalea assured the footman unsteadily. "I know you are all busy. I shall just sit here until my husband returns." Waiting for the ax to fall... Perhaps she should leave now, alone, run, and hide in Grizelda's spare bedroom. She could not face anyone else. But then, she could not even bring herself to move, and in any case, she owed Eric the explanation.

He had kissed her, she remembered dazedly, forcing herself not to touch her still-tingling lips. But even if he still loved her...

She became aware that the footman was gazing at her in anxious expectation. He must have asked her something.

"I'm sorry, what did you say?"

"Shall I send for your carriage, my lady?"

"No need," Eric's voice said from the stairs as he descended briskly and accepted his hat from the footman. "We'll walk, and the air will hopefully clear her ladyship's head."

"I hope so," she said fervently, for at the moment, she seemed unable to think of anything. However, it appeared she could stand and even walk across the hall, through the door and down the front steps, and along the side of the deserted square. "What were you even *doing* there?" she wondered aloud.

"Making sure you were safe," he said shortly.

She turned her head, frowning. "You saw me leave?"

His lips twisted under the light of a lamp. "I told you recently I was not a complaisant husband. I suppose I did not say I was a jealous one. And then I imagined you were only enjoying some fresh air."

"I have never enjoyed anything less."

A carriage rumbled past them. Azalea did not even glance at it, although Eric tipped his hat. He must have known the occupants.

"Who is he?" Eric asked abruptly. "And what did you give him?"

She closed her eyes. Her hand was on his rigid arm once more, but she didn't really care if she walked into anything. She thought she would welcome the pain. "I don't know who he is. I gave him money."

In the following silence, she was aware of his head turning toward her. She opened her eyes as he steered her around a group of amiable but wobbly drunks, trying to outdo each other in civility but staggering and giggling whenever one of them bowed.

"You may regard it as a silly question," he said, "but why were you giving money to a stranger? In secret? I would not have classed him on first acquaintance as *deserving poor.*"

"No," she said candidly, "I have a horrible feeling he is a gentleman, at least in name though clearly not in practice." She drew in her breath. Only the truth would serve now, whatever the consequence. "I am being blackmailed."

CHAPTER NINE

I N THE DEAFENING silence, his gaze burned into her face. She waited patiently for outrage to break through his astonishment. For him to push her hand off his arm. She would have to live with his disgust, at least until the truth was uncovered. And by then, how much damage would have been done? How much of her marriage, of her love or his, would be salvageable?

"Why didn't you tell me?" His voice was low, almost husky. "Why did you not come to me?"

He could always surprise her, this wonderful husband of hers. She could barely see through the tears suddenly filling her eyes.

She gestured with one helpless hand. "How could I? We had just begun...to reach each other again. We were going to Trenchard to be together, to try and close the distance that has grown between us. I could not bring myself to spoil that by confessing my sins. Although it was clearly a foolish impulse, because I have only made it worse, even more suspicious."

"You had better tell me all of it."

He did not sound remotely angry. She turned her head to look at him, but he was gazing straight ahead. They were in Mount Street, walking past other people's large houses toward their own.

Unexpectedly, his gloved hand covered hers on his arm. "When we are inside," he said, "and you are warm."

"It isn't the cold that's making me shake," she blurted, but she couldn't say more, for her throat ached too much with suppressed tears that were about to overflow if she relaxed for an instant.

It was oddly soothing that he could be his old self again, greeting the servants, asking for the fire to be lit in the library. When he removed his gloves, he did not appear to notice the split knuckles on one hand.

The library had always been his territory, but it was a pleasant, comfortable room, smelling of old books and something elusive that was peculiarly Eric. In the early days of the marriage, she had often joined him to talk or simply to be in his company while they both read. She wondered if he had chosen it for that reason tonight or because it gave him some kind of advantage in whatever was to come. In matters of business, he was a calculating man.

Business, dear God!

Abandoning any attempt at dignity, she went and knelt, shivering, by the recently lit fire. Her skirts billowed around her like a protective blanket.

As he had done in the drawing room after Gunning's ejection, Eric poured two glasses of brandy and brought her one. She took the glass in both hands as if it could somehow warm her, while he pulled his chair nearer the fire and sat down.

"Tell me everything," he said. His gentleness surprised fresh tears, which she hastily blinked away.

She took a reviving sip of brandy. "I don't know where to start."

"The beginning?" he suggested.

"I suppose the beginning was the letter I received in the post, the morning after we dined alone. It demanded money for silence in the matter of incriminating love letters written by me, now in the possession of the blackmailer. It said if I didn't pay him five hundred pounds, he would give the letters to you and the newspapers."

A quick glance at Eric showed him frowning faintly. "There was five hundred pounds in that packet tonight?"

"Oh no, I'm afraid there was…a thousand," she hurried into explanation. "It was my pin money, plus some I had not spent from previous quarters, and a little of my grandmother's inheritance."

He swallowed. "Perhaps we should come back to that later. Did you give him the five hundred first?"

"No, I gave him *one* hundred and told him there would be no more until he sent the letters to me. It was Grizelda's idea."

His eyes were fixed, opaque. "You told Grizelda?"

"I asked her and Dragan to investigate it for me," she admitted with difficulty. "They are good at puzzles, and I wanted him found rather than paid. His instructions were to leave the money in our theatre box…"

"Ah. So that is the real reason we went to the theatre and that quite ordinary comedy."

"And why I felt I could not go to Trenchard as soon as we had agreed." There was no point in keeping any of it to herself now. "Anyway, I left a hundred pounds and my own demands in the box, and when we left, Griz and Dragan doubled back to see who collected it. But he had actually climbed *out* of the box and into another, so they missed him. The next letter demanded a thousand pounds more but at least sent me a fragment of a letter in my hand. That thousand is what you caught me delivering."

Eric dragged his gaze free and looked into the fire instead. "To return to these love letters. To whom were they written?"

"I don't know that either," she whispered.

His mouth twisted. "You have written so many that you cannot even narrow it down?"

"Oh, it is not like that!" she pleaded, then emitted a sound between a laugh and a groan. "At least, I don't think it is."

"You don't appear to know much about any of this," he said neutrally.

"I don't," she agreed. "I don't recall writing love letters to anyone, not even you, and certainly not the fragment the blackmailer sent me. Dragan is comparing the handwriting to see if there are differences, in case the letter is forged."

"Is he?" Eric said with odd deliberation. "To be frank, Azalea, I am having difficulty believing you cannot remember to whom you wrote a letter of love that is worthy of blackmail."

She nodded. "I know. That is the other reason I did not tell you. You would not believe me innocent. But that is the root of the whole problem, the reason why I cannot risk all this coming out. I don't know that I did *not* write such things because…because there are blanks in my memory, things I cannot remember doing, people I apparently met but don't recall. I hid that from you, too, from everyone. I felt foolish, ashamed, afraid I was becoming like Great Aunt Matilda, who forgot everything, including her name. And then at other times, I was sure it was an aberration, an oddity that would stop and not matter, but it seems it won't stop."

He was looking at her once more, the frown etched deeply into his brow.

"I saw Dr. Gibson," she said hurriedly. "Once I realized the importance. He says it is merely my nerves, and I should rest, get away from the hectic activity of town."

"To forget things of such importance?" Eric said, carefully controlled. "I think we will obtain another opinion."

"To be fair, I did not tell him the importance of some of the things I could not recall. Dragan says some traumatic event could have caused me to wipe everything associated with it from my mind. He has come across soldiers with head injuries who did so."

"You have a head injury?" he said quickly.

"No. But Dragan still thinks this is possible." She took a deep breath. "Gunning, whom I thought I barely knew, seemed to think I had invited him that afternoon for some kind of assignation. I cannot think why I would have done such a thing. His touch repelled me.

And...and the Royston's ball that I asked you about? I cannot remember being there at all. I cannot remember going or coming home." She forced herself to withstand his gaze. "That is why I paid. I cannot be sure of anything I have done or said, and I could not bear such things to be public and hurt you. Hurt us."

"It is not the publicity that would hurt me."

She felt her shoulders slump in misery and had to make the effort to straighten them. To her surprise, his hand closed over one in a gentle, steadying grip.

"The most important thing you have told me about is your health. Your blackmailer, our problem with trust, come well below that."

"*Our problem with trust*," she whispered. "You do not trust me."

His hand fell away. "You do not trust yourself. Beyond that...there was a time when you would have come first to me with any problem, and we would have solved it together."

She felt the blood drain from her face, leaving it icy cold. "But you must see why I could not, how this..." She broke off, lifting one helpless hand in dismissal.

"How this concerns me? Us? And how you trusted *not* me but your sister's husband, whom you have known barely three months?"

A single tear escaped. She could not wipe it away without drawing attention to it, so she let it roll.

"That is not a criticism of you," he said with a lightness that sounded oddly forced. "Merely a comment on the state of our marriage. A comment I have no right to make after asserting the most important matter is your health. Like the blackmail, our relationship will wait."

"Isn't that the problem, Eric?" she burst out. "We waited and waited for things to get better, and neither of us *did* anything."

Something blazed in his eyes that caught at her breath. His lips parted in hasty response before he closed them, and his eyelids drooped, hiding his emotion. But it was too late. She understood what he would have said.

"*Apparently, you did?*" she said in a flat, hard voice. "Is that what you were going to say? You needn't hide it. There is nothing you can say on the subject I have not already asked myself. But there's the rub. I do not know if I did or not."

For an instant, her own misery was mirrored in his eyes. "We will find out," he said calmly. "But Zalea, I will not be excluded anymore."

"No," she whispered, both defeated and bizarrely comforted.

He took the barely touched glass from her hand and set it on the hearth, then stood and drew her to her feet. "Come, you need to rest. And tomorrow, we will go together to call on the Tizsas."

She rose obediently. Despite the relief in having told him, she felt his terrible distance like a pain. Common sense told her she had delivered several shocks that he would need time to get over. And infidelity was no doubt an insurmountable hurdle. She hung onto the hope that there had been no infidelity and tried to summon yet another batch of patience.

More than anything, she longed to spend the night in his strong, comforting arms. Just for his presence, without even the passion. But the plea stuck in her throat. He barely touched her as they walked together upstairs. And when they parted at her door, he only touched her cheek in a quick, distracted caress one might give a child.

"It will be well, Azalea," he said gently, distractedly. "We will sort it out." And then he turned away and walked back to his rooms. The tears rolled unchecked down her face as she blundered into her room.

It was some time before she could even bring herself to ring for Morris to help her undress.

"MY LORD." MORRIS'S soft voice drifted into Azalea's wakening consciousness. It came from the outer room, distant and familiar.

"Is her ladyship awake?" That was Eric's cool, lazy voice, wrapping her in warmth from the same distance.

"I'm not sure, my lord," Morris replied. "If you wait one moment, I'll just go and find out."

"No need," Eric said. "I'll see for myself."

It was an instant before the meaning of his words penetrated her sleepy, appreciative brain. She sprang into a sitting position just as Eric sauntered into the bedchamber, resplendent in a heavily braided dressing gown of dark green and gold.

"Ah, you are awake," he observed and closed the door between the rooms.

"Eric," she said, still somewhat befuddled. "Morris will think—" She broke off, blushing.

His lips quirked provocatively. "What?" He sat casually on the edge of her bed. "That I have come to make love to my wife?"

After eight years of marriage, she refused to let him embarrass her. "Enticing as you are in that magnificent dressing gown?"

"Isn't it gorgeous?" He lifted his forearm to admire the velvet fabric and the gold braiding around the wide cuffs. "A gift, if I recall, from your parents."

"Ah, then you wear it for protection?"

"Yes, but not from you. I came to suggest an early morning call upon Griz and Dragan. Just to make sure they have not vanished into one of their adventures for the rest of the day."

"Very well," she agreed.

"Can you be ready in half an hour?"

"Of course."

His lips twitched. "Including coffee and breakfast?"

"Of course. I can drink and eat toast as I dress."

"What a marvel is the human species, when pushed." The faint teasing smile in his eyes faded. He shifted, and his hip pushed against her thigh. Even with the bedcovers between them, she liked that.

"How are you?" he asked quietly.

"I'm quite well and remember everything about last night," she managed, meeting his searching gaze.

"Then it was not too traumatic?"

"Apparently not."

His lips quirked again. "You must forgive me. I am not used to playing the heavy-handed husband, and I don't think I like it. Shall we be partners instead?"

In spite of herself and the fact that she couldn't even tell if he was joking, she smiled back. "Yes, please."

"Good." He stood, much to her disappointment. "Half an hour then."

CHAPTER TEN

A LITTLE LESS than an hour later, Azalea led her husband up her sister's garden path. Emmie, who was polishing the brass handles and locks, smiled cheerfully and let them walk straight in.

"They're both in the drawing room," she informed them. "Shall I announce you?"

"Oh, I don't think that's necessary," Eric replied smoothly. "You carry on."

Azalea led the way upstairs. At the door, she hesitated, raising her hand to knock. After all, she did not wish to discover the newlyweds in an embarrassing display of affection.

Eric, however, clearly suffered from no such discretion. He merely reached around her, allowing her a pleasant whiff of Eric-ness, and opened the door. Inevitably, perhaps, Vicky, the little greyhound, bolted toward them.

At once, Eric and Azalea whipped themselves into the room and closed the door to prevent the dog from bolting downstairs and past Emmie, into the street; and Vicky launched herself at them instead.

Griz and Dragan, although at opposite ends of the table, each looking at separate mounds of paper, looked as guilty as if they had been caught *in flagrante*.

"Zalea!" Griz exclaimed, leaping to her feet. "Eric, how are you? Have you come to discuss important matters with Dragan? Why doesn't he take you to his study while Azalea and I—"

LETTERS TO A LOVER

"He knows, Griz," Azalea interrupted. "There's no need to hide anything, anymore."

"Ah." Griz shook off her brief flush of embarrassment. "Well, thank God for that. What brought you to your senses?"

"Lack of choice," Eric drawled, kissing Grizelda's cheek. "You look well, Mrs. Tizsa."

Griz flushed rather endearingly. "So do you, Lord Trench. Are we having tea, or did you come to scold us?"

Eric raised one eyebrow. "Why would I scold you for helping my wife?"

"What happened last night?" Dragan interrupted, looking at Azalea.

"I left the money on the bench," Azalea said, "and was just rushing back to watch from the window when Eric charged across the square and punched my blackmailer in the face."

Grizelda's eyes sparkled with unexpected approval. "Did he, by God?"

"Sadly, my wife then grabbed me by the arm, and our man escaped," Eric said. "With the money."

"Who was he?" Griz demanded, waving aside the money. "Did you see?"

"I saw a man's face more or less hidden by a top hat pulled low and a woolen scarf pulled high. It didn't leave much."

"Then you don't think you know him?" Dragan asked, apparently disappointed.

"I hope not."

"What intrigues me," Azalea said, seating herself on the sofa, "is how that hat clings to his head. It didn't fall off, according to your theatre usher, when he climbed out of the box nor even when Eric hit him, and he bolted across the square."

"He must have taken some added precautions to keep it on his head," Dragan replied quite seriously. "Which means he is afraid of being recognized."

"He should be," Eric murmured.

"Yes, but it does not help us identify him," Griz pointed out.

"It narrows things down," Dragan disputed. "It means he is afraid of being known by you or your circle of acquaintances."

"With respect, Dragan, that hardly narrows it at all," Griz retorted. "Azalea and Eric know *everybody*."

Dragan picked up a pile of his papers from the table. "But everybody was not at the particular area of the theatre we are interested in last Wednesday or at Lady Royston's ball."

"You still think the ball is connected with the blackmail?" Azalea asked quickly. She was glad Eric sat beside her.

"I spoke to Rosemary and Gordon, who were there, too," Griz said. "And Annabelle. They all said you seemed your usual self through most of the evening, but that after supper, you seemed...off. Annabelle said disinterested. Rosemary said dazed."

"She said nothing of the kind to *me*," Azalea said indignantly. "And I asked Rosie about the ball!"

"You inquired about which gown you wore," Griz said wryly, "and she told you. She didn't bring up anything else because when she asked you at the ball if you were well, you bit her head off."

"I did?" Azalea frowned. "Who was I with? Who did I dance with?"

Griz grabbed her notes from the table and sat down. "Before supper, you danced with Lord Royston, Mr. Lawrence Hammond, Lord Darchett, and Sir Jeremy Naseby. You went into supper with Sir Jeremy, and afterward, you danced with Gunning and Mr. David Grant."

Azalea leaned forward in some excitement. "Sir Jeremy was there last night! He left the salon just before I did! He could easily have been our blackmailer."

"He went straight to the cloakroom," Eric said apologetically. "And I noticed him in the salon again when I made our excuses to

Lady Braithwaite. His jaw did not appear to be bruised."

"Oh, well," Azalea said philosophically. "I suppose I quite like Sir Jeremy, so I'm glad it's not him. But Gunning...that is interesting. I danced with him when I was, in Rosie's opinion, dazed. I wonder what I said to make him imagine I wished to begin a liaison with him?"

"Some men take common civility as an invitation," Eric said with a very superior curl of his lip.

"That is true," Azalea allowed. "Which is why I am usually perfectly plain about my intentions. Or lack of them." She broke off, aware that Eric was frowning at her. "What?"

"You have...much to negotiate at parties of pleasure."

"Women do," Griz said unexpectedly. "Very beautiful women, even more so."

Eric closed his mouth, apparently appalled.

"What were the other names you mentioned?" Azalea asked hastily.

"Lawrence Hammond and David Grant."

"I've known Mr. Hammond for years, but David Grant?"

"Ah," Griz said, "well, that is the name of the man you later encountered at the Exhibition with Timothy Worth and Gordon. So if you were only introduced to him at the Royston ball, that explains why you didn't recognize him later."

"Hmm. But why did he seem so embarrassed to meet my gaze at the Exhibition? And then try to speak to me, only to run off when Darchett got in there first?"

"Perhaps he is shy," Dragan suggested. "A bashful admirer."

Eric turned to Dragan, fixing him with his gaze. "You really think something happened to Griz at the Roystons' ball?"

Dragan shrugged. "It's possible. But unless or until she remembers, we can't know for certain."

"It's also difficult to ask the Roystons and their other guests without drawing unwelcome attention to Azalea," Griz added. "But there seems to be no gossip doing the rounds either about her or anything that went on there—at least not beyond the who danced with whom and how Lord Darchett managed to lose so much money at cards while pursuing the Fenner heiress."

"Fenner?" Eric said, suddenly frowning.

"Catherine Fenner," Dragan said. "She is the daughter of your associate, George Fenner. He and his wife also attended the ball. Do you think it matters?"

"Beyond the fact that he is one of the people I asked you to investigate for me, I don't see that is it does. Coincidence."

"You all move in the same wealthy social circles," Dragan said. "Though Fenner is hardly aristocracy."

"No, but he's very thick with Verry, who is," Eric said.

"We entertained them for dinner, once, did we not?" Azalea said.

"Yes, about a year ago."

"Did I speak to them at the ball?" Azalea wondered.

Griz glanced at her notes. "Not that we know of."

Azalea stared at her. "You have a list of people I spoke to?"

"Of those Rosemary, Gordon, or Annabelle noticed you conversing with for any length of time," Griz corrected. "Plus, those that you danced with. We've been comparing the list of dance partners with those who attended the theatre, with boxes near enough to yours to be suspicious. It isn't infallible," she added defensively, though no one had criticized, "but we thought it could at least eliminate suspects."

Eric shifted restlessly. "You may well be right, but I'm more interested right now in what happened to Azalea at the ball."

"If anything did," Azalea intervened.

"As you say. But *if* it happened, it is very unlikely to have been while you were dancing or talking in full view of everyone else in the ballroom."

Blood seemed to surge in her ears, dizzying. "Unless I made an assignation with Gunning and was so disgusted with myself that I decided to forget it."

"It seems somewhat trivial to make you forget an entire evening," Dragan observed.

"It isn't trivial to me," Azalea said bitterly.

"No, but why would you have done so?" Griz demanded. "It isn't in character for you, the man makes your flesh crawl, and he's unlikely to have threatened you into it anywhere so public."

Azalea risked a glance at Eric. How bizarre to be discussing such matters with her husband.

"On the other hand," Dragan said heavily, "you seemed to vanish after supper. Annabelle and Rosemary both saw you leave the supper room early and alone, and neither they nor Gordon saw you again until the second dance after that."

Azalea's heart beat uncomfortably hard. "Then where did I go?" she said slowly. "It's a long time to spend in the cloakroom. Did I poke around the house? Take the air?" She frowned. "There is a small, ornamental garden at the side of Royston House, accessible from the ballroom."

"Did you go there during the ball?" Eric asked steadily.

Azalea squeezed her eyes shut. "I don't know. I don't remember any of it."

Eric's hand covered hers, strong and reviving.

Dragan said, "Don't try. We will try to find out more from the servants, who might have seen where you went. In time, something could jog your memory, and it will all come back."

She rubbed her forehead. "I hope you are right. Though I'm not sure why we are concentrating so hard on the ball. In my missing hour, or half-hour, did I sit down and write one or more love letters to someone I had only just met?"

"Unlikely, I agree," Dragan said. "But the ball is the period in time you can't recall, and when you were behaving strangely enough for other people to notice. The blackmailer could have noticed, too, and either made something up or worked out later that you couldn't recall him or what he had done or made *you* do."

Eric shifted on the sofa, a small yet violent movement. His fingers curled convulsively around hers, and she pressed back instinctively to comfort him.

"Did you look at the letter fragment he sent?" she asked in a rush. "Do you think it really *is* my writing?"

"If it isn't, it's an excellent forgery," Dragan said with a shade of awkwardness. He delved among his papers and brought out the familiar fragment. "The letters are all formed much as you usually do. You see the distinctive tails of your y and g, the way you write w, are all the same. I could find no real discrepancy. The only oddity is that many of the words are joined by a faint line, as though you were in too great a hurry even to lift the pen properly off the paper. And the writing is on a faint slope. Neither of these seems normal for you, so they may just be consequences of writing in a rush."

"Why would I write a love letter in a rush?" she wondered. Her lips twisted. "Or at all." She waved one hand in sharp dismissal. "To the devil with it. Thanks for looking, Dragan."

She drew in a reviving breath. "*So*, you have a list of suspects. People from the Roystons' ball who were also at the theatre on Wednesday and could have been in the vicinity of Grosvenor Square last night."

Dragan passed her a piece of paper, which Eric read aloud over her shoulder.

"Lord Royston, Naseby, Fenner, Verry, Lawrence Hammond, Gunning, Lord Darchett, David Grant. They were all at all three places?"

"Well, we cannot yet prove they were not," Dragan admitted. "They were all at the ball. Fenner is listed largely because he is a suspicious character, and he probably knows you don't like him. Verry for the same reason. Gunning has a grudge, and Darchett is short of money besides saying such odd things to you in the park."

"Yes, but blackmail is hardly gentlemanly conduct," Azalea pointed out.

"I think we all know birth does not necessarily bestow virtue," Dragan said wryly.

"Radical," Eric accused with a faint, sardonic smile.

"To the core," Griz agreed. "But also, a gentleman by birth and otherwise."

"Indisputably," Azalea agreed, amused in spite of herself to see her sister jump so quickly to her husband's defense.

"In any case," Dragan continued, calling the company to order with a frown, "now that you have come face to face with him, you must have noticed something that can help us shorten the list."

"I didn't see his face or even his hair," Eric protested. "And despite the lamps in the square, it was quite dark by that bench."

"I'm sure that's why he chose it. That and the fact it was on the far side of the square from Braithwaite House. You couldn't possibly have made out his features from the window as you planned, Azalea."

"No," she agreed with a sigh. "It was a silly idea, though I did get closer than I imagined I would when I tried to stop Eric hitting him again."

"I wish you hadn't done that," Dragan said thoughtfully. "However, you may both have formed useful knowledge. What did you notice about this man besides his hat and his scarf? Was he young? Old? Fat or thin? Tall or short?"

"Tall," Eric said as if surprised by the memory. "Almost as tall as me. And thin."

"Almost lanky," Azalea added with growing excitement. "He seemed all legs and hat as he sprinted across the square."

Eric nodded. "And he was certainly spry enough to run, so I doubt he was old, but otherwise, I could not tell his age. Nor did he speak, so we couldn't describe his voice."

"Still, Mr. Grant is not a tall man," Azalea said eagerly, "so we can eliminate him. And Darchett is more *solid* than thin."

Dragan took back the list, scribbling something in pencil beside the names.

"Lord Verry is stout," Eric observed. "And Naseby too slight."

"Who are we left with?" Azalea asked eagerly.

"Lord Royston. Hammond, Fenner, Gunning," Dragan read.

"I cannot believe Lord Royston guilty of such a thing," Griz said doubtfully.

"Being a friend of His Grace's doesn't make him a saint," Azalea argued. "Though I do see your point. I can't quite imagine it either."

"We should not eliminate him yet," Dragan decided.

"So what do you suggest we do next?" Eric asked him.

"Griz is going to visit the Roystons, see what she can learn from them or their servants. I thought I would speak to Fenner and Verry about investing money I don't have in their building ventures. I shall imply you are too rigid for my tastes."

"Thus, pursuing two investigations at once," Eric approved. "I take my hat off to you. I can speak to Gunning and Darchett."

"I can take Lord Darchett," Azalea offered.

"No," Eric said flatly. "I don't want you near any of them."

"Don't be silly, Eric! I can't just sit at home chewing my nails while the rest of you do all the work. I'll go mad."

"Do it together," Griz suggested brightly.

"That way, Azalea is protected," Dragan said with a nod of approval. "Two impressions are better than one. And it's just possible one of them may jog your memory. If it does, then it's best Trench is there with you."

Azalea did not argue. Having spent years, it seemed, proving that she did not mind whether or not her husband accompanied her anywhere, she was secretly glad of the excuse to be together. It was just sad that either of them needed an excuse.

"Good," Griz said, springing happily to her feet. "Now I'm going to see what gossip I can extract from barrow boys and girls on my way to call on Lady Royston."

Azalea caught her hand as she passed. "Griz? Don't go poking bears, my fearless little sister."

Griz only grinned. "Not unless I have Dragan with me," she promised.

⇛⇚

"So, WHERE ARE we most likely to meet Gunning or Lord Royston?" Azalea asked as they walked together back toward Mount Street.

"I imagine the Roystons will be at your parents' dinner party."

"Ah, yes, that is probable! When is it? Can you remember?"

His lips twitched. "Tonight."

"Well, that is fortunate! We had better compare engagements for the rest of this week, too. Drat, is that a spot of rain?"

It was indeed, inspiring them to walk briskly for the rest of the way, for Azalea had forgotten her umbrella. They ended by running along Mount Street and bolting up the steps and into the house together.

"My engagement diary—" she began breathlessly when she had divested herself of her damp short cape and hat.

"Don't you want to change first?" he asked.

"Lord, no. My bonnet got the worst of it, and one thing about such massive skirts is no matter how wet, they never cling to your legs. I think my diary is in the morning room. Where is yours?"

"In my head."

Of course it was. His astonishing memory was one of the things that had first impressed her. With his sleepy eyes and indolent expression, he never seemed to pay a great deal of attention, and yet he could remember everyone who entered a room and what each said in his hearing.

It was a long time since he had spent much time in the morning room, and his sheer size and masculinity seemed to dwarf it, especially when he shrugged off his damp coat and threw it over the back of a chair. For some reason, she felt flustered as he lounged on the delicate sofa. Hastily, she pulled the little book from her desk and sat beside him, opening it in her lap.

"You are quite right. Her Grace's dinner is tonight. Tomorrow is Sunday, so I have no engagements except church if I choose. On Monday, there is an al fresco luncheon in Hyde Park, followed by an excursion to the Exhibition, both arranged by Mrs. Ellesmere. I could never quite make up my mind whether to accept or go to Anne Gaunt's at home. But now I think about it, I believe Gunning is a friend of the Ellesmeres."

"Gunning may not want to talk to us, of course." Eric was frowning at a rag nail on one finger.

"Because I poured tea over him?" Azalea said, trying not to laugh at the memory.

"Well, that and…I may have threatened him."

She smiled. "Did you?"

"You needn't sound quite so delighted. I am not a violent man."

"Which is why it is so alarming when you are. Impressive, but alarming."

He glanced up, a provoking expression in his eyes that caught at her breath. "Well, now that we have two engagements at least on our joint calendar, what would you like to do with the rest of the day?"

The heat from his eyes seemed to burn right through her clothes. The suggestive curve of his sensual mouth tugged at some invisible thread to her lower body, arousing, attracting. A responsive smile trembled on her lips.

But before she could speak, the door burst open, and Michael and Lizzie flew in, exclaiming in delight to have found them both together.

Elsie toiled breathlessly behind them, effusive in her apologies.

Eric's humorous gaze met Azalea's over their children's heads. "I believe the matter is out of our hands."

CHAPTER ELEVEN

AZALEA DRESSED FOR her parents' formal dinner party that evening with a certain frisson of excitement. Part of it was a desire to be doing something for herself and pursuing the villain. She had paid to prevent scandal, but she was not giving up. And that she was doing it in partnership with her husband gave her a warm, fuzzy feeling in the pit of her stomach.

Her mood was improved, too, by having spent a large part of the day with Eric and the children. They did not need to go to Trenchard to spend time together. It was perfectly possible in London, too.

Handing her into the carriage, Eric was at his most urbane, the perfect town gentleman escorting his lady. And if his eyes smiled, it seemed to be meant only for her.

But was it a smile of closeness or sardonic amusement at expending such civility on a wife who had betrayed him? Why could she not tell the difference?

Because the situation was so odd, neither of them really knew how to behave, except to discover the truth.

Familiar footmen at Kelburn House let down the carriage steps and welcomed them into the house, directing them upstairs to the drawing room.

The Duke and Duchess of Kelburn greeted Azalea with their usual slightly distracted pleasure. They were, she knew, always pleased to see her, but there were also too many other things going on in their lives for them to notice a great deal, which was how Griz had managed to live more or less a double life for years without them noticing. Even when she had first met Dragan.

Griz was not here tonight. The guests were mainly political allies of His Grace, or those he was wooing for that purpose. Azalea knew she had been invited to dazzle and persuade and Eric to add the leaven of wit to heavy conversations.

Her brother, the Marquis of Monkton, was also present, but her two brothers who still lived at home were notably absent, no doubt because Horace worked all the time, and Forsythe would have been bored silly.

The first person Azalea noticed when she had greeted her family was Lady Royston. Smiling, she sat immediately by the baroness. "Lady Royston, how do you do?"

"Exhausted, my dear, utterly exhausted. So delighted to be here because I swear to you until this moment, I have not sat down since I last saw you!"

"Too much gaiety, ma'am?"

Lady Royston sighed. "Indeed. I must be getting old, but it is not just that. Geraldine, my eldest, has not been well, my cook is threatening to resign because she swears she saw a mouse in the kitchen, and on top of that, one of the footmen has vanished into thin air just when I need more help, not less."

"Vanished?" Azalea repeated, smiling. "You mean he has taken a position somewhere else?"

"No, I mean he has vanished without a word. Did not trouble to give notice or even take his few things with him. No one knows where he's gone or why. My butler and housekeeper are both distraught."

"Oh dear," Azalea said, distracted from her troubles by this fresh mystery. "When did this happen?"

"Oh, a week or so ago. We noticed the very day after the ball when *everyone* was needed to clear up."

Azalea paused, lowering her lashes to cover her sudden interest. "Have you spoken to the police?"

"My butler did, but they know nothing. In fact, I was saying to your sister, dear Lady Grizelda, only this afternoon, that I should ask her clever husband to find the boy. Did he not discover the fate of one of Her Grace's maids in the spring?"

"Why, yes," Azalea said, startled, "but I do hope *your* footman's fate is not so grizzly!"

"There is no sign of it," Lady Royston said dismissively. "And I would not like you to think he took the silver with him! There will be some girl at the root of it, I daresay. But it is most inconvenient."

"Indeed," Azalea agreed. She hoped it wasn't even more inconvenient for the girl in question.

"But how are you, Lady Trench? You seemed a little faint just at the end of the ball."

"I was a little," Azalea said easily. "Like you, perhaps I am exhausted by the gaiety of the Season. But I feel perfectly well now.

Lord Royston, she noted, was talking to Monkton and a young Member of Parliament. And, oddly enough, entertaining a few of the wives was young Lord Darchett, rumored to be courting the wealthy daughter of Eric's dubious business partner, Mr. Fenner. He was hardly a figure of political importance, but he must have escorted his mother, an old friend of the duchess's and a former political hostess of some renown.

And then they were summoned to dine. By good fortune, Azalea found herself seated beside Lord Royston, who talked happily to her about politics and the benefits of the Great Exhibition. She did not try very hard to steer the conversation to the recent ball since Griz had already been asking questions on that score. What she really wanted to do was to ensure his attitude to her had not changed. In truth, she could not imagine him stooping as low as blackmail. Nor could she think of a reason. Certainly, he was tall and thin as the man Eric had struck last night, but he bore no signs of assault on his face, and he spoke in his usual avuncular manner.

"I was sorry to hear Geraldine is unwell," she said once, as the conversation flagged,

"Kind of you," Royston said wryly, "but I don't believe she is. Her mother will fuss, but if you ask me, it's all attention-seeking because she wanted to come out this year, and we put it off to next."

"I remember being impatient for my debut," Azalea said with a certain amount of sympathy, but suddenly her head was buzzing, for it had struck her they hadn't considered any of the Roystons' family. Their eldest son, Beresford, was willowy in build, like his father, though only eighteen years old. Neither he nor the seventeen-year-old Geraldine had been at the ball, but they must have been in the house, and they had both attended the theatre with their parents. Beresford, at least, would have been able to slip out of the family home and be present at Grosvenor Square at ten o'clock last night. And climbing between the boxes was surely a young man's trick, as the usher had told Griz.

Of course, he had no more motive than Lord Royston, as far as Azalea could see. Unless it was sheer mischief, born of boredom. Perhaps Beresford and the impatient Geraldine had simply been playing some trick on her.

The idea that anyone could have so turned her life upside down for a mere prank boggled her mind. And could they really have frightened her so much that she had blanked her memory? Of course, the two were not necessarily connected. Still, she wished she could remember more about the children, but she had had very little to do with them.

Fortunately, Lord Royston's attention was taken by the lady on his other side, and he did not notice her sudden distraction.

On the other side of the table, Eric was dividing his attention between the Dowager Lady Darchett, who was looking very frail, and a

Mrs. Pickard, whose husband was about to stand for Parliament with the duke's backing. Their eyes met for an instant, and he twitched one humorous eyebrow, acknowledging her as he had used to when they were parted at formal events.

The fleeting gesture warmed her. If only they could get this blackmail business behind them, and if only she had not done anything too dreadful, perhaps happiness was still possible. At the moment, those felt like very large *ifs*.

At last, the ladies left the gentlemen to their port, cigars, and heavy discussions, and made themselves comfortable before joining Her Grace in the drawing room. Azalea was not quick enough and found herself hailed by her sister-in-law, Augusta, the Marchioness of Monkton.

"Azalea. What was the matter with you at the Roystons' ball?"

Azalea sighed. "I don't know, but I feel sure you are about to tell me."

Augusta cast her a sharp glance, as though suspecting the barb but missing it, "You walked right past me, pale as a sheet when I spoke to you."

"I beg your pardon. I did feel a little faint that night. But thank you for asking. I am now quite well." That was a barb, too, since August had waited two weeks to inquire after her health. But again, the marchioness missed it. There was really no point, so Azalea merely asked. "How are you, Augusta?"

"In perfect health, as always. Tell me, have you seen anything of Grizelda or that ramshackle husband of hers?"

"Why, yes, I called on them only this morning. But I don't believe she would thank you for the epithet *ramshackle*."

"Monkton," Augusta said grandly, "does not like him."

"Trench," Azalea replied, "does. So do I. More to the point, he makes Griz happy, so let's leave them be. How are the children?"

It was some time before the gentlemen rejoined the throng in the drawing room, wafting in on a breeze of brandy and recent cigar smoke. Eric veered toward her, leaning down to murmur, "Anything?"

"Bits and pieces. You?"

"Likewise. But I have learned that young Darchett is an intimate of our friend Gunning, and he looks petrified whenever I speak to him."

"Does he?" Azalea said, startled. "I wonder why? He did make those odd remarks to me in the park. What are you going to do?"

"Speak to him some more," Eric said blandly and strolled away toward Lord Darchett.

The younger man saw him coming and did indeed look like a frightened rabbit. When Eric fell gracefully onto the sofa beside him, she thought he would actually bolt. Although it wasn't really funny, a surge of laughter escaped her, which she turned into a cough and apology.

⟫⟫⟩⟨⟨⟨

"Well, what did you get out of him?" she asked impatiently when they finally shut the door of the carriage to go home.

"Darchett?" he said, immediately understanding. "Nothing, really, except that he says Gunning was at his club with him the night we went to the theatre. And later, they went on to some cockfight."

"Do you believe him?"

"I'm not sure. I'd say he's definitely covering something. But he may just have heard about Gunning's behavior and how we dealt with it. What did you learn?"

"I can't believe it was Lord Royston, though it did strike me it could be his children. Do you know Beresford and Geraldine?"

"No," he replied thoughtfully, "but perhaps we should consult with Griz about them."

"Oh, and one of their footmen is missing. Vanished without a word, which is odd, though I can't see how it's relevant."

111

"Missing since when?"

"Since the day after the ball."

He met her gaze. "That *is* interesting. Though like you, I cannot see how it would connect to our problems."

"Perhaps he was aiding the children in their trickery and took fright. Or helping some unknown man who is our blackmailer. After all, it is not forced to be one of Griz and Dragan's suspects."

"No, but it does make sense to be someone close enough to you to know your likely engagements and—"

"And what?" she prompted as he broke off and lapsed into silence.

He shrugged. "And the state of our marriage."

She felt it like a blow in the stomach, which she covered involuntarily with one hand.

"I mean that we are not often together," he added. "That neither of us truly knows what the other does from day to day."

"And that I am reckless and fast? You really have been talking to Augusta."

"I have, and she did indeed begin on how I should curb your madder starts before... Well, I'm not quite sure what dire eventuality will befall either you or me, but she certainly advises the curbing. More importantly, she is an excellent source of gossip about other people."

"Such as?" Azalea asked, distracted.

"Such as Lawrence Hammond has financial woes. Gunning has been cut out of his great-uncle's will. And the Roystons cannot afford their daughter's social debut this year."

Azalea frowned. "So, they are short of money. But my thousand pounds, surely, would not be enough to change the lives of such expensive men! Or their heirs," she added, thinking of Royston's son.

"Well, the thousand pounds was never likely to be the last demand," Eric pointed out. "Although we might have scared him off. Why would you pay any more when I know everything?"

"To keep it out of the newspapers?"

"I think, between us, the duke and I can manage that. At least the ones that matter."

She stared, then closed her mouth with a snap. "You mean I paid all that money for nothing? We were never in any danger of exposure?"

"I wish you had trusted me."

So do I. She could not speak. Her throat was blocked with tears and self-anger.

In the silence, he leaned across from the seat opposite and took her hand in a firm hold. "I'm not blaming you for this, Azalea. How could I?"

"How could you not?" she whispered. "Whatever I did or didn't do, I have made such a mess..."

"We both have. It would never have happened if my pride had not let this distance form between us."

She clung to his hand. "I don't want the distance, Eric."

"Neither do I."

The carriage stopped outside their home, and reluctantly, it seemed, he released her.

As they alighted and climbed the few steps to the house, Azalea knew how such evenings ended. For the last two years, on the few occasions that they attended and left an event together, they walked upstairs together. Usually, Eric would leave her on the first landing with a civil, "Good night, my love," and head off to his library. Lately, she had longed to be invited to go with him, as in the early days, but without his indicating a desire for her company, she had refused to inflict it—more pride.

Once or twice, when it was very late, they had actually climbed to the next floor together, and her heart had raced with hope. But he had usually left her at his own bedchamber door, and desire and hope had crumbled just the same.

He was right. Foolish pride had let this distance flourish until neither knew what she had actually done in her unhappiness. Their evening together after the incident with Gunning had been his idea. Now it was her turn.

"Shall we go to the library to plot tomorrow's adventures?" she asked lightly. *Please don't say, 'It's late, you need to rest'...*

He didn't even think about it. "Excellent plan."

And at once, her dropping spirits rose immeasurably.

When they entered the library, Azalea turned up the lamps enough to make the room welcoming, while Eric went to the decanter and frowned. "There's only one glass. Ring the bell, Zalea."

"There's no need," she said, unwilling to be interrupted. "I don't really want a drink."

She knelt once more by the empty hearth, and for a time, they discussed the theory of the blackmail being a careless, callous prank by the Royston children.

"The trouble is, I don't remember seeing them leave the theatre," Azalea said. "I was more interested in who Griz and Dragan were going to find collecting the packet from our box. I don't know if there was any time Beresford wasn't with them."

Eric sat down with his brandy in the same chair he had occupied last night. "No, and it does seem a very young man's trick to be climbing out of one box and into another. On the other hand, it's a *mean* trick. Children can go their own way, but is it really likely in the Roystons' offspring? What on earth could they have against either of us?"

"Nothing. Just opportunism."

"Well, until we can rule them out, we shall bear them in mind." He sipped his brandy thoughtfully. "And on Monday, you think Gunning might appear at Mrs. Ellesmere's al fresco?"

"Yes, but it will be difficult for either of us to question him direct-ly."

"I shall endeavor to speak to a group of friends that includes him.

Perhaps we can learn more about where he was and what he was doing at the relevant times." He took another sip of brandy, then, to her surprise, offered her the glass.

Her gaze flew to his, for it was reminiscent of an old ritual from the early days of their marriage, when they shared a wine glass, and he made sensual play of drinking from exactly the same place her lips had touched.

His eyes gave nothing away. But pride, or the pretense of it, had been no friend to either of them. She took the glass, just brushing his fingers, and turned it toward the light to find the mark of his mouth.

Deliberately, she held his gaze over the rim of the glass and drank. His eyes darkened as the fiery, fragrant liquid spilled over her tongue and burned its way down her throat. Desire rose to meet it. Slowly, she held up the glass to return it.

He reached down. Both his hands closed over hers on the stem of the glass, and she couldn't breathe. He lowered the glass and her hand and kissed her.

It was not a long kiss, just enough to melt her bones, and then he straightened, the glass once more in his sole possession.

"Tomorrow evening is Lady Gaveston's ball," he said, as though nothing had happened, "where we might encounter several of our suspects. Did you accept the invitation?"

"I did," she managed. "I think even Griz did, more to prove she is not ashamed of Dragan than because she actually wants to go, but at least we should be able to confer there."

"Then we shall have a busy day ahead of us."

But not until Monday. Sunday was a quiet day. Nothing between her and Eric would or could change all at once. They had already spent more time today in each other's company than at any time for more than two years. And that, surely, was enough to build on.

"We shall," she said, rising to her feet before he could move to help her. "And I believe I shall sleep well, in spite of everything." She touched his shoulder to keep him in his chair. "Don't get up. Good night, Eric."

With a fleeting smile, she walked toward the door, realizing almost with surprise that she was not sad at this parting. She turned back to find him watching her from the chair.

"Thank you," she said softly.

He stared. "For what?"

"For being *with* me. For helping me."

His lips curved. "My dear, I will always help you. I will always be with you."

And that, she thought, as she ran upstairs with her heart full, was the sweetest of goodnights.

CHAPTER TWELVE

Azalea's optimism was still strong as she and Eric walked through Hyde Park at midday on Monday. Sunday had been a quiet but agreeable day. She and Eric had gone to church together at St. George's in Hanover Square, and they had spent the afternoon largely with the children, at home and in the park.

To spend the day as a family had been bittersweet for Azalea, reminding her how lucky she was and how much she loved her family. But also forcing her to acknowledge how much she had to lose. She had pushed such anxiety to the back of her mind, enjoying the present.

She still was, walking arm-in-arm with Eric in the sunshine. They came upon the Ellesmere party, light-hearted and loud by the banks of the Serpentine.

The arrival of Lord and Lady Trench caused quite a stir, and Mrs. Ellesmere welcomed them with heightened color and somewhat gushing words. Azalea took it all in her stride, for she was a social realist and was well aware her fashionable presence and that of her distinguished husband was something of a coup for their hostess. Although perfectly respectable, Mrs. Ellesmere's husband was in trade and not of gentle birth. But the lines between old and new money were blurring, and in any case, Azalea had no patience with such snobbery. Eric, for example, was of old, landed aristocracy, but most of his wealth came from financial and trading ventures. Lawrence Hammond's father had been awarded a knighthood for his services to trade, and his family was accepted by the highest in the land.

She glimpsed Mr. Hammond with a group of young people sitting on a blanket and throwing bread to the ducks. Some older people sat on trestle chairs, some getting quietly intoxicated, others still the center of their circles.

Gunning was sprawled on another blanket beside Lord Darchett and two very young ladies—giggling debutantes by Azalea's guess.

"The dark one is Miss Fenner," Eric murmured in her ear. "And Fenner himself stands with his wife and Verry in the group just behind them."

"I remember them. I wish we had spoken to Griz and Dragan first. How annoying if we ask the same questions. They will suspect something."

"Does that matter? If we frighten them into revealing themselves, I, for one, will be happy."

"And I, now you mention it. Shall we go first then to the Fenner party?"

"If you can stand Gunning's company."

"I might giggle. He is forever in my mind with wet tea leaves running down his neck."

A breath of laughter hissed between Eric's teeth. "That's my girl. Just don't stray from the circle in his company."

They approached the older group first.

"Ah, Trench," Lord Verry greeted them. "Lady Trench, your servant. Are you acquainted with Mr. and Mrs. Crookston?" He introduced Eric as a business associate of himself and Fenner, which Azalea could tell her husband did not like, however true.

After a little polite conversation, Mrs. Fenner was addressed from the nearby blanket by her daughter, who was then also introduced, along with her friend, Miss Jones. And Azalea had the opportunity to sit down with the younger people.

The girls looked awestruck. Gunning appeared wary, but Darchett seemed to have got over his unease of the other night and gallantly presented her with a glass of wine and a plateful of nibbles. Footmen were passing among the various groups around blankets and trestle tables, offering more substantial fare.

Azalea smiled at the tongue-tied young ladies. "So, is this your first Season in London?"

"Yes, my lady," Miss Fenner replied.

"I am not really part of the Season at all," Miss Jones said in a rush. "But Catherine invited me since her sister is indisposed."

"What a good friend you are," Azalea said, struggling for a response to this confidence. "But I hope your sister's indisposition is not serious, Miss Fenner?"

She was sure Miss Fenner actually giggled before covering it with a shaky throat clearing. "I'm glad to say it is not."

"A spot," Miss Jones explained. "On the end of her nose."

Miss Fenner kicked her friend. Lord Darchett grinned openly. Azalea did not glance at Gunning, let alone Eric, who must have overheard.

Instead, keeping her voice as steady as possible, she said lightly, "I *almost* long for those youthful days. At least aging has some benefits. So, will you both be attending Lady Gaveston's ball this evening?"

"I will," Miss Fenner said, then, perhaps for revenge on her sister's behalf, she added, "Miss Jones does not have a suitable gown."

"I wasn't invited," Miss Jones blurted.

"Never mind. It's bound to be a shocking squeeze, though we shall all love it. What has been your favorite party so far, Miss Fenner?"

"My first ball was like a fairytale," Miss Fenner said naïvely. "At Lady Verry's."

"That was the first time I met you and danced with you," Lord Darchett put in, with a quick smile that made Miss Fenner blush.

Azalea gathered that the dance with Darchett was part of the fairytale.

"I don't believe I was at Lady Verry's," Azalea said. "Lady Royston's the other week was special, I think. But I don't recall seeing you there." That at least was true since she didn't recall anything about it.

"Your ladyship had no reason to notice me," Miss Fenner said meekly.

Which meant she had been there and her father, too, no doubt.

"I do also enjoy the theatre very much," Miss Fenner offered, eager to extend the conversation.

Azalea smiled, since it saved her bringing up the subject. "Do you prefer tragedy or comedy? Or opera, perhaps?"

"All of it," Miss Fenner declared. "I love being lost in the story."

"My youngest sister is just like you," Azalea said. "She won't chat during the play or pay attention to fashion or gossip but sits glued to the stage, whatever the noise around her. And I'm not even sure she discriminates between the good and the bad. Why, only the other day, she dragged us to some very pedestrian comedy at Haymarket, and she was riveted. What was it called, Eric?" she called to her husband. "That dull play Griz made us go to?"

Eric obliged with the name before carrying on his conversation.

"There, you see?" Azalea said with amused pride. "My husband remembers everything."

"We saw that, too," Miss Fenner declared.

"Did you like it?"

"Oh yes, though it wasn't, perhaps, very funny."

"I should have thought that a minimum requirement for comedies," Gunning murmured.

"Not necessarily," Darchett argued. "The story could appeal while the humor does not. I presume that is what you meant, Miss Fenner?"

"Indeed," the girl said fervently, with a grateful smile at Darchett.

Azalea was glad and slightly surprised to see him trouble to protect her from so mild a criticism. According to rumor, he was pursuing her for her fortune, encouraged by her father, who wanted the aristocratic connection.

Gunning sneered, excused himself, and got up to wander off toward another group.

Azalea was not sorry to see him go. She turned her attention to Darchett. "You and Mr. Gunning are good friends, I gather?"

Darchett's smile was a little rueful. "We have got up to a lot of mischief together over the years. We were at school together."

"And he saw that same comedy," Miss Fenner said, "for he was your guest, too. He smiled enough at the time."

"Perhaps I did not pay enough attention," Azalea murmured. "I am too easily distracted. At any rate, I look forward to seeing you at Lady Gaveston's this evening."

⸌⸌⸌⸍⸍⸍

"WELL?" ERIC MURMURED as they met during the mingling after luncheon.

"I think it's Gunning," Azalea said triumphantly. "He was in Darchett's box when we were at the theatre, which is in the same passage as ours, only four farther away from the staircase. And Miss Fenner, who is a very useful source of information, told me he was not with them when Darchett saw her and her parents to their carriage."

"And Fenner did not leave her side?"

"She doesn't think so, though, to be honest," Azalea admitted, "she was paying no attention to him. She is much more concerned with Darchett, who seems quite genuinely taken with her, and it was quite hard to get her to talk about anyone else. Did you learn anything interesting?"

"Only that Fenner is not discomposed by my presence or yours. He is a little too loud in associating me with his ventures, but that is to do with business. And he does not like Gunning, thinks he is a bad influence on Darchett."

"Darchett told Gunning off for some mocking comment he made about Miss Fenner's opinions."

"Well, perhaps there is hope for all of them, then. Hammond, how do you do?" he added, and Azalea turned to see Lawrence Hammond approaching them with his amiable smile.

Azalea did not believe for a moment that Mr. Hammond was her blackmailer. For one thing, although he had the right build to match the man Eric had punched in Grosvenor Square, he was much too stately, not to say staid, to be easily imagined climbing in and out of high theatre boxes and sprinting through streets.

And he was, she had always thought, a decent man with a quiet sense of humor. But she went through the motions of trying to discover where he was at the times in question.

"I have not seen you since the Roystons' ball, have I?" she said. "For you were not at Lady Braithwaite's soiree."

"Alas, no, I had to go out of town that day. My father summoned me to Kent. Did I miss anything?"

"A very fine pianist," Eric said. "I trust your father is well?"

"Alarmingly so. His message had sounded urgent, but he only wanted to lecture me on investments, which could easily have been done at any time. Ah, I believe we are moving toward the Exhibition at last! Have you been before, Lady Azalea?"

"Oh yes, we attended the opening, and then we took the children a couple of times, but I have still not seen half of it."

In sprawling groups and couples, the party began to make its way from the river toward the Crystal Palace, so dubbed because it was made mostly of glass and steel, a huge and unique edifice, housing the most diverse exhibits one could imagine.

The building was oddly beautiful, too, in the sunlight, shining and welcoming.

"Lady Trench."

She blinked up at Lord Darchett, realizing she had veered off the path and away from Eric and Hammond.

"My lord."

"I hope I'm not interrupting. You seemed a little lost in your thoughts."

She smiled. "Dazzled by sun on the Crystal Palace! I believe I shall miss it when the Exhibition is closed."

"Indeed. Lady Trench, I wonder if I might have a word?"

"Of course."

He glanced around and lowered his voice. "In private."

Intrigued, she veered further off the path, away from straggling members of their party, although it brought them closer to other people, all swarming toward the Exhibition.

"I wish to apologize," he muttered, "and I really do not wish others to overhear."

Azalea glanced toward Eric, some distance ahead with Hammond and a couple of ladies. But Darchett was young, unthreatening, and not one of their suspects since he was the wrong shape. Moreover, he might well be about to give her the information she needed.

So, she turned her footsteps away from the swarm, toward a little grove of trees.

"You intrigue me," she said when there was no one within hearing distance. "What are you apologizing for?"

"For my behavior at Lady Royston's," he said, low. He took her arm to help her negotiate a rough, muddy patch of grass, and something seemed to connect in her mind like a bolt of lightning. She just didn't know what it was, but it was something to do with the Roystons' ball, a grip on her arm...

She stared at him, convinced suddenly that it was also to do with *him*. Blood began to sing in her ears.

"I should have said it long since," Darchett said, "for I have been ashamed since the incident itself. I had the insolence to speak to you before, when we met in the park, to ensure your discretion over my sins, but that was to miss the point. I apologize for that, too."

He drew a deep breath and blurted. "Lady Trench, you were quite right to slap me. I did not know how to look your husband in the face on Saturday evening, and yet today you are so pleasant to me and kind to Catherine Fenner. I just had to speak. My lady, are you quite well?"

No. No, she wasn't well at all. That same sense of panic she had felt when Gunning had touched her surged once more, and with it came a blast of images. Darchett by her side, the night sky, her hand flying toward his face. And revulsion, terror, blood.

"I want you to know I apologize sincerely and unreservedly…" Darchett's voice meant nothing. It was fading, and she was falling, aware only that hands she did not want anywhere near her were holding her in a frightening grip, and she was alone, fighting them off.

➤➤➤◄◄◄

HAMMOND SEEMED MORE interested in discussing investment, particularly in Trench's housing projects, so it wasn't easy to keep steering him back to where he was and who he had seen on certain evenings over the last two weeks. Azalea was much cleverer and subtler in such matters, but she had wandered off.

A quick glance through the crowds found her with Lord Darchett, moving through a swarm of people.

"There is no room in either of those ventures," Trench said. "But there will be others, and I will certainly call upon you…" Unease twisted through him, for Azalea and Darchett were moving farther away, not just from him and the rest of the Ellesmere party, but from everyone.

And something about her posture, even over that distance, was wrong. And now, too, many people were in the way. He could no longer see her.

"Excuse me," he said abruptly and moved away, striding across people's paths. They kept getting in his way, blocking his view of his wife. Once he glimpsed her looking up at Darchett while the man grasped her arm.

How dare he? Enraged, he broke free of the crowd, aware he was drawing too much attention, but Darchett now clutched Azalea in his arms, and she was lashing out at the startled baron.

Even in his fury, he saw the moment Darchett spotted him.

"It's not what you think!" Darchett cried. "Please, she is not well. Take her!"

Trench almost snatched his wife from the other man. Immediately, she stopped struggling, but her face was white, her eyes wild yet almost unfocused.

"Eric," she whispered, clutching his lapel, pressing against him. "Don't leave me, don't..."

"I won't," he assured her, his voice shaking with mingled fear for her and fury at her attacker.

Darchett blanched and took a hasty step back, though interestingly, he did not try to flee.

"What did you do?" Trench asked between clenched teeth, keeping his voice low for Azalea's benefit, though he did not trouble to disguise the menace of his glare over her head.

"Nothing," Darchett assured him. He looked appalled, hunted. "I tried to apologize to her, and she seemed to faint, only when I caught her, she lashed out at me. I could neither let her fall nor calm her."

Azalea was trembling in Eric's arms, but her eyes seemed to have refocused. "He didn't touch me," she said weakly. "Well, only to hold me up. I was remembering."

Trench swallowed. "Perhaps we should discuss that later. Darchett, drop your coat under that tree so that she can sit for a little."

Obediently, Darchett shrugged out of his coat and spread it on the ground. Trench lowered his wife tenderly to sit and crouched by her side. She seemed reluctant to release his hand, which she clutched in a vise-like grip.

Trench glanced up at the anxious Darchett. "What happened?"

"I thought only to make things better, to do the right thing. I never dreamed it would upset her to this degree that—"

"Tell me," Trench interrupted.

"I was apologizing to her," Darchett said miserably. He glanced around, then dropped to a crouch, too, though keeping Trench between himself and Azalea.

"For?" Trench asked coldly.

Darchett's eyes veered away, then came back to Trench's with conscious courage. "For a stupid wager I made with Gunning, and for acting on it. In truth, I knew neither of us stood a chance with her, but we were drunk, and I'm short of money, as the world knows. So I accepted the bet as to which of us...could..." he swallowed convulsively, "...seduce Lady Trench."

Trench's eyes narrowed in cold, icy fury. "That is the most despicable thing I have ever heard. To even bandy the name of—"

"I know, I know," Darchett said in what appeared to be genuine anguish. "There is no excuse. All I can say in our defense is that at least we had enough decency left to make it private between ourselves. In any case, when I saw Lady Trench leave the supper room, I followed her onto the terrace, managed to detach her from her friends, and tricked her into the secluded little garden, where I tried to kiss her. She slapped my face, quite deservedly, which at least sobered me up. I was already ashamed when she walked away from me."

"Where did I go?" Azalea asked unexpectedly.

Darchett blinked, frowning at her.

"It's hazy in my mind," she said. "I suppose I was enraged. Did I go straight back into the house?"

"No, you walked farther into the garden, which I thought rather magnificent of you. It was I who slunk back into the house. And I have been trying to find a moment to apologize to you ever since. Especially after Gunning told me he had called upon you, as if the wager was still on. I assured him it was not."

Trench met Azalea's gaze. Whatever had happened to her, she now showed no fear of Darchett or any further confusion. Her eyes, in fact, sparkled with speculation.

Trench turned back to Darchett. "Was Gunning really with you on Friday evening?"

Darchett looked surprised. "Yes, at my club. There was a group of us playing cards."

"And he was there all evening?" Trench asked.

"Well, yes, until about midnight when we all went on to see the cockfight." Darchett frowned and scratched his head. "Though he did disappear for a while when I think about it. Probably drank too much, to be honest, but he can't have gone far because he was definitely with us when we left at midnight." He dropped his hand to his knee. "You asked me about that on Saturday, too. Look, we were entirely in the wrong about Lady Trench, and we both know it. We spoke, after you sent Gunning about his business and agreed the wager was canceled. There will be no more."

"Then I think we are even," Azalea said briskly, "since I fainted and panicked over you, and you faced the wrath of my husband."

"You are so kind," Darchett said humbly. "I can't believe we were so vile as to treat you in such a way."

"I would definitely eschew the brandy," Trench drawled. "If not the company you keep."

Azalea took his hand and rose to her feet. He did not release her while Darchett picked up his coat and shook it out.

"I hope there are no mud or grass stains," Azalea said. Trench did not care.

"What is another scold from one's valet? I would let him go if only I could afford to pay him." Realizing, perhaps, that he was babbling, Darchett bit his lip and donned his coat. Then with a deep bow, he muttered, "Forgive me," and marched away.

CHAPTER THIRTEEN

"**W**ELL," AZALEA SAID, taking her husband's arm. "What do you make of *that?*"

"That at least he did not hurt you," Eric said grimly. He paused, his eyes raking her once more. "Did he?"

She shook her head. "No. I do think he was just desperate to apologize."

"In case you dropped a word to Miss Fenner, no doubt."

"Perhaps that had at least something to do with it. But as soon as he took my arm, Eric, *something* frightened me. I *did* start to remember things. I remembered being in the garden with him, slapping his face for trying to touch me, even his ludicrous expression afterward."

"But he implied you walked away as if you *weren't* frightened, leaving him to slink away with his tail between his legs."

"No, I wasn't frightened *then*, and Darchett didn't frighten me this afternoon. Something in my memory did."

He placed his hand over hers on his arm and gripped. "What?"

She squeezed her eyes shut, then shook her head with frustration. "I don't know. I can't remember that. But I can recall fragments of the evening now. Dancing, supper, walking with Darchett in an indulgent kind of way, then slapping him…and then it's blank."

Eric's eyes narrowed. "Then you don't remember if he came after you?"

"I don't *think* he did."

"Come, shall we walk home, or will I send someone for a cab?"

"Oh, no, let's go to the Exhibition. I feel fine now." She smiled. "Actually, I feel wonderful because at least I've started to remember. I don't feel that evening is lost forever. Dragan is right. I just need something to jolt my memory."

"And rest," Eric reminded her.

"Just for an hour," she pleaded. "To show the world that I am well, and you did not feel it necessary to thrash Lord Darchett. Besides, I want to see this bed the children were talking about after you took them to the Exhibition. The one that's attached to an alarm clock and actually throws you out of bed at the required time. And *then* I promise I will rest before the ball."

He hesitated. "You will stay with me while we are in the Exhibition?"

"Yes." God knew it would be no hardship. She wondered if he could sense her genuine pleasure. They began to walk toward the Crystal Palace once more. "Eric?"

"Yes?"

"As soon as you were there, as soon as I recognized your arms, I knew I was safe."

"I should have been there when it mattered," he said bitterly. "With you at the Roystons' ball."

In spite of all the people milling around them, she rested her head against his shoulder. "You are here now."

>>><<<

THE EVENING'S BALL was a grand affair. Azalea's parents, the duke and duchess, no longer attended such events, but a large part of her family was there, including the Monktons, Rosemary and Gordon, Horace, and Forsythe. And, Azalea was glad to see Griz and Dragan, looking carelessly beautiful and causing many heads to turn. Not that Griz would care about such attention, if she even noticed.

But it seemed she did. "Have I a smut on my nose or torn my gown?" she asked Azalea when she had caught up with her.

"No, my dear. You just look beautiful. And you are seen so little in Society that your presence is marked. Your hostess is preening."

Griz looked startled. Then, being Griz, she reverted to the practical. "We need to have a conference. Do you suppose we can find a quiet spot here?"

"Of course," Eric said. He had always been wise in the ways of secluded spaces at parties. "But not immediately. We have to dance a little first. Perhaps you would do me the honor, Lady Grizelda?"

"Thank you," Griz said, with something like relief. She did not like dancing with strangers.

"Will people find it odd if we dance together, too?" Dragan asked Azalea.

One couldn't always tell when he was joking. "Not unless you stand on my toes. Besides, I want to talk to you."

"Then, please, dance with me," he invited.

He was a good dancer, graceful like Eric, and he led well. If there was a little more drama to his waltz, well, he could be forgiven as a Hungarian.

"I started to remember things today," she murmured and told him about the incident with Lord Darchett.

He listened carefully. "Then it was his touching you that set off both the memory and the sense of panic?"

"Yes, I think so. But I remembered that *particular* sense of panic. I felt it before when Gunning lunged at me, only not so badly."

"Because Trench interrupted sooner?"

"Perhaps," she admitted.

"But you do not appear panicked now," he observed, moving his hand at her waist to show what he meant.

"Because dancing is different," she said at once, then frowned. "Or because the man is."

"Perhaps we should talk more about that later. Have you remembered any more since this afternoon?"

"No, I don't think so."

"It will come," Dragan said comfortingly.

She hoped so, and yet... How horrible would the elusive memory be if it had already caused her to forget so much?

〉〉〉〈〈〈

THE BALLROOM OPENED onto a small terrace, from which narrow steps led down to an unlit patch of garden. Neither seemed ideal for a private discussion in ballgowns. So Trench found a small room next to the supper room, where some dishes were already being set out.

The smaller room was not lit for use, but Trench doubted his hosts would either notice or object if he lit one lamp and closed the door.

The four slipped away from the ballroom after the third dance of the evening, and when they were in Trench's chosen room, he closed the door.

"I think Gunning is the blackmailer," Azalea said, almost at once. "He could easily have been in Grosvenor Square on Friday evening, for he was not with Darchett at his club the whole time. He could have left and come back. He is the right size and shape. He bears a grudge against us, and he is short of money."

"But we can't rule out Fenner, either," Trench pointed out.

"But why would he?" Azalea demanded. "What does he gain from it?"

Trench shrugged. "Trying to distract me, perhaps, from what he's up to with my building projects."

"But the blackmailer is assuming I will not tell you!"

"Well, I think that cat's out of that bag since Grosvenor Square. Perhaps he doesn't want you luring Darchett away from his daughter.

After all, Darchett was paying you considerable attention at the Roystons' ball. He had a wager with Gunning," he flung at Griz and Dragan, "as to who could seduce my wife."

"It would be pathetic if it weren't so distasteful," Azalea remarked. She eyed her sister and then Dragan. "You're not saying much."

"Trying to fit what you found out into what we did," Griz replied.

"Oh, I had another thought," Azalea said, "about the Royston children." She frowned. "And one of their footmen is missing, though I have no idea how that could fit into any of this."

"Ah, you discovered the footman, did you?" Griz said, apparently pleased. "He was stepping out with Franny the housemaid, who is terrified of something but seems to have no idea where he is. And there was a stain of something very like blood on the garden wall. What?" she asked, frowning as she noticed Azalea and Trench both staring at her.

"It probably has nothing to do with either the blackmail or your memories," Dragan added. "But I am trying to find him."

"Lady Royston's servants seem to be quite unaware of anything odd happening at the ball," Griz continued. "Though Franny might know something, she is saying nothing, and according to the other servants is merely distressed over Ned's disappearance. Ned being the footman, who is tall and strong."

"I see," Azalea said. "We just seem to collect more oddities and suspects rather than finding the *one*. What do you think of the Royston offspring, Griz? You are closer in age to them than I."

"Not that much closer. Beresford is only eighteen, and I never had much to do with him. I would say he's a bit of a smirking bully, and Geraldine was petulant and attention-seeking. But people grow up."

"I think, perhaps I should call on Lady Royston and inquire after Geraldine, who is supposed to be unwell," Azalea said thoughtfully.

"If we consider alliances," Trench said, "like the Royston children, what about Gunning and Darchett together? Or Fenner and Verry?"

Azalea groaned. "Then we've ruled out no one! But surely Darchett could not be involved? He was so open and apologetic this afternoon, I really did believe him."

"Perhaps he's sorry for the blackmail as well as the wager," Trench said sardonically. "I don't see any signs of regret in Gunning."

"Gunning," Dragan offered, "was ill in the cloakroom of Darchett's club while you were in Grosvenor Square."

Trench raised his eyebrows. "So, neither he nor Darchett can vouch for each other that evening after all?"

"No, but others can. Darchett did not leave the table for longer than a few minutes. Though he could still be working with Gunning, who could possibly have slipped out of the club and back without anyone noticing."

"You don't think it's likely," Azalea guessed, sighing. "I want it to be him because I don't like him."

"We can still search his rooms," Griz offered.

"Grizelda!" Azalea exclaimed, appalled.

"Well, how else do you find evidence?" Griz demanded. "And a set of rooms is easier to search than an entire house."

"Dragan, you won't let her do such a thing?" Azalea appealed.

"I would rather do it myself, but a girl is less suspicious. She would go in disguise," Dragan explained.

Seldom had Trench seen his wife lost for words. "But what if she is caught?" Azalea managed at last.

"I shall keep watch for her."

"No," Azalea said firmly.

Griz stuck out her tongue and smiled.

Trench laughed. "You won't change those two. Let them do it their way. And you and I shall call on the Roystons."

Azalea jumped to her feet, pacing the room. "I feel we are going in circles," she fumed. "And no further forward."

"That isn't true," Trench said. "We are immeasurably further forward. Who knows? We may even have finished with the whole mess in time to go to Trenchard next week, after all."

She paused, glancing at him and a funny little smile dawned in her eyes. "I hope so."

"In the meantime," Trench said, rising, "since there is little more to do tonight, I suggest we simply enjoy the ball. Shall we give the world something to gossip about, Zalea, and actually dance with each other?"

Her full lips curved. "Why not?" she said carelessly.

But Trench was not fooled. He saw the faint rise in her color, sensed her pleasure, both in his asking and in the anticipation of the dance. As they led the way back to the ballroom for the supper dance, her fingers lay lightly on his arm. They both greeted passing acquaintances with a nod or a few words, apparently ignoring each other except for that formal touch on his sleeve. But awareness sizzled between them, perhaps because they were so close to admitting in public what they had avoided in private.

That they longed for each other.

He understood his own yearning only too well. He just hoped he was right that she felt it, too. Ignoring the rest of the guests, who could snicker and mock if they wished, he walked onto the dance floor, proud to have her as his partner and as excited about taking her in his arms as if he were a boy in the throes of first love.

But he was not a boy. He had the grace to bow and smile and to hold her with the respect due to the situation. And then the dance began, wrapping them in anonymity.

"How long has it been," he asked softly, "since we last danced together?"

"In public? Eight years."

"Before we were married," he observed. "And in private?"

"Three."

"You have been counting."

"I remember it distinctly because it was the evening we decided to go to London for the Season."

"It was the first time I had seen you smile for months," he recalled.

She smiled. "It reminded me of fun and gaiety and love."

"In London."

"Why not? London was where I first fell in love with you."

"Were you not still in love with me?"

Her smile faded but did not die. There was sadness in her eyes that made him ache, and he spun her, taking her by surprise to cover the fact she might not answer. But her feet were still nimble. She didn't miss a step but followed with incomparable grace.

"Of course I was," she said. "It was a dark time, and you were my only light. I don't know where I would have been if you had not been there. If you had given up and left me, even for a month, a week. You were always there. I always relied on your being there. And then one day, maybe a year ago, now, I realized that you were not really there at all."

"You did not need me anymore," he said with difficulty.

"I always needed you. My fear was—is—that you no longer need me. Or want me."

He stepped forward, and she back in perfect time, and yet as they turned, she was somehow closer in his arms. Had he achieved that, or had she?

"Oh, I want you," he said huskily. "I never stopped wanting you, and I never will."

Her beautiful eyes darkened. He could feel the heat on her silken skin, where his fingers reached up over the low-cut gown to her naked back. She shivered, and they smiled together. She had always had that ability to dazzle and smolder at the same time. "Prove it."

He smiled. How could he not?

"Prove it," she repeated. Her head lifted, bringing her face just a little nearer and allowing him a stronger, more alluring waft of her scent. "I dare you," she whispered. "Take me to bed tonight. I am your wife."

He bent his face even closer. How tempting to kiss her, here, in front of everyone. "You are my wife," he agreed softly. "And I can take you anywhere I choose."

And with that, he danced her off the floor and whirled out of the open terrace door.

CHAPTER FOURTEEN

Y OU ARE MY *wife. And I can take you anywhere I choose.* His words inflamed her body even before her mind had quite grasped them, and by then, somehow, she was on the terrace with the cool night breeze on her cheeks.

She had been more than flirting. She had been seducing for later, and she should have known he would more than accept the challenge.

Without releasing her, he cast a quick glance around the terrace to make sure they were alone, and then he sank his mouth into hers in the most sensual kiss she could ever recall. Fire and glorious weakness and utter happiness...

"We choose," she whispered against his lips.

His mouth stilled, drew back a fraction, though she could still feel the heat of his breath. "What?"

"You can take me anywhere *we* choose," she clarified.

His breath hissed out in something close to laughter. "I always grant the right of veto. What about here?"

"We would be seen!"

"Very true." He walked her backward to a narrow set of steps, where the light barely penetrated and swung her down a couple of steps. At the same time, his mouth came down on hers again, and his hand swept over her breast in a tender, arousing caress.

"Here?" he mumbled between kisses.

Oh God, yes, no more waiting... "Still...too...danger...ous..." she managed, grasping on to her failing common sense.

Again, she was swung through the air, and this time, she landed in almost complete darkness, with her skirts bunched between them and his arms hard around her.

"Here," he growled, and kissed her breathless while she clung to his neck and tugged at his hair in need.

Her heart thundered as she realized his hands were busy at the fastening of her gown. *Oh, my, he's really going to do it. We're really going to…*

Her gown hung around her elbows and billowed about her legs and his. Until he swept it down over her hands and simply lifted her out of it. She had never thought to be quite so glad that its wide petticoats were sewn into the gown. Clad only in her shift, stays, and stockings, she stumbled back against the wall, still holding desperately onto him. She swept her hands down his back and around, trying to reach the fastening of his trousers while his hands stroked her hips and thighs as though recalling every contour.

He was hard and more than ready in her hand. Triumph only added to her urgency. And then she gasped aloud as his caressing fingers glided inward toward the fire between her thighs, and he uttered a wild, breathless groan, quickly smothered in her mouth as he nudged against her and drove home.

Oh, God, thank you…

But this was like no other loving. Even in the early days, before and after their wedding, there had been an unhurried grace and care in his every caress. This was quick and wild, the pleasure relentless and so blindingly sharp that she would have collapsed had he not been holding her up and following her hard over the edge of bliss.

His breath rasped into her mouth as she kissed him, shuddering. Every inch of her trembled with wonder. She hadn't known she could reach such joy so quickly. She hadn't known he could.

"Forgive me," he whispered, "if I was rough. I have been patient too long."

"So have I," she breathed, and she felt the smile on his lips as he kissed her deeply. From upstairs in the ballroom, the stately waltz music continued.

He lifted her again, and though she didn't know how he could see, she landed in the center of her discarded gown. Somehow, he found the open neck and drew it upward, helping her find the armholes.

While he fastened the back of her gown, they heard voices above them.

"My lord, I should not be out here alone with you." Surely that quick, nervous voice belonged to Miss Fenner?

"One kiss," said a male, husky voice. *Darchett?*

Eric kissed Azalea's nape, and she moved her head in pleasure, aroused all over again. But he stepped away, adjusting his clothing.

"Now we can go back inside," Darchett said on the terrace above, and Miss Fenner gave a pleased little giggle. "It is time for supper."

The music had come to a close. Azalea ran a hand through her husband's wild hair, combing it into some semblance of order, then made sure his necktie and collar were respectable. He caught a few locks of her hair and wound them round pins already there.

"It needs work," he murmured and led her out into the dim light from the terrace, where he checked it was empty before dusting down her skirts with his hands. She liked that, too.

"The ballroom should clear, and we can use the cloakrooms there before we go up to supper," she said, lifting her skirts to climb the narrow steps.

"What an excellent planner you are."

She caught his hand and glanced up at him. "I didn't plan this."

For an instant, his eyes were serious. "Do you regret it?"

"Never."

A warm smile curved his lips. "Then let us go and brazen it out like an old married couple perfectly used to copulating outside ballrooms."

A shock of laughter took her by surprise. "Well, we are now," she said, taking his arm. And oddly, as they strolled across the terrace and into the emptying ballroom, she felt no embarrassment at all, just a certain smug triumph.

"And when we go home," he said in her ear, "we'll see if we can't make the pleasure last a little longer."

This time, she definitely blushed.

⋙✳⋘

SINCE GRIZ AND Dragan had walked round from Half Moon Street, Azalea offered them a seat in the Trench carriage to go home.

The rest of the ball had been curiously fun, eating, talking, dancing in the warm glow caused by what she had just done with Eric. She felt very contented and pleased with herself—like the cat who got the cream.

"I think," Dragan said to Eric, "you might want to look into the work currently being done on your building sites. The firm you contracted is the same as was involved in Fenner and Verry's previous projects. There seems a shortage of materials being ordered for the money they've drawn. I need to get a look at their accounts to be sure, but if I were you, I'd send your architect round to see what they're doing."

Eric didn't seem surprised. "I will. My solicitor's already looking into how we can eject one or both of them from the partnership. What do you think is going on?"

"Much as you suspected," Dragan replied. "I think the builder is cutting costs on foundation, water supply, drainage, load-bearing walls. I suspect he'll take the money for the original specification and split the difference with Fenner and possibly Verry."

"And our building will be no better than the slum it replaces." Eric's frown cleared. "But that is a worry for tomorrow. Thanks, Tizsa."

"How did you come to be involved with these people?" Azalea asked him.

"Impatience," Eric said ruefully. "I was looking for quick investment in order to get started. I knew Verry socially, was glad enough to take his money, and he brought Fenner with him. I ignored the rumors. But it seems our contract is already broken. I shall start again."

"Will you lose much?" Dragan asked.

"Not enough to matter if I act quickly."

Something was nagging at Azalea's mind as the carriage stopped to let Griz and Dragan alight. Something about a contract. Only as the horses started forward once more did she realize why it bothered her.

"I still don't know what I did," she blurted.

"When?" Eric asked.

"When I wrote that letter," she said, distraught once more. "When I was at the Roystons. I knew from the moment I first read the blackmail letter that any reconciliation...any *mending* between us would have to wait until we knew..."

He took her hand in his firm, warm clasp. "Knew what?" he asked gently.

"Whether or not I betrayed you." She forced the words out, yet her fingers clung to his fiercely.

"You didn't."

"Oh, Eric, we don't *know* that!"

"I know you. If someone tricked you or forced you into anything, whether in word or deed, that, too, will be added to the reckoning."

She stared into his face. "You would forgive me?"

"There would be nothing to forgive."

"But if I'm guilty...of *something*, you might regret that, Eric, regret what we did this evening. I was right about keeping some distance between us until—"

"No," he interrupted, unexpectedly fierce, as indeed he had been during the delicious incident she referred to. "That isn't how marriage works. We are partners."

"So are you and Fenner."

He blinked, catching her train of thought. "You and I are not a business transaction. We are *life* partners, and we will go forward together, Azalea. These bizarre events have given us the kick we needed, and I, for one, will not lose it. I will not waste another day, another hour of loving you. We will deal with this together."

Enchanted, she could only gaze at him in wonder as the horses came to a halt once more, and he handed her down from the carriage. A little buzz of happiness seemed to surround her as she walked inside with him. Her husband.

"Are you tired?" he asked.

She shook her head. "No. I should be. But I feel I could dance for another three hours or run across fields like a child." She halted at his bedchamber door, her heart beating loudly. "If you are not tired either..." Her voice broke, and she finished huskily, "you could come to my room."

His fingers brushed her cheek. In the dim light, his eyes were warm and clouded, but his free hand was already reaching for the door. She tried to smile, though the disappointment was heavy. She still had the evening. And tomorrow...

"Mine is closer." The door gave under his hand, and before she had understood his meaning, she was whisked inside. "I've grown to hate this room," he said softly, taking her in his arms. "I think it's time we created some pleasanter—much, much pleasanter—memories here."

She smiled, lifting her face for his kiss. "What an excellent idea."

TRENCH WOKE TO the sound of his bedchamber door opening and hastily closing again, as Ford no doubt spotted his master was not alone and retreated. They had not even bothered to close the bed curtains.

Trench smiled and stretched like a large, contented cat. His fingers encountered soft hair on the pillow.

In truth, he was almost surprised to find her still here. The night had been memorable, not just for the wild and hasty interlude at the ball but for the much longer, sweeter loving in the dawn light. It had felt like a new beginning. A long, hot beginning of sensual delights. He had almost forgotten the way her skin seemed to ripple in response to his every caress, her open, generous passion, her joyful smile as she shuddered and trembled in the throes of climax...and her tender triumph as she brought him to his.

The bedclothes were rumpled, barely covering her nakedness. His arousal grew. Though he knew she needed to sleep, he could not resist just one butterfly caress from her lips to the base of her throat.

She sighed in her sleep, but an instant later, her eyes opened, and she caught his hand, sliding it to her breast. And so, although he had meant to rise, he loved her again.

In the end, it was almost midday before they rose and moved to her sitting room to enjoy coffee and toast in fresh surroundings.

"Although I certainly look more favorably upon that bedroom than I used to," he observed.

Morris left them to privacy, and Trench rather enjoyed the domesticity of being handed coffee and offered toast by his wife. He was even prepared to take his mesmerized gaze off her for long enough to read his post in a lazy, contented kind of way.

On the other side of the small, intimate table, Azalea picked up her own little pile of post and shuffled the letters. And then they fell from her grasp onto her plate.

Eric glanced up, an amused quip forming on his lips—until he saw her expression. She was gazing down at the top letter, which was unopened.

"Every time," she said unsteadily. "Every time I start to believe all will be well—" She broke off, swiping the letter onto the floor with unusual violence.

"All *will* be well," Trench said firmly. But he rose and picked up the rejected letter, placing it in the middle of the table before he sat back down. An uneasy suspicion had formed. "How does this offend?"

"It's from *him*," she said with loathing. "The blackmailer. I recognize his writing."

"Then he is giving us another clue as to his identity. Do you want me to open it?"

Her gaze flickered to his face, then back to the offending letter, which she snatched up and tore open in one disgusted movement. She scanned it. Then her lips twisted, and she passed it wordlessly across the table.

My lady.

Although you have not played fair with me (involving your husband after I expressly forbade it), I believe you have at least paid a fair price for your incriminating letters. Therefore, I will return it to you this evening (Tuesday) at No 70 the mews behind Berkley Square. Be there, alone, without your husband, at ten o'clock, with a mere five hundred pounds, and I will return the letters to you. Our game will then be over.

However, should you involve your husband or anyone else, I can promise you only misery such as you have never dreamed.

I trust this will be our last communication on any subject.

"Do you?" Trench murmured. "Well, I really don't think it will be." He tossed the letter on the table and reached for his coffee.

Azalea said hopelessly. "What shall we do?"

"*I* shall keep the assignation. Without any money whatsoever. And we shall see who gets the better of that tussle. We are already agreed we can stop him publishing anywhere that really matters, and if he does publish some rag or other, well, I'm not sure I care a great deal when you and I know the truth. Now, what was on our agenda for today?"

She stared at him, almost angered by his carelessness. Then, slow-ly, her expression began to lighten. "We are going to call on the Roystons, and hopefully meet their children."

"And the maid who was stepping out with the missing footman," Trench added.

"Yes, that is odd, too."

"And tonight, we should discover who this opportunist is."

She picked up the letter and reread it. This time, she sounded al-most gloating as she said, "You gave him a fright in Grosvenor Square. That is why he's calling off the blackmail, with one last money-grab, giving us no further reason to pursue him. Otherwise, he would be trying to milk me for years." She frowned. "You know, I cannot really believe the Royston children could be involved in something like this. I don't *know* anyone quite that nasty."

"Apparently," Trench said, "you do."

She frowned again in fresh anxiety. "You can't go alone. I think we should all be there, even if only hiding, ready to step in and help you capture him."

"Hmm. Well, I'll not deny Tizsa will be a useful ally. He was a soldier, after all. But I would be happier with you and Griz safe at home."

"If you imagine Griz will sit tamely at home during such an excit-ing event, you are delusional. And I believe, for once, she will be in the right of it. Besides, what if he is watching the place and sees you turn up instead of me? He needs only to walk away, and we still won't know who he is or solve the mystery of the wretched letters."

Privately, Trench acknowledged the truth of that, and it worried him. For it went entirely against the grain to allow her to walk in to meet such a villain alone. Perhaps a little more ingenuity was called for.

"After we've been to the Roystons'," he said, laying down his cup and reaching for the toast, "I think we should call in on the Tizsas."

CHAPTER FIFTEEN

N O HOSTESS WAS ever "not at home" to Lord and Lady Trench, so Azalea was not surprised to be immediately admitted to the Roystons' house and welcomed by their butler.

While depositing outer garments, Eric exchanged some half-jocular horse-racing tips with the butler, and Azalea wandered further toward the stairs, looking about her.

A maid scuttled through the green, baize door from the servants' quarters and hurried across the hall before she caught sight of Azalea and stopped dead. Even over the yards between them, Azalea could see the blood drain from the girl's face. She looked terrified.

In quick concern, Azalea took a step toward her, and the girl hurried over, clearly meaning to speak to her.

"This way, my lady, my lord," a footman said.

Azalea hesitated, but the maid veered away, rushing into the nearest room as if that had always been her destination. Perhaps it had.

Reluctantly, Azalea let her go and accompanied Eric and the footman upstairs to Lady Royston's drawing room. However, the maid's startled face stayed with her, and with a jolt, she realized why.

I've seen her before! From the window, hanging around Mount Street, near Trench House. She had almost gone down the area steps. Azalea had imagined she was looking for work, but perhaps… Had she spoken to this girl the night of the Roystons' ball? Did she know something?

Azalea dredged her memory, for many small details had come to her since the incident with Lord Darchett. She remembered arriving at the house with her brother Forsythe, who almost immediately deserted her in pursuit of some long-suffering young lady. She remembered speaking to various people and even dancing. She recalled the faces of several servants who had taken her cloak and presented her with champagne. But she couldn't remember that particular maid, except in Mount Street.

They were fortunate enough to find Lord and Lady Royston both in the drawing room where, Azalea suspected, Royston had been reading his sullen son a severe lecture. At the footman's announcement, he broke off abruptly, smiling a jovial welcome to his guests.

"Well, well, what a pleasure, my lady! How do you do, Trench?"

While his parents greeted them, young Beresford showed a tendency to gawp at Azalea. And when introduced—or at least reintroduced—he turned bright red and uttered something incoherent. He might have been overawed and tongue-tied. Azalea did have that effect on some young men. Or he might have been embarrassed at discovering his victim in his mother's drawing room.

"Just been trying to drum into the cub how important it is to study," Royston said to Trench. "He's going up to Oxford this year but seems more interested in chasing the petticoats at Covent Garden."

Lady Royston kept smiling and pretended not to hear. So did Azalea.

"And how is Geraldine?" Azalea asked, taking the seat offered her. "She was not well when I spoke to you last. Is she recovering?"

"She seems quite well, now. Thank you for asking after her! Oh, Beresford, ring the bell and ask them to send Geraldine down to meet her ladyship. It will do her no harm," the proud mother told Azalea, "to see how far she is from the grace and maturity of a fashionable lady."

"Oh well," Azalea said, "one cannot expect young debutantes to behave quite like old married women."

"Oh, no, but it gives her something to *aspire* to. For *next* Season."

It was not the most scintillating half-hour Azalea had ever spent. Between the gawping Beresford and the awed but petulant Geraldine, she found it unusually difficult to make conversation. Eventually, she hit on the idea of asking the girl if she played the pianoforte.

"Indeed, she does," Lady Royston beamed. "That is, she is coming along. Play something for Lady Trench, my love."

With much better grace, Geraldine jumped up and went to the piano in the window. "Beresford, turn the music for me," she ordered.

Beresford opened his mouth, clearly about to deliver a blistering refusal when he caught his father's choleric eye and closed it again. He rose to his feet. "Very well. But only if I might perform the same service for Lady Trench afterward."

Azalea only laughed and crossed her fingers in her skirts, hoping Geraldine was not too awful.

In fact, she played surprisingly well and, moreover, lost her vaguely resentful look while she did so. Azalea had no qualms about asking for another piece.

Undercover of the music, and Eric's casual voice asking about Beresford's outings during the last week, Azalea asked her hostess about her missing footman.

Lady Royston sighed. "Still missing. But I have asked your brother-in-law, Mr. Tizsa, to help find him. Such a useful man to know!"

"Indeed, I believe it is a *profession* in much demand," Azalea said with delicate emphasis, just to remind her ladyship that Dragan should be paid for his discreet services.

They could not, in all civility, linger very much longer after Geraldine's second piece came to an end. And if Azalea had not learned much from the visit, she still hoped to run into the maid again downstairs.

She was in luck. The girl must have been lurking in wait, for she all but ran toward Azalea with her wrap. Her huge, anxious eyes gazed up in something very like fright. "My lady, have you heard anything?" she almost whispered.

Azalea took the wrap. "About what?"

The girl's eyes widened impossibly. "About *him*. Ned."

"No," Azalea said, honestly enough. "Have you?"

"No, thank God."

"Franny," the butler reproved, making the girl jump.

She sketched a hasty curtsey. "I'll never forget what you did. Thank you."

Azalea almost reached out to call her back. *What did I do?* But impossible to ask here with the butler and the footman hovering. Guests did not converse with the maids in hallways. So, with an odd mixture of frustration and excitement, she nodded graciously and left the house.

"That girl *knows* something," she almost hissed at Eric as she took his arm, and they turned their footsteps toward Half Moon Street.

"Geraldine?"

"Franny, the maid. She thanked me, said she'd never forget what I did. And asked if I'd heard anything about Ned, who is the missing footman."

"Did she say why you might have?"

"No, but she seemed pleased I hadn't. That footman is connected with our problem, you know. I just can't work out how."

"Perhaps he is the blackmailer," Eric said thoughtfully. "We have not even looked at the servants of our suspects."

"Well, servants don't have a great deal of freedom of movement," Azalea argued. "Unless they disappear from their employers, of course." She frowned. "Or are acting for their employers. Drat it all, Eric, the waters are muddied even further. Did you learn anything useful?"

"No, except that I doubt very much Beresford was the person I punched in Grosvenor Square. He's too...insubstantial."

"And his face isn't marked. I think we have to rule out the Royston children. Neither of them seem malicious, just discontented."

"Never mind," Eric murmured, glancing up at the sky. "It's a lovely day for a walk."

Distracted, Azalea smiled at him instead and squeezed his arm. "So it is."

➤➤➤❮❮❮

THEY DISCOVERED GRIZ in her garden, sitting in the sunshine and casually throwing sticks for Vicky, the little Italian greyhound, to bring back to her. Azalea didn't notice Dragan at first, but he sat on the ground at Grizelda's feet, his back against her legs, while he gazed over several pieces of paper and occasionally made a brief mark in his ubiquitous notebook.

It was an idyllic scene. Even yesterday, it might have caused Azalea a hint of painful jealousy amongst her pleasure in her sister's deserved contentment. Today, with her own growing happiness glowing about her, she felt merely loathe to interrupt them with the ugliness of blackmail.

It was Vicky who noticed them first, though the game was clearly too important to do more than glance at them and wag her skinny tail even more enthusiastically. At least that made Griz look up and smile.

"Aha. You've come for a conference," she said. "Good timing, for Emmie will bring tea soon."

Dragan laid aside his notebook and set trestle chairs for his guests before resuming his position at his wife's feet without any embarrassment. Nor did Griz appear to mind.

"I got into Gunning's rooms," she confided, much like a mischievous child confessing it had managed to raid the biscuit tin. "Disguised as one of his ladybirds."

"He must have a very relaxed landlady," Eric said, amused.

"Landlord," Griz corrected. "A retired gentleman's gentleman, who winked at me and told me not to rush, for His Nibs would be back within the hour."

"How," Azalea asked, distracted by her sister's workaday gown and spectacles, "did you manage to disguise yourself as—er—a ladybird?"

"Emmie altered a horrid, pink, frilly gown Mama made me wear once when I was fifteen. I knew it would come in useful one day. And it did, with a cheap matching umbrella and pink flowers in my old bonnet. I kept my spectacles in my reticule and batted my eyelashes, so I could hardly find my way upstairs to his rooms."

Azalea smothered a snort of laughter. "Did you find anything?"

"Nothing incriminating," Griz said, sounding disappointed, "but I did steal a note that he must have left for his landlord one day. We're comparing it to your blackmail letter."

"Ah, well, we have another of those," Eric murmured, delving into his pocket.

Dragan glanced up, frowning, and took it from him, while Griz read it over his shoulder.

"*It*," he pounced, pointing at the tiny word. "He says letters, plural, at the beginning, then says he will return *it*."

"We thought it just a mistake," Azalea said.

"It probably is, though it may stem from the fact that there *is* only one letter."

They all thought about that for a moment. "I'm not sure that's any better," Azalea said at last.

"But it might be more believable that you forgot one letter."

Azalea wasn't sure believable was good in that case, either. Neither, she suspected, was Eric, who swiftly moved on.

"Is that Gunning's note?" he said, nodding to the scrap of paper on Dragan's lap. "It looks to be a completely different hand."

"It does," Dragan agreed. "But it's always possible the blackmailer has enough sense to disguise his writing. In which case, there might be little things to give him away—distinctive loops or tails they forget to disguise sometimes and match with their usual writing."

"And are there any such giveaways?" Azalea asked.

Griz took the stick from Vicky's mouth and threw it again.

"Not that I have discovered," Dragan admitted. "I don't think it's Gunning. And Griz was pretty thorough in her search, including under loose floorboards and the mattress. There were no stolen letters. And besides, I think Gunning is too...*entitled* to bother hiding such things."

"You're probably right," Eric said. He pointed a toe at the other documents scattered around Dragan. "What are these?"

"Samples of Darchett's writing, Fenner's, Royston's, and Lawrence Hammond's."

Azalea stared at him. A breath of admiring laughter hissed between Eric's teeth.

"Where," Azalea asked faintly, "did you get those?"

"Various places," Dragan replied "There are no obvious matches, but I'm still looking. What do you plan to do about this?" He tapped the newest blackmail epistle.

"We haven't decided yet," Eric said restlessly. "Originally, I thought of going instead of Azalea and capturing our blackmailer. But as Azalea pointed out, he could easily see it was me and just not meet me. In which case, we might have lost our last chance to catch him."

Emmie appeared then with a tea tray and extra cups for the guests. The scones were still warm. Vicky was banished to lie down with her stick several feet away.

Dragan buttered a scone and took a huge bite of it, while Griz passed around cups of tea. "What," he said when he could speak again, "if we start early? Watch him watching us?"

"You mean hide early in the vicinity and wait for him to arrive?" Eric said thoughtfully.

"Azalea would still need to meet him," Dragan said, "but as soon as there is any exchange, we can pounce on him. In fact," he added, gathering up his papers and getting to his feet, "why don't we go and reconnoiter now? Spy out the lie of the land and make plans accordingly?"

"We're coming, too," Griz announced. "Vicky needs a walk."

"No, she doesn't," Dragan argued. "She's been running round the garden for hours. Besides, ladies in the mews would cause notice, even if our man doesn't happen to be there at the time. And, for his benefit, when you arrive this evening, you have to be looking for the right place, not marching right up to a familiar stable."

"Hmm, perhaps," Griz said grudgingly.

"Who lives in Berkley Square?" Azalea asked suddenly. "Who owns the mews in question?"

"We can find out about the mews," Dragan said.

"But none of our suspects actually live in Berkley Square," Eric said in frustration.

Dragan threw his arm around Grizelda's shoulder and kissed her on the lips without embarrassment. "He doesn't have to live there, just stand still long enough for us to catch him."

Eric rose to follow him. "That is true." Passing behind Azalea's chair, he brushed his knuckles lightly across the back of her neck, which made her shiver. A strange, warm shiver of pleasure. She twisted her head to smile up at him. And then he was on his way.

"It's an odd thing," Griz observed after some minutes of thoughtful silence, "but since all this blackmail nonsense began, you actually seem happier."

"Did I seem *un*happy before?" Azalea asked lightly.

"No," Griz admitted, then, "Yes, in comparison. I didn't notice." She glanced at her with a faint, self-deprecating smile. "I always thought you had everything. Everything you always wanted, all that Their Graces wanted for you. You were the shining example held up to Rosemary, Athena, and me. I didn't want the same things as you, and yet I envied you."

"Did you?" Had she known that? Certainly, there had been odd, ungracious moments that Azalea had pushed aside as just another of her little sister's eccentricities. "Why? Because I found Eric when I was so young?"

Griz shook her head. "No. No, I think… I always thought everything was easy for you. Approval, social success, adulation, wealthy, adoring husband and children. Your husband isn't even boring."

"Should he be?" Azalea asked, amused. "Am I?"

"Of course not," Griz said impatiently. "I am observant by nature, but I never truly observed you. It wasn't always easy, was it?"

Azalea looked away, conscious of a lump in her throat. She shook her head. "Social success comes at a price. Oh, I enjoyed it and took every advantage, but at the beginning, I also had to face the spite of envious girls, the tricks of some of their mothers. That hurt. And I had to learn how to deal with over-amorous and entitled men. That does make one cynical and perhaps a little hard."

She drew in her breath, giving herself time to clamp her mouth shut and stop talking. But it seemed she couldn't. "I told you that after Lizzie, I was…sad. I had no reason to be, and yet I could not pull myself out of it. I really thought I must be insane." She waved that aside with one, impatient hand. "Eric was wonderful, although I knew he was so worried. So I was inspired to make a push. I think I went through the motions of being happy again until I actually *was*. Only… I don't know. I shone too brightly, lost part of myself in the pretense, and Eric and I…"

She broke off. "It is better now. We're doing this together, and he trusts me more than I trust myself. I don't just *know* I love him. I feel it again. I remember why. And I'm talking nonsense, aren't I?"

"No." A fleeting smile crossed Grizelda's face. "You were always my favorite sibling. Shall we go inside?"

✦✦✦✦✦

THE MEWS IN question ran the whole length of Berkley Square from Charles Street, with another mews lane leading off it to the left. Both lanes were wider than most and busy. Trench and Tizsa found Number 70 near the end, which opened onto Charles Street. Unlike most, the door was closed, and Trench could see no movement.

All around them were grooms and coachmen, the rumble of carriages and horses clopping along the cobbles. Some of the stables were being mucked out; at others, horses were being groomed. Outside a few stable boys lounged, talking or playing push penny against a wall.

Tizsa wandered over to the nearest such group. "Is Number 70 free to rent, do you know? My friend is looking for extra stable space."

"Been empty for at least two years," said a snubbed nosed stable boy. "Belongs to the old lady in Charles Street. She might rent it to him."

"Nah," said another. "My guv'nor tried to get it off her to keep the missus's new carriage in, but she weren't having it. Dog-in-the-manger like. She got no use for it now—don't keep a carriage no more—but won't let anyone else have it neither."

"Wouldn't let *your* guv'nor have it," the first stable boy argued with a grin. "She probably don't like him any more than you do. Might let *him* have it, though."

"I wonder if she'd let me see inside it," Trench mused. "Just to see if it suits before I call on her."

"The stable door ain't locked," said the second boy. "So help yourself. Won't be able to see the room above, though."

Under the amused eye of the stablemen, Trench and Tizsa wandered back to Number 70 and pushed open the door.

There wasn't much to see. It still smelled vaguely of horses, overlaid with damp. A small pile of old straw lay in one narrow stall. Some empty hooks for tack lined the walls. To one side of the door stood an old stool with a grubby cushion. The hairs of some long-gone horse still clung to it.

Despite the stable's proximity to people and passing horses, it felt isolated and cold. Trench didn't like to think of Azalea coming in here alone in the dark.

"At least there aren't many places for him to lie in wait unseen," he said grimly.

"Nor for us," Dragan murmured, wandering in and out of the stalls.

Trench moved toward the inner door at the back of the stable. Presumably, it led upstairs to the living quarters, so when he pushed it, he didn't expect it to open.

It did.

He found himself in a tiny, gloomy hallway. A short, narrow passage on the right led into what must have been the carriage house. Another door, directly opposite the one he'd just come through, proved to be locked. This would be the door to the living quarters upstairs.

"I could hide here," Trench said as he sensed Tizsa standing behind him.

"So could he."

"Then I could step back into the carriage house out of his way."

"If he doesn't look there, too. Wait. Stand behind me."

Obediently, Trench swapped places with Tizsa, who was drawing from his pocket a piece of wire and something that looked like a surgeon's instrument. Before his startled gaze, Tizsa crouched down and actually began picking the lock.

"I'm not even going to ask how you learned such a trick."

"I once shared a prison cell with a thief. He imparted only a fraction of his knowledge before we escaped." The lock clicked. Tizsa turned the handle and pushed. "But it was enough for simple work like this."

Over Dragan's shoulder, Trench glimpsed a bare staircase leading upward.

"We'll leave this door unlocked," Tizsa said, closing it and straightening. "That way, if our man does look around, you can back onto the stairs until he retreats again."

"I suppose he will assume the stair door is locked and inaccessible."

"Let's hope so."

As they walked back through the empty stable, Tizsa murmured, "I suppose you will want to be in here. Griz and I will find another spot outside to wait. That way, we should be able to trap him."

They emerged into daylight. Trench waved to the watching stable lads, who suddenly jumped to their feet as a carriage began to approach from the other end of the lane.

"There will be people around all the time," Trench murmured. "I can't see where you and Griz could remain inconspicuous. The chances are our man would recognize Griz, at least, and bolt."

"Amorous servants lurking in the darkness are not so unusual."

Trench regarded him with amusement. "I suppose you should be allowed some compensation for a long wait."

CHAPTER SIXTEEN

T RENCH STOOD IN his wife's sitting room, anxious to be gone and yet agonizingly reluctant to leave her.

"You mustn't even glance at it in more than passing," he said. "But I shall be behind the door at the back of the stable, just waiting to grab him."

"I know," Azalea pointed out from the armchair. "You told me."

He smiled ruefully. "I'm repeating myself. The truth is, I hate the thought of you walking in there alone."

"I shan't be alone. You will be there, and Dragan and Griz will follow."

"Unfortunately, I can't tell you whether he will be waiting for you in the stable or come in after you."

She rose and went to him, winding both arms around his neck. "I know that, too, and it doesn't really matter."

He held her tightly against him, pressing his cheek to hers, loving her scent and her softness. Anxiety threatened to become a pain under which he could not function.

"I wish there were another way," he whispered.

"There isn't," she said, taking his face between her hands. "I will be careful, as should you. And Griz and Dragan. But I'm not afraid. And in a few hours, it will all be over."

He kissed her fiercely, so moved by her instant response that he nearly forgot he was meant to be leaving.

He tore himself free, mocking himself for thinking of a soldier going into battle. In reality, he felt more like a wife must watching her husband march off to danger. He didn't allow himself to look back.

The mews behind Berkley Square were much quieter as he strolled along at about seven that evening. He did indeed glimpse an amorous couple of servants, who were not Griz and Tizsa, and who ignored him.

He adjusted his speed to allow the carriage ahead of him to turn into Charles Street, then, he slipped through the door into the stable of Number 70. Closing it behind him, he raised his fists, ready for an attack.

None came. The stable was as empty as before. Knowing he would have a long and uncomfortable wait for ten o'clock, he considered the musty cushion on the stool beside him. God knew what was living in it. With regret, he walked past it, to the inner door, checked the equally empty carriage house, then closed the door to the stable.

His little hallway was gloomy even at this time of the early evening, so he opened the stair door to let in a smidgeon of light from above and sat down on the first step. Taking from his pocket a small book and the sandwiches made by his puzzled cook, he settled down to assuage his hunger and wait.

AT ABOUT NINE o'clock, Griz and Dragan took up position at the mews gate nearest Charles Street. She wore the old, grey gown she generally wore for her charity work in St. Giles, together with the white cap of a maidservant. Reluctantly, since she wanted to see what was going on, she removed her spectacles. They made her too recognizable. And besides, they had a tendency to steam up when kissing.

Kissing Dragan had never been a hardship. Nor was being held in his arms and nuzzling his neck. Her only worry was that she might get distracted from the main purpose and miss their quarry or, worse, the arrival of Azalea.

"Perhaps he's here already," she murmured into his ear.

"It doesn't matter if he is. Trench is there, too."

"I hope he can keep still."

"He is a still man. We've been here long enough. Slip through the gate into the garden, and we'll emerge a little further along."

They did that a few times. Sometimes Griz took off the cap. Sometimes, Dragan wore a hat and a bright kerchief. Servants rarely had the time to spend an hour kissing in an alley, so for the benefit of any watchers, they wished to appear as several different couples in different places, from all of which, they could see the door to the Number 70 stable.

After about twenty minutes, when they had just arrived at their third spot on the other side of the lane, Dragan breathed, "Look."

She peered over his shoulder, too short-sighted to see more than a blurry shape in the gloom. He walked quickly from the Charles Street direction, a tall thin man with a top hat pulled low on his head. He seemed to be contemplating his feet rather than the way ahead, so she doubted even Dragan could see his features.

In any case, he veered suddenly right and in the stable door of Number 70.

FROM HIS STEP, Trench heard the door creak. He stood, hastily and soundlessly, closing the stair door. Then he crouched, putting his eye to the keyhole, and listened.

It was too early to be Azalea.

The footsteps were heavy but unhurried, easily heard echoing about the empty stable two doors away. This was the blackmailer, making certain all was well.

After a little, the door between the tiny hallway and the stable opened. Trench held perfectly still as a tall, thin figure walked past his keyhole. He couldn't see the man's face, but he heard him moving to the carriage house, pausing and returning, again flashing past Trench's keyhole. He closed the stable door behind him.

As the footsteps receded, Trench realized his hands were clenched. How badly he wanted to knock down, to seriously hurt this man who dared to threaten his wife. Whoever he was. From what he had made out, the blackmailer's coat had been well made and well-fitting.

The outer door creaked again and closed in silence.

Trench left the stairs, closing the door behind him, and leaned against the wall of the little hallway to wait.

"HE'S COMING OUT," Dragan murmured.

They were hiding now behind a tree at the bottom of one of the gardens behind the stable buildings. It was almost dark, so Griz could only hope they were not visible. With her spectacles back on, she peered around the tree and saw the hatted figure walk back the way he had come.

Only he didn't walk as far as Charles Street. He stepped smartly through a garden gate and vanished.

"He's hiding, watching for Zalea," Griz breathed. "Is that good?"

"I don't know. I'm just glad Trench didn't leap out and murder him."

Which gave Griz another bad moment. "What if *he* murdered Eric?"

"No," Dragan murmured confidently. "He is determined, not stupid."

At TWENTY MINUTES to ten, Azalea, dressed in an ivory silk evening gown with matching wrap, walked down the front steps of Trench House and into her waiting carriage. Bravado had chosen her gown. She did not plan to linger for long in a grubby stable, and she wanted the blackmailer to know he was despised and she unafraid.

"Berkley Square," she said pleasantly to the coachman on her way inside.

During the short journey, she sat bolt upright. Her heart beat too fast, and there was a twist of nervousness in her stomach. But she was glad to find she was not afraid. She wanted this man taken, and her letters returned, and she had the feeling that once they were, everything would come back to her about why she had written them and what had happened at the Roystons' ball.

"Where in the square, my lady?" the coachman asked through the speaking tube.

The carriage had just turned into Berkley Square and was heading toward the corner of Hill Street. No vehicles had stopped on this side of the square, although a hackney passed them at a fast trot, and another carriage was moving along the far side.

"Here is fine," she replied. "Wait, if you please. I should not be long."

The coachman's boy jumped down as soon as the carriage halted and let down the steps for her. Since she had brought no escort or footmen, they must have assumed she was visiting one of the elegant houses on the square. She didn't disabuse them. She just hoped that if they noticed her vanishing into Charles Street, they did not try to follow.

She hoped, too, that they would see nothing odd in her unhooking the dainty lantern from inside the coach and taking it with her.

She heard no following footsteps, saw no dangers in the well-lit square or in Charles Street as she hastened toward the mews lane. The mews were lit, too, some by lanterns outside the stables.

She knew from what Eric had told her that Number 70 was on her right, but she looked at both sides as she proceeded, past a couple of high garden gates and mews buildings, until she found the right one. Every hair on the back of her neck stood up. She felt a thousand unseen eyes watching her. Further down the lane, a groom was soothing a restless horse, trying to persuade it into its stable.

Mentally squaring her already rigid shoulders, Azalea turned toward the stable door and pushed it open.

She lifted her lantern, glad and slightly surprised to find that her hand did not shake. The stalls were empty, like the rest of the dingy room. The only furniture seemed to be a stool beside the door topped by a dingy cushion. But she did not feel like sitting down.

She walked forward, wanting to call out, *Eric, are you there?* But she did not dare. The blackmailer could be hiding behind that door at the back, or he could be watching her from outside the open door onto the lane.

She walked slowly, circling the room, listening intently. *Come, you worm, hurry up and show your cowardly face...*

The quick footfall from the lane almost took her by surprise.

She spun around to face the open door.

The silhouette of a man in a top hat stood there, the flaring light of his lantern distorting what was visible of his features above the scarf which covered his mouth. Clearly, he still didn't wish to be recognized.

Bad luck.

The man stepped inside. One thing she and the others had feared was that he would bolt the door from the inside, but he did not even trouble to close it. He just stepped inside and bent to set down his lantern on the floor.

She held out her hand. "My letters."

He didn't speak, just picked up the musty cushion from the stool and began to walk toward her. Her heart leapt. Had he hidden the letters inside the cushion?

Certainly, he was holding it to his chest as though it were precious. But his other hand was also delving deep into his coat pocket. The oddity brought a frown to her brow.

"Zalea, down!" Eric's voice cried suddenly. Uncomprehendingly. For he had burst through the door behind her and crashed into her, just as a muffled crack echoed and a sudden, searing pain pierced her arm.

A patch of scarlet bloomed on the sleeve of her ivory gown, growing... and mingling suddenly with another image in her mind—of blood spilling over a knife that slid so easily into human flesh. Pain and noise engulfed her, and the world tilted and darkened.

TRENCH ONLY REALIZED what was happening when it was too late.

Through the same crack in the door that he had seen Azalea arrive and walk around, he also saw the tall, thin figure of the blackmailer enter and pick up the cushion. It was such an odd gesture that Trench watched the man's other hand, realizing he was using the cushion to hide what he was doing, what he was taking from his pocket. The letter?

A weapon.

He didn't see it, not then, but understanding flashed through his mind, even as he burst into the stable in a desperate bid to save his wife.

The blackmailer had had enough. Since Trench had punched him in Grosvenor Square, he'd known the game was over. He had even said so. He was now tidying loose ends with a cushion to muffle the sound of his shot.

Although Trench shouted to her to get down, she didn't understand what he meant. How could she? He heard the muffled crack just as he snatched her, throwing her down on the floor with him. She emitted a funny cry of surprise, but it wasn't at his rough handling. He had already seen her arm jerk, and the dark spot of scarlet on her pristine sleeve was already visible when her lantern fell and went out.

The blackmailer dropped the cushion and fled.

Trench barely noticed, for he was cradling his wife in his arms.

"Azalea," he whispered in shock. "Azalea, for God's sake, speak to me…"

Her eyelids fluttered. Her staring eyes came into focus, blinking. "Eric, what happened?" She winced, pain flooding her eyes.

"He shot you," Eric said grimly, ripping the sleeve of her gown to see the damage.

"Trench?" That was Tizsa's voice rushing toward them. He must have snatched up the lantern from the door, bringing it nearer. "He's bolted, right—Dear God, what's happened?"

"He shot her," Eric said again, the words still sounding unreal, unfathomable.

Dragan pushed him aside. "I'm a doctor, remember? Go after him."

"No!" Eric objected. "My wife is—"

"*My* wife has gone in pursuit!" Dragan said savagely. "I'll look after yours if you look after mine."

Unexpectedly, a hoarse laugh broke from Azalea. "Do it, Eric, it makes sense, and I won't be shot for nothing."

Feeling as if he was being torn in two, Trench leapt to his feet and across the stable. He felt like screaming.

"Which way?" he flung over his shoulder.

"Charles Street," Tizsa barked, already wiping blood from Azalea's arm.

Trench bolted outside, more than half of his mind still on his wife, so that he almost ran into two horses pulling a carriage along the mews at a fast clip. Forced into awareness of his surroundings, Trench veered back into the wall and began to run once more.

Beyond the carriage, he could see the figure of a woman standing at the end of the mews and looking to her left along Charles Street.

"Griz?" he demanded when he caught up with her. By then, she had turned left into Charles Street and was walking briskly past the first of the terraced townhouses. "Where is he?"

"He vanished again," she muttered in frustration. "How does he keep doing that?"

"He doesn't. He simply goes somewhere else. Where can he have gone this time?"

"He definitely came this way," Griz said. "Turned left from the mews, but by the time I got here, there was no one."

Trench, still wrenched apart by competing urges to return to his injured wife and to lay savage hands on the man responsible, stopped under the street lamp. "How far could he have gone in the time it took you to get here? Could he have got as far as Berkley Square? Crossed to the other side of the road?"

She shook her head impatiently. "No, I'd have seen him. I'm sure he couldn't have got further than one of these first two houses." Neither had gardens to hide in or a route to the back except through the house. "I heard a sound, like a door closing," she recalled with sudden excitement, and she began to stride onward. "It can't have been the first house, or I'd surely have seen the movement. I think it's the second, *this* one."

"Could he have gone down the area steps?" Trench demanded.

"I heard no sounds of that. Only swift, *level* footsteps."

And both front doors opened off the street. As Griz strode up to the second front door, he caught her arm. "Wait there," he said grimly. "The man is armed." He hadn't even told her that her sister was shot. *Don't think of that. Catch the bastard!*

His hands were clenched and ready as soon as he struck the knocker. It felt tarnished under his fingers. The paint on the door was peeling in places.

Hurried footsteps sounded inside, and the door opened little more than a crack.

"Yes?" said a breathless maid. Her gaze widened as it swept over him, and she added, "Sir. Her ladyship is indisposed and won't be receiving callers for a few days. Besides," she added severely, "it's late to be calling uninvited."

"You are entirely right," Trench allowed. "Perhaps I have the wrong house? I was looking for whoever owns the empty mews building—Number 70, just around there. And I thought I saw someone from there come in here."

She regarded him as though he were mad. "No one's come in here at all since seven o'clock! Good evening, sir." And she closed the door in his face.

"That went well," Griz observed. "Well, we're not going to catch him there tonight, short of breaking in or fetching the police, which I doubt would work... Eric, where are you going?" She had to run to keep up with him, for he was already striding back toward the mews.

"I should have told you," he said abruptly, without slowing. "He shot Azalea."

CHAPTER SEVENTEEN

"HE SHOT ME?" Azalea repeated to Dragan. Her mind felt oddly sluggish. *It must be the shock.* "With a cushion?"

"*Through* the cushion to muffle the noise. It upset his aim, thank God, for the bullet seems only to have grazed you. Still, I think it will need a stitch or two. For now, I'm going to bind it."

Fascinated, she watched him make a pad of his handkerchief and some other fabric that looked like her embroidered petticoat.

"It is," he said apologetically, reading her thoughts.

She smiled faintly. *Don't think about the blood.* He pressed the pad firmly to her wound, causing her to hiss with pain. In truth, her arm throbbed like the devil. One-handed, he removed his necktie, and with swift efficiency, bound the dressing tightly in place.

"Where is Eric?" she demanded.

"He went after Griz. And our man. I'm sorry. We were still yards away when we heard Trench shout, and he bolted out the door. I never expected he would leave again so quickly, never imagined *anything* like this."

"He tried to kill me," Azalea said, understanding at last. She stared at Dragan's grim, anguished face, impossibly handsome in the lantern's glow. "I won't die, will I?"

"No. No, you won't die. But I won't say the same for the monster who did it. If ever I've seen murder in a man's eyes, it was in your husband's when he left. Is your carriage in Berkley Square, as we agreed?"

She nodded.

Dragan took a flask from his pocket and unscrewed the stopper. "Take a mouthful of this."

She swallowed obediently. "Brandy."

"Good for shock and dulls the pain."

"Not sure you have enough for that," she said shakily, handing him back the flask.

"No, I'll give you something better for the pain once you are safely home. Can you stand?" He rose carefully, helping her with his arm at her waist.

She seemed to be shaking. Her legs were certainly wobbly, but they proved to be capable of carrying her out of the musty stable into the mews.

Dragan released her but pulled her good arm through his. "Hold on to me," he commanded. "And tell me if you feel faint again."

As she concentrated on putting one foot in front of the other, she was aware of Dragan looking constantly around them, to each side and behind. He tensed as two figures appeared at the end of the mews, then relaxed as they broke into a run. Eric and Griz.

She had never seen Eric frightened before. He had risked his life to save hers and stared down at her with such stark fear. That fear was still there now, mixed with hope and relief that she was walking, and something else so turbulent that it brought tears to her own eyes.

She leaned forward and against his chest, and though she hadn't felt Dragan release her, it was Eric's strong arms that closed around her. And despite the huge mess that still surrounded their lives, despite the spectacular failure of their plan tonight, she knew everything would be well in the end.

"WE NEED TO think about involving the police," Griz said more than an hour later.

She, Dragan, and Eric were all perched on Azalea's bed, while Azalea, herself, after the torture of having her wound thoroughly cleaned, stitched, anointed, and rebandaged, reclined against the pillows, wide awake and eager to talk.

"We can *think* about them," Eric agreed, "but I'm not sure I want them blundering about in this. Unless you think we could persuade them to search that house in Charles Street?"

"Unlikely," Griz said, producing a calling card from the pocket of her gown. "I've just discovered who it belongs to—by rifling among the truly spectacular number of cards you have in your desk drawer, Zalea."

She reached forward and placed the card on the covers over Azalea's lap.

"Lady Darchett," Azalea read, astonished. "Darchett's mother! But that means…" She frowned. "What does that mean? Aren't we already sure Darchett is not our blackmailer? Are we wrong?"

"He didn't seem much like Darchett to me," Eric said. "And it is certainly not his mother!"

Azalea frowned. "Couldn't it be? After all, it was a woman dressed as a man who killed poor Nancy Barrow."

"This is different," Griz said. "She made a young, elegant, slightly effeminate man. This person, our blackmailer, runs like a man. And he is far too tall to be any woman that I know."

"Lady Darchett is not as tall as me," Azalea remembered reluctantly. "And unless she is pretending, she is somewhat too frail."

"One of her servants?" Eric wondered.

"One who has a key to the front door," Griz reminded him.

"We don't even know if she has a butler or any other manservants," Eric said discontentedly. "We only saw that maid who opened the door. I think we need to speak to Darchett, quite urgently."

"I think you're right," Dragan agreed. "Does he live with his mother?"

"Actually, no," Eric said, thoughtfully scratching one ear. "He lives in the official residence in Grafton Square."

"Which must be one reason he is short of money," Griz observed. "The upkeep of two establishments in London must cost a fortune."

"The outside of the Charles Street house did not look to be in good condition," Eric agreed.

"Perhaps we should also consider Gunning?" Dragan said abruptly. "The chances are he's been in that house with Darchett, would know about the empty mews building and its unlocked stable door."

"And I wouldn't put it past him to purloin Darchett's key," Azalea commented. She tried to concentrate on the figure she had glimpsed in Grosvenor Square and again in the stable, picking up the cushion. "*Could* that have been Gunning?"

They all thought about it.

"I wouldn't rule him out," Eric said.

"Neither would I," said Dragan and rose to his feet. "You should sleep now, Azalea. The laudanum will help. I've left some," he added to Eric, "in case she needs it during the night. I'll be back in the morning to make sure the wound is still clean. Feel free to call in your own doctor, of course." His lips quirked. "I'm still not qualified."

"Nor will be if you never have time to study," Azalea commented, holding up her good hand. "Thank you, Dragan. And Griz."

"We *will* sort it out," Griz assured her. After an instant hesitation, she bent and hugged her fiercely. "Don't frighten me like that again."

"I'll come down with you," Eric said, rising from the bed.

Considering someone had tried to kill her and she had a throbbing gunshot wound in her arm, Azalea felt curiously contented. That would be the laudanum, she supposed, combined with relief at the ending of the added pain Dragan had inflicted with his cleaning and stitching. And if she was honest, it had felt good to have everyone sitting so casually around her bed with the sort of camaraderie that never seemed possible after childhood.

What evil monster lurked beneath the hat and scarf? Could it have been Gunning? His image swam into her mind, young, good-looking, entitled. She remembered him covered in tea and smiled. She remembered him at the Ellesmeres' al fresco, still more resentful of the result than ashamed of his own conduct.

And yet, she had given him no real reason to hope for an assignation. For the first time, she remembered dancing with him at the Roystons' ball. She had felt slightly dazed, very distant. She had smiled at most things he'd said because she hadn't really taken them in, hadn't known what to reply.

Except he had asked once, "May I call on you?"

She had smiled at that, too, and his eyes had sparked. She had felt dizzier, turning in the waltz so often.

"Alone?" he had asked.

And she had laughed. "Probably."

Why had she said that? What had she meant? She had felt despairing, afraid, appalled, but she couldn't remember why.

Eric came back into the room, and her heart lifted once more. "I've been remembering," she said at once. She didn't want to forget again, and she didn't want to hide anything from him ever again.

While she told him about dancing with Gunning, he took off his coat and sat on the bed once more, kicking off his shoes and unwinding his necktie.

"The rest will come," he said gently. "You're remembering more every day." He touched her cheek. "And you know, I think Tizsa is right. You are so afraid of what it is you've forgotten that your mind doesn't want to remember. You mustn't be afraid, Zalea. Whatever it is, you are alive, and I love you. And we'll face it together."

She caught his hand, carrying it to her cheek.

After a moment, she said, "Will you stay with me tonight?"

"I was going to sleep in my room to be sure of not hurting you by accident."

"You won't hurt me. I'd...I'd rather you were here. If you don't mind."

He smiled. "Mind? Zalea, there's nowhere I would rather be. Ever."

And so, as her eyelids finally began to give in to exhaustion and the drug, Eric removed the rest of his clothes and climbed into bed beside her good arm. He lay curled against her, her hand clasped in his, his face against her hair. Solid, physical, and at this moment, her whole world.

⇒⇒⇒⤜⤜⤜

SHE WOKE TO pain in her arm, and Eric's low voice in the sitting room, answered by Morris. Daylight seeped through the bed curtains. Eric's quick, firm footsteps came closer, and the curtains were drawn back.

"Good morning," she greeted him, struggling to sit.

At once, he was there, easing her up by the waist and placing pillows to support her. "Morris has brought you coffee and toast." He placed his hand on her forehead.

"Excellent. I don't feel fevered, Eric. I'm fine."

"You seem to be, but we'll await Tizsa's recommendation before you get up." He brought a tray from the table and placed it over her knees, then poured a cup of coffee for each of them before perching once more on the side of the bed.

She could easily get used to seeing him there again.

"Also, the weather is dull and rainy," he said with unusual satisfaction, "so there is less incentive for you to go out. Which brings me to more important matters."

"What?" Azalea asked, sipping her coffee with relish.

"Someone tried to kill you."

"I know. I was there."

"The point being, whoever he is, he will know soon enough that he failed."

She paused in the act of selecting a piece of toast. Her gaze flew up to his. "You think he will try again?"

"It's possible."

"Oh, no, surely he will be so appalled by you and Griz chasing him that he will give up? He cannot hope to get away with such a murder, for there would be a *huge* noise."

"That did not appear to deter him last night. He must have assumed there would be nothing connecting him to your shooting. No one should have seen him entering Lady Darchett's house. In any case, what we *don't* want, is him thinking up new ways to try again. So, for that reason, as well as for the sake of your wound, you should not go out for the next few days."

She stared at him. "Not go out? But I have to visit Lady Darchett! You can come with me," she offered generously.

"Thank you. I believe I prefer to take Grizelda."

She eyed him. "No, you don't."

"In this case, I do."

"But I shall be bored! Why don't we wait to hear what Dragan says when he has looked at the wound again?"

"You are a stubborn wife."

"I am."

"I haven't agreed," he pointed out. "In fact, we were talking last night when I showed Griz and Dragan out, and we think it might be a good idea to pretend you are—"

"Not dead!" she exclaimed. "Think of my poor parents!"

"Not quite dead," he said apologetically. "But if we put it around that you are—er... at death's door, then our man is less likely to come after you. It should give us some time to act."

"You're still not thinking of my poor parents!"

He shrugged impatiently. "I can have a word with them, assure them you only have a cold or something, while to everyone else, we'll insist you are terribly ill."

"No, no, that's a dreadful idea! *Augusta* will come."

"My dear wife, when have I ever given you cause to believe that I am not capable of dealing with Augusta?"

"Never," she admitted, drinking more coffee. "It is I who cannot deal with her."

She munched her toast in silence, glaring at her husband, who seemed blissfully unaware of her threatening stare. Only she knew he was not.

Fortunately, a distraction occurred, in the shape of the children tumbling into her room and jumping on the bed. Eric was quick, scooping them up in each arm.

"One moment, wriggling creatures," he said severely. "Mama has a very sore arm—*that* arm—so you must not touch it under any circumstances. You must be gentle around her. No bouncing, bumping, or over-enthusiastic hugs until the arm is better. Promise?"

They had both stopped wriggling.

"Promise," Michael said at once.

"Pomiss," Lizzie agreed.

Eric set them down on the bed, on Azalea's good side, and she hugged each of them with her right arm.

For the next half hour, while she finished her coffee and toast, the children helped distract her from the pain and the lurking unease that the blackmailer who had tried to kill her could indeed try again.

What if he attacked her when she was with the children? What if he came into the house, endangered all her family and servants, and the new governess who was due to begin tomorrow? She had almost forgotten about her in the chaos of the past few days.

Morris stuck her head around the door. "Lady Grizelda and Mr. Tisza want to come up, and Elsie wants to know if she should take the children?"

"Oh, yes, send them up," Azalea said eagerly. She glanced uneasily at the children. "And children, you should go to Elsie now. Uncle Dragan is going to help my sore arm get better. Oh Morris!" she added as the maid shooed the laughing children toward the sitting room. "Tell Elsie to keep the children indoors today."

"Don't think that will be much hardship," Morris muttered, glancing at the rain-soaked windows.

Griz had raindrops on her spectacles, though she immediately took them off to dry and polish them on her handkerchief.

Azalea wondered if it was to avoid looking at her, afraid to find her worse. "I feel perfectly well this morning," she said brightly. "The arm hurts, but less, I think, than last night. And I have taken no more laudanum."

Dragan set down his medical bag and asked Eric to send for boiled water. "The cleaner we keep the wound," he told Azalea, "the less chance of infection and fever, and the quicker you will heal."

Unwinding the bandage, he inspected his neat handiwork. He did not look displeased, though he bathed it carefully when the clean water arrived, reanointed it, and put on a fresh dressing.

"Will I do?" Azalea asked lightly.

"So far," Dragan said with a warning glance at her as he tied off the bandage.

"We have lots to tell you," Griz burst out, "if you're up to it, Zalea?"

"More than up to it," Azalea assured her. "Tell me instantly."

"Dragan has found the Roystons' missing footman!"

"I *might* have found him," Dragan corrected. "Since Griz found traces of blood on the garden wall, it seemed likely someone was injured, so I've been asking around the physicians of my acquaintance if they've treated any injured young men called Ned for severe cuts. It was a bit of a long shot, you might say, but I finally met someone this morning who had. I have an address for this Ned—at least if he is still alive. The physician has not seen him since."

"Well, the Roystons will be pleased you've located him," Eric remarked. "Do we know, then, if his vanishing has anything to do with us?"

"Not yet, but two such dramatic events as a severe injury and Azalea's loss of memory are unlikely to be a coincidence."

Azalea's stomach was uneasy. "What was his injury? What happened to him?"

"He told this doctor he was in a fight while drunk. He had a knife wound to the stomach."

A knife sliding through flesh like jelly. Blood, pools of blood...

"The wound was infected," Dragan said. "Although it had begun to heal. The doctor had to open it again, to remove—Azalea, is this distressing you? Shall I go on?"

Eric took her hand in a strong clasp, and she clung to him, banishing the image of blood and the sickening sliding of a knife.

"Yes," she said determinedly.

Dragan kept his gaze on her. "I mean to go there now and see if this is definitely our missing Ned."

"Franny, the maid, seems glad he's gone," Azalea contributed. "I'm not sure he should be restored to the Roystons."

Dragan shrugged. "We won't know until we talk to him. I can look at his wound, too, see if I agree with my colleague that it was inflicted around the time of the Roystons' ball."

Azalea swallowed, afraid to let in the bloody image. She let it come, anyway, sickening and frightening. But that was all there was, no before, no after, no context.

"I need to come with you," she blurted.

"Zalea, we need the blackmailer to think you are at death's door," Eric reminded her.

"Then I'll go in disguise, like Griz does, but I think I have to see this man." And she told them about the disconnected image in her mind, of blood spilling over a knife.

"So you might know what happened to him," Dragan said slowly. "And through him, remember what happened to you. With luck, it will bring us closer to the blackmailer's identity, too."

"But is she up to going out?" Griz asked Dragan worriedly.

"In the carriage, perhaps. I'll make you a sling to keep your arm still, and we can smuggle you in and out of the house. Trench?"

"Please, Eric," she whispered, squeezing his hand.

His lips curved. "You are very brave," he said unexpectedly.

She didn't feel brave, but she liked to hear him say so.

CHAPTER EIGHTEEN

M ORRIS WAS SUMMONED and instructed to help and to pretend to everyone else that her mistress was unwell. While the maid helped Azalea to dress, Eric swept the others downstairs to inform the housekeeper and butler that Lady Trench was too ill to receive callers today.

By the time a veiled Azalea descended the deserted stairs—without Morris's help—the carriage had been summoned.

"It's a little fine for Cheapside," Eric said cheerfully, "but it hardly matters since it's Mayfair we're hiding from."

"The carriage is too fine?" Azalea asked. "Or my understated dress? I assure you, this is quite the dullest gown I possess, and the skirts are no wider than Grizelda's."

"It doesn't matter what you wear," Griz said, "except for the veil. Shall we go?"

Traveling east along the side of the Thames was not a route Azalea had often taken. Nor was the maze of narrow streets behind the Cheapside warehouses. Bad smells of rotting meat and sewers invaded the carriage, even before the door was opened. A vague fog seemed to hang in the air, heavy and threatening.

"Is John armed?" Azalea asked nervously about the coachman.

"Yes," Eric said easily, lifting her down by the waist.

Dragan led the way as though he knew where he was going. He did a lot of work among the poor, Azalea knew, with patients who could not pay. She did not envy him coming here or other such places. She could only pity those forced to live in such squalor.

For the first time, as she entered a filthy tenement building that smelled of urine and stale cabbage, she began to seriously understand Dragan's radical politics. Only birth decreed she and Eric lived in elegant mansions, while the young couple with a baby she glimpsed through an open door lived in one tiny room and coughed their lungs up.

Picking up her skirts, which would probably need burned when she got home, she followed Dragan and Griz up a narrow stone staircase, where young children sat sullenly staring at them.

Dragan paused on the first landing and knocked loudly. There seemed to be a lot of shouting beyond the door, two women screeching at each other, so perhaps it was not surprising no one answered. Dragan knocked again and kept it up until the door suddenly flew open, and a blowsy woman said, "What?" in a thoroughly annoyed tone of voice.

She wore a dirty bodice with her hair spilling from its pins, and she reeked of some low form of alcohol. Gin?

"We're looking for Ned," Dragan said politely. "If you please."

The woman's jaw dropped, and she emitted a cackle. "If I please, eh? And if I don't?"

"I'm a doctor."

Her eyes narrowed and darted beyond him. "Are you? And the toffs behind you?"

"Charitable ladies and gentlemen," Dragan said smoothly. "May I see Ned?"

"If your charity covers his friends."

Eric reached around Dragan and handed a coin to the woman, who looked awed and stepped back out of the way.

"Got any more of them?" she asked hopefully.

"Once we've seen Ned, I might find another," Eric said.

"He's in there." She pointed to a door with a boot-sized hole in it. "Ain't fevered no more, but he's weak as a kitten, thank Gawd. Here! You ain't the same doctor who was here last time!" she appeared to recall suddenly.

"No," Dragan agreed, walking purposefully across the cluttered room to the broken door. "I'm a colleague."

Azalea followed, glad of Eric at her back, for another hungry-looking couple sat at the other side of the room, their expressions speculative.

Dragan knocked on the broken door and opened it. Only after a quick glance inside, did he open the door wider and step in. "Ned, I believe? My colleague Dr. Lyle asked me to call in on you. I hope you don't mind my...observers."

"We're charitable," Griz assured him.

As they all filed into the small room with peeling wallpaper and a heavy stench of human waste, Azalea saw the patient, thin and pale, on his bed. She couldn't recall ever seeing him at the Roystons, but then, he was hardly at his best.

"Come to prod me some more?" Ned said aggressively.

"Just to look," Dragan soothed. "I understand you almost died."

"Felt like it," the patient said, hauling himself into a sitting position, which seemed to exhaust him. "This won't cost me, will it?"

"Not this time," Dragan assured him. "This was from a nasty fight, I understand. May I see the wound? My friends will turn their backs."

But Ned was paying no attention. He had caught sight of Azalea and was staring at her, not with the awed admiration she was used to, but with abject terror. Her heart bumped.

"You brought *her*?" he exclaimed. "Get out! Get out right now and take that *bitch* with you!"

Shocked, Azalea could only stare at him, uncomprehending. No one had ever spoken to her like that. She had never given them cause to.

Eric eased past her and loomed over the injured man. "You will keep a civil tongue in your head," he said softly. "Being injured and weak will not save you indefinitely."

The man was a bully. Franny, the maid, supposed to be his sweetheart, was afraid of him. But perhaps the habits of service were hard to break. He knew a nobleman when one confronted him. His eyes slid away, avoiding both Eric and Azalea.

"Oh, I'm mum," he muttered. "Always the way of it. No one cares that it was she put me here. She sticks me, and *I* have to run!"

Blood seemed to rush into her head, and she reached out blindly for support. A knife, sliding into flesh, blood spilling over the knife and the hand that held it.

The hand was hers.

She reeled. Eric's arm was there, catching her, drawing her across the squalid room to the window. Griz was on her other side, anxious or appalled or both, opening the grimy window to let her breathe.

She heard a hoarse moan escape her throat and tried to swallow it back with the memories forcing themselves to the front of her mind.

Something, the windowsill, was at her hips, supporting her. Dear God, she did not want to know this, she did not want to remember, for it would ruin everything, her life, Eric's, the children's. And Eric would look at her not with love but...

He was looking at her now, steadily, urgently. "Let it come, Zalea. Let it come."

She gasped and clutched his arm, and then it flooded her, harsh, dreadful, unchangeable.

Behind the wall of Eric and Griz, she could hear the faint murmur of Dragan's voice and Ned's response. The world seemed red, terrifying, and yet she had to tell.

"I told you about Darchett at the ball, enticing me outside. When I dismissed him, I walked farther into the ornamental garden to prove, I think, that he was nothing to me, that I would go on taking the air until I chose to return to the ballroom. I walked right through the garden, almost to the path that runs between it and the kitchen garden. And just at the edge, I came across..."

Her breath seemed to get away from her. Her fingers tightened convulsively on Eric's hand, but he didn't wince or draw it away. Not yet.

"I saw *him*." She nodded toward the man in the bed, whom she could not see and did not want to. But God help her, she did know him. "He was with a girl. A maid. It was Franny. He was holding her in one arm, so that at first, I thought they were lovers, and I meant to slip back the way I had come without disturbing them. It was none of my business how Lady Royston's servants conducted themselves. But then, I heard her *whimper*."

The mists in her mind cleared as all the outrage she had felt then flooded back. "He was not caressing her. He was *pinching* her, cruelly hard, squeezing her skin, *torturing* her, defying her to cry out. And she didn't, beyond that whimper. But for that, he punched her in the stomach, not once, but twice. She fell to her knees, her mouth open in pain, silently retching, weeping.

"I could not allow it," she whispered. "I did not even think about it but went charging toward them. Neither of them saw me at first—I was in the darker part of the garden, while they stood in the light flooding from the open kitchen door, and a lantern hung on the wall. I saw his face, and it was terrifying. I have never seen an expression so...*gloating*, and yet so angry. He was furious with her, felt quite justified in what he was doing, and yet I could see he enjoyed her pain and his power over her.

"And then I saw something gleam in his hand. A kitchen knife. He had been grasping it all the time he held her. When she fell, it dangled by his side. He crouched down, seizing a handful of her cap and hair, I suppose, and he showed her the knife, holding it close to her face, threatening her with cuts, mutilation, and scars."

She swallowed her fear and continued, "Neither of them saw me coming until I snatched the knife out of his hand and ordered him away from her. At least I think I did, for he sprang up and back. But I can't actually remember my precise words. I had never been so angry, so appalled in my life. He stared at me, open-mouthed, for I was no servant. I was a guest of his mistress, and he must have known I would not let this go. I put my free arm around the girl, helping her to her feet. I told him we were going straight to Lady Royston, that everyone from his lordship to the police would be informed of his disgusting, violent conduct. That he would go to prison."

She frowned, trying to piece together the movements that followed, that led to the final act. "I don't think he even threatened me. I think he was pleading, for he was no longer the one with the power. *I* was. But he came right up to me, talking. It was *he* who looked appalled now. He was even genuinely sorry for what he had done to Franny, and he reached for her, to embrace her, I think, but I drew her away, jerking myself between them. And he lunged at me, whether to threaten or plead some more, I will never know, for the knife I was still holding slid straight into his stomach."

She stared up at Eric, at Griz. "It went in so easily," she whispered. "His mouth fell open—ludicrously surprised—and he clutched his stomach and stared at me as he backed away, leaving me holding the knife. There was blood all over it, all over his hands and mine. *I've killed him*, I thought. *I've killed him*. The angry, outraged part of me insisted he deserved it, but I knew that wasn't true. I had stopped one act of violence and committed a worse one. He turned and staggered away."

She frowned. "Not into the house, for that is the way we went, Franny and me. Our positions had changed. Franny took the knife from me, led me through the door into a scullery, where she washed the knife, and a spot of blood on my gown, and I scrubbed and scrubbed at my hands." She closed her eyes. "*Out, damned spot*, like

Lady Macbeth. That was why my wrist was sore. There was a splash of blood on it, and I scrubbed it too hard, too long. No one hurt me. I hurt myself."

"Oh, Zalea," Eric whispered.

What must he think of me? What must anyone think of me? She pulled herself together. "I was worried about Ned coming back, hurting her again. I wanted to tell the housekeeper and Lady Royston. But Franny said he would be dead by now, that we couldn't tell anyone in case I got in trouble about the knife, about what I did…"

"*We'll both be in trouble,* she said. And I knew that was true. *But don't worry,* she said. *I won't tell them you were even there. Why not?* I asked her. For I knew she would suffer more than me, even though it was I who did it. It's the way of the world."

Eric squeezed her hand.

"She said, *No one's ever stuck up for me before. It was an accident, my lady, and I won't forget that.*"

Azalea swallowed convulsively, staring in anguish from her husband to her sister and back. "But the thing is, I…I was so angry with him, that I had wanted to hurt him, wanted him dead for what he did."

A silent sob wracked her.

The man was not dead. She had not murdered him. But she knew her life was over just the same, for Eric could never look at her now, not with love.

To her astonishment, his arms came around her, careful still of her wounded arm. "Oh, my poor girl," he murmured, "my poor, brave girl."

And then the tears came like a flood.

AS THE CARRIAGE rumbled west through Cheapside, Griz clutched her hand fiercely. Eric and Dragan sat opposite, both deep in thought.

Azalea felt curiously light. The unseen darkness that had haunted her was out in the light. And Eric had not deserted her.

Not yet. He had held her, soothing her until she had control of the anguished tears. Then he had asked Griz to take her back to the carriage. She didn't know what had been said or discussed with Ned and didn't much care at the moment.

"He won't die, will he?" she asked Dragan suddenly.

"No, I don't think so. The wound is healing well, amazingly enough considering the filth of that place." He met her gaze. "For what it's worth, he told the same story you did. It wasn't the first time he had beaten the maid when she offended him. By talking to another footman, by smiling at someone, or talking back to him. And I think he'd been draining the glasses collected from the ballroom. You were interfering, and he knew he was in trouble. He isn't very sure whether he was trying to intimidate you or plead with you for silence, both perhaps, but he told me he walked into the knife."

She frowned. "Why would he say that? Doesn't he want to get his own back?"

Dragan's lip curled. "He isn't the sort of man who can accept being defeated by a woman. If it was an accident, he can live with it."

"Is that what he will tell the police?"

"He won't tell the police anything," Eric said. "Any sentence he got for what he did to Franny would be trivial. It isn't worth dragging your name into such a mess. When he's stronger, he'll leave London, and he'll never go near Franny."

She licked her dry lips. "Do you believe him?"

"Yes. I don't think the incident is one he cares to remember."

"And Trench can really be quite...frightening," Dragan added.

"So...so we just sweep it all under the carpet?" It felt *wrong* to Azalea, unfinished.

"I think so," Griz said firmly.

"There are men like him in every walk of life," Eric said, gazing

LETTERS TO A LOVER

out of the window. "Bullies. Who reserve their most violent tenden-
cies for the women who love them, who can't and won't fight back.
You fought back for the maid. Any damage that came to him from that
is his own fault. And perhaps he will think twice now before he repeats
such behavior. Perhaps."

There was a certain truth, a certain sense in his words. But it
would take time for him to look at her again in the same way. If he
ever did.

Griz squeezed her hand. "I'm glad you remembered."

"So am I." It was true, despite all the chaos that came with it. She
frowned suddenly. "But *he* didn't blackmail me. He's bedridden. And
besides, the fragment of the letter I was sent had nothing to do with
violence."

Eric turned back to her, his gaze unreadable. "What did you do
when you left Franny in the scullery? Where did you go?"

"I...I left with her. By the kitchen door." She pinched the bridge of
her nose and rubbed it distractedly. "I think we turned back toward
the ballroom...but it's hazy. I can't...I can't remember."

"What is the next thing you remember?" Dragan asked her. "After
leaving the kitchen with Franny?"

She tried. Tried hard. "Seeing Augusta in the ballroom," she said in
frustration. "Why can I not remember what went between? Surely
there is nothing *worse* that my mind is refusing to remember?"

"Of course not," Dragan said comfortably. "What happened with
Ned is clearly the source of your memory loss. The rest will drift back
to you as the other pieces did. Give it time."

"We don't have time," Eric said flatly. "Not when the blackmailer
is trying to kill her."

"Franny," Azalea said. "I need to speak to Franny. Without drawing attention to her."

"And how will you do that?" Eric asked. "Remembering you are—
er...at death's door?"

"I'll write to her," Azalea decided. "Morris will take it to her at the servants' hall at Lady Royston's. She will have enough respect there to see Franny and tell her verbally if the girl cannot read."

"Tell her what?" Griz prompted.

"To come to Trench House and ask for Morris. Morris will bring her to me."

"To us," Eric said mildly.

CHAPTER NINETEEN

"What will Dragan tell Lord Royston?" Azalea asked Griz. "About his missing footman?"

They sat in her sitting room, waiting for Morris to return from the Roystons' servants' hall. Eric and Dragan had gone off in search of Lord Darchett, hoping to find out about his mother's servants and who exactly had a key to her front door.

Griz shrugged. "I expect the truth. That he found the man in Cheapside, recovering from a wound he says was sustained in a fight. That he was afraid to return to his employers in such a state and tenders his resignation. It will set their minds at rest and open the way for them to engage a replacement footman."

"If they bother. Do you think they postponed Geraldine's debut for financial reasons? Or because she is not ready?"

"A mixture probably. I suspect things are a little tight for them, but all the servants are paid on time. I don't think they're on the verge of financial disaster."

Azalea nodded and shifted restlessly in her chair. "Shall we have tea?"

The door opened, and Morris came quietly into the room.

Azalea jumped up. "Did you find her? What did she say?"

"She read your letter, my lady, changed color a few times and said she had no evening off for several days. I said to come then. But she asked me to wait a few minutes and dashed off. The upshot is, she's managed to swap evenings off with another maid and will come *this* evening at seven."

"Oh good! Well done, Morris."

"And she knows to ask for you rather than Lady Trench?" Griz said anxiously.

"Of course, my lady," Morris replied with dignity. "I believe we all understand the need for discretion. Is there anything else, my lady?"

"Ring for tea, would you? You had better wait to receive it, so the other servants don't see how healthy I am."

Morris gave a small smile that was almost conspiratorial.

While they drank tea and ate cake, Eric and Dragan returned.

"Franny is coming round at seven," Azalea told them. "How did you get on with Darchett?"

"Couldn't lay hands on him," Eric said in frustration. "He wasn't at home or at either of his clubs. Apparently, he has gone out of town, but he is expected for a dinner engagement at White's this evening, according to the porter. We can beard him then."

"Will you have dinner here?" Azalea offered. For some reason, she was nervous about being left alone with Eric. She didn't want to see the disappointment in his face when he looked at her. "That way, you could see Franny, too."

"I doubt she would be comfortable with such a crowd of us," Griz said. "No, Dragan and I will leave you now, and you can let us know what she says."

"You should rest," Dragan told her. "Do you need another drop of laudanum?"

"No, I think I need to be able to think."

He finished his tea and rose with Griz. "Then I'll be back this evening to change your dressing. We can exchange news then."

"I'll walk down with you," Eric said casually.

And although she had been nervous of being alone with him, she was foolishly hurt that he was so eager to leave her. It was, she thought miserably, the beginning of the revulsion she fully expected. Whatever his kindness in Cheapside, or his comforting words in the carriage, what she had done inevitably added a huge strain to that of the letters. It all had to make a difference.

Yet her heartbeat quickened when he walked in once more.

"I've spoken to Mrs. G., Morris will bring your dinner on a tray to keep up the appearance. I'll dine with Tizsa at the club in order to catch Darchett more quickly."

"That makes sense," she said calmly, while disappointment twisted through her. Had she not wanted a little time alone, to come to terms with the memory she had just recovered? "Except, it contradicts the appearance of a distraught husband whose wife is at death's door."

His lips curved. It wasn't quite a smile. "Not at all. I shall look anxious and morose. Everyone will assume Tizsa has dragged me away from your sickbed because I am useless there."

"Of course they will."

"Is Griz coming back to be with you when Franny is here?"

"No, I don't think so."

"Then if you receive her here, Morris must stay in the bedchamber, alert for your call."

Azalea's eyebrows flew up. "You suspect *Franny?*"

"Not really. If I did, I would not go out. But on one level, I suspect everyone, and I refuse to take any more chances with you."

"She is too small to be our blackmailer," Azalea argued.

"She could be an accomplice."

Then stay. But she had never wanted him to stay because she asked it.

"I doubt it," she said aloud. "She would have to be the best actress in the world."

"All the same, Morris must be close by."

"Whatever you say."

He regarded with the hint of a real smile in his eyes. "You are humoring me."

"I am an obedient wife."

For an instant, fire flared in his eyes. He even took a step nearer her, then paused. "I should go and deal with a few matters before I meet Dragan. I'll say goodbye when I go. Why don't you take a nap?"

"I might," she said lightly.

He came and kissed the top of her head and then strode away.

⫸⫷

IN THE END, Franny arrived early, and Morris brought her straight up, so Azalea did not see Eric before he left.

"Franny Wilson is here, ma'am."

"Thank you for coming, Franny," Azalea said as the young maid dropped a deep curtsey. "Sit here, please, so that we can talk. That will be all, Morris, thank you."

Morris inclined her head and walked into the bedchamber, closing the door behind her.

Franny's hands twisted together in her lap. She was clearly both eager and apprehensive.

Azalea began. "I wanted to tell you that my brother-in-law found Ned. He is still weak, but he will recover. He has officially left Lord Royston's employ and will leave London as soon as he is able. I'm assured he will bother neither of us again. Unless you wish to make charges against him."

"Lord, no," Franny said fervently. "If we got away with it, I won't rock the boat."

"Don't ever accept such behavior from a man," Azalea said seriously. "Whatever his expressions of love or regret. Tell the housekeeper, your employer. Or come to me. I will always help you if I can. I just don't want you in that position again."

"You're so kind, my lady," Franny whispered, wiping her eyes.

"And I know what happened to Ned was an accident, but he deserved it. I been worried about you, my lady. I tried to pluck up the courage to ask in your kitchen how you were, but I thought it would cause too much talk."

"It's you who are kind," Azalea said warmly. "And as you see, I am quite well."

That was the easy part of the conversation dealt with. Azalea shifted in her chair. "Actually, I would have contacted *you* earlier, but the truth is…I had trouble remembering everything that happened. My brother-in-law, who is a physician—almost—thinks my mind blocked the memory because it was too horrible. I have lived a sheltered life, as you probably guess, and I had never seen violence of any kind before."

Franny's eyes were wide and attentive.

"I'm remembering more all the time," Azalea persevered, "but there is still some time I can't account for at the ball. At least, I think there is. I remember washing my hands with you in the scullery and then walking with you back outside. But that's where it fades. Until I was back in the ballroom. Did I go straight back?"

"No, my lady," Franny replied, and Azalea's stomach twisted. "You needed time to recover from the shock of what happened, but I couldn't take you through the kitchen. Everyone would have seen you. So, I took you back outside and in through a side door to the garden room, and from there up to the library, where I knew no one would go."

Azalea tried but could remember no such journey. "Did you stay with me there? You must have been in some pain."

"I was, a little," Franny admitted. "And I did stay with you for a bit. If we were discovered, we agreed to say you were feeling unwell, and I was looking after you."

That rang a vague bell for Azalea. She had a flash of a private library, lined with bookshelves and leather chairs. "And then?"

"I felt too guilty being away from work, so I left you there."

"What was I doing when you left?" *This is it. This is the question I truly need answered.*

"You were going to write a letter, my lady."

⟫⟫⟪⟪

IN THE ELEGANT dining room at White's club, Trench and Tizsa took their seats at a table from where they could both see the door. It was still early, so there were not many other diners.

"Lord Darchett here yet?" Trench asked the waiter.

"No, my lord, but his party is expected soon." He poured them each a glass of claret and departed.

Trench gazed thoughtfully into his glass, wondering how and why his wife had achieved distance between them once more.

"It will take her a little while to adjust," Tizsa murmured.

Trench blinked, wondering uneasily if he had actually spoken aloud. Then he picked up his glass and drank. "Sometimes, I can't make up my mind whether you are too perceptive or just too insolent."

"Both," Dragan admitted. "She is grappling with a huge mess of violence and guilt and shame. You know that, so I will just say...no one thinks of your wife or mine as particularly vulnerable. But they are. I daresay you've noticed Grizelda often hides hers beneath determined eccentricity or even aggression. She finds it hard to believe anyone could find her beautiful, charming, or delightful. Azalea was the unreachable heights of perfection she was encouraged to aspire to, so she finds it difficult to grasp that this paragon might have vulnerabilities of her own."

Trench regarded him with a practiced hint of ice. "I'm sure you have a point, Tizsa, but I do hope you are not going to explain *my* wife's vulnerabilities."

"I wouldn't presume," Tizsa said promptly. And did. "Because of her poise and beauty, they are harder to see, but it seems to me, she is a little like Griz. Except, where Griz does not believe she has any beauty, Azalea thinks no one can see anything else. And beauty is little defense against assault or adultery or feelings of guilt."

Trench stared at him, understanding perfectly well what he was implying. "If it were any of your business, I would tell you I have no intention of abandoning my wife. She has done nothing wrong. On the contrary, I am proud of her. She already knows that whatever she has done, or not done, makes no difference to my...to me."

"You might need to keep telling her for a little," said the unbearable Tizsa. "And on cue, just before you hit me, here is Darchett."

"You're not afraid of anything, are you?" Trench murmured, tearing his gaze away to the party of boisterous young men entering the dining room.

Tizsa laughed. "You could not be more wrong."

At least the laughter attracted Darchett's attention, and Trench left quizzing his wife's impertinent brother-in-law until later. He lifted his hand in a friendly manner, gesturing Darchett to join them.

Obligingly, Darchett excused himself to his friends and walked across to Trench, saying cheerfully, "How do you do? Quiet dinner today?"

"Quieter than yours, by the look of things," Trench said with an amiable gesture toward the slightly rowdy companions now sitting down at the large table at the back of the room. "I'm giving my wife a little peace since she is unwell. We were wondering," he added, through Darchett's civil good wishes for her speedy recovery, "if you could answer a few questions relating to that?"

Tizsa pulled out a chair he had thoughtfully added to their table earlier, and Darchett, looking bewildered and slightly alarmed, sat in it mechanically. A passing waiter set an extra glass on the table, and Tizsa poured some wine in it, pushing it toward their guest.

"Questions relating to your wife's ill-health?" Darchett said warily.

"In a manner of speaking," Trench replied. "I won't beat about the bush here, Darchett. There is a nasty campaign against my wife, and I need your information and your discretion."

"We understand," Tisza put in, "that your distasteful wager with Mr. Gunning was no more than that, but I'm sure none of us here would like it to come out, let alone be misconstrued as part of a much more sinister plot leading to trial and prison."

"No, indeed!" Darchett paled, his eyes wide. He took a reviving gulp of wine. "What is it you want to know?"

"A few odd questions concerning the Dowager Lady Darchett's house in Charles Street."

Darchett blinked. Clearly, he had not expected that. "What about it?"

"Do you have your own key to the front door?"

"Yes, but what does this—"

"Who else has one? Lady Darchett's servants?"

"Not to the front door. They use the area door to the kitchen. The housekeeper does not even keep a latch key, only the deadlock key. Why—"

"Does Lady Darchett own the mews property Number 70, in the lane running behind Berkley Square, between Charles Street and Hill Street?"

"Yes, but it's been empty for years. She doesn't keep a carriage anymore. Can't afford it, to be frank. In fact, between ourselves, we can't really afford the house, but she refused to stay in Darchett House after my father died, and she won't go anywhere less expensive." Perhaps realizing he was talking too much, he compressed his lips.

"Did you know the door to the mews building is not locked?"

He shrugged. "The lock's been broken forever. It doesn't matter, there's nothing in there. The other folk down there make sure the door is at least closed. And last I checked, the living accommodation is still secure—not that there's anything up there either, but don't want anyone sneaking in and making themselves at home. Why all this interest in my mother's property?"

Trench glanced at Tizsa, who gave an infinitesimal nod. For the sake of urgency, they had to make a decision to trust that Darchett was not involved and that he would not warn whoever was.

Trench said, "An attack was made on my wife last night, an attack that could all too easily have killed her."

"Dear God!" Darchett exclaimed in genuine horror. This was clearly news to him.

"The culprit fled," Trench went on, "into your mother's house in Charles Street, either using a key to get in or having an accomplice there to admit him."

Darchett's jaw dropped. "But that's impossible. Last night, *I* was at my mother's house. She isn't well either. What time did all this happen?"

"Around ten o'clock. Were you still there?"

"I stayed the night to keep her happy. I don't understand why she doesn't just come back to Darchett House, though I suppose once I am married..." He broke off again, clearly yanking his wayward thoughts back to the matter under discussion. "I heard no one rushing in. The servants would have told me."

"Did you go out at all during the evening?" Tizsa asked.

Darchett shook his head.

"Tell us," Trench said, twirling the stem of his wine glass between his fingers to quell his impatience, "about your mother's servants. What manservants does she have?"

Darchett looked from one to the other, baffled. "None, save the boy who stokes the kitchen fire. It's a house of women. They're cheaper to employ."

Tizsa threw himself back in his chair, clearly frustrated. "Any of them unusually tall for a female?" he asked without much hope.

"No," Darchett said flatly. And then paused with his glass halfway to his lips.

CHAPTER TWENTY

"I WAS ABOUT to write a letter," Azalea repeated, gazing at Franny while her heart drummed with excitement. "In my host's library during a ball?"

"Yes, my lady, that's what you said. You sat at the desk, drew a sheet of paper, and picked up the pen. That's how you were when I left you."

"But who on earth was I writing to at such a time?"

"I don't know, my lady. You didn't tell me."

Azalea rubbed her forehead, willing herself to remember. "Did we meet again that night, Franny?"

"No, my lady. I tried to look out for you leaving, but I was kept too busy. Everyone was annoyed with Ned for vanishing during the hard work. I kept my head down and said nothing."

"And were there letters waiting to be posted that night?"

"Oh, no, the table where they're left was empty that night and the next morning. I looked especially because of *your* letter."

"I don't suppose," Azalea said without much hope, "that you went into the library to see if I had left it there?"

"Actually, I did, just before I went to bed. There was nothing there. You must have taken it with you."

"I might have." But somehow, it had ended in the hands of a blackmailer. Quite aside from why she would have written such a letter—she must have been temporarily insane—there was a very limited time when she could have lost it.

She knew because she had asked when she first realized she had forgotten the ball that her carriage, driven by the trusty John, had brought her home. If she'd dropped the letter in the carriage, or in the house, John or one of the house servants would have brought it to her. So she must have lost it at the Roystons. No one was likely to have taken it from her. Ned, who might have imagined she was accusing him to the police, had vanished into the night, severely wounded. Franny would not have protected him by stealing it.

But someone else could have stolen it. They had already ruled out Lord Royston, who could not have been present in all places the blackmailer had definitely been.

"The servants..." she murmured. "Franny, do you trust your fellow servants at Royston House? Particularly the manservants?"

"Mostly," she said doubtfully. "Don't particularly like some of them. They let Ned get away with too much. Matthew even began to talk like him, kind of bullying, you know?"

"What does Matthew look like? Is he tall and thin?"

"Tall, yes, but not thin, my lady. Big. Muscley, like footmen are."

"Are any of the servants tall and thin?" she asked with fading hope. "Any of them own a silk hat?"

That drew a smile. "No, ma'am. Not even Mr. Thompson—he's the butler—though he is tall and quite thin."

"Is he indeed?" Azalea sat up. "I don't suppose he was out yesterday evening?"

"Oh, no, my lady. It's not his evening off until Monday. He was counting bottles most of the evening and fuming because he thought someone had been pilfering."

"Even at ten o'clock?"

"He'd calmed down by then and was having a cup of tea with Mrs. Gently, the housekeeper."

Azalea sighed. It had been a faint hope. "I think," she said carefully, after a few moments, "the letter I wrote the night of the ball got lost or was stolen somewhere in Royston House."

"Well, if it was lost, it would have gone to Lady Royston eventually, and if she knew it was yours, she would surely have given it back to you."

"I must have signed it," Azalea said. After all, the blackmailer knew it was hers. "So it must have been thrown out with the rubbish or stolen."

"I didn't take it, my lady," Franny said in sudden fright. The instant fear of the servant that they would be accused before their betters.

"I know you didn't," Azalea replied at once. "But someone must have. Franny, do Mr. Beresford or Miss Geraldine frequent their father's library?"

Franny smiled with genuine amusement. "Lord, no, Miss Geraldine isn't interested in books, and his lordship can't entice the young master in there to study, no matter how hard he tries. It's really his lordship's own room."

"Were there guests staying the night for the ball?" Azalea asked hopefully.

"No, my lady."

The Roystons' ballroom was built onto the back of the house, on the ground floor. It had its own supper room, and the cloakrooms for both men and women were also on the ground floor. None of the guests would have had reason to go upstairs to the library. Which didn't mean none of them did.

Only who?

"I have run out of suspects," Azalea said ruefully. "It seems no one in the house that night—apart from you and I—would have had the time or the inclination to stray from the ground floor or go anywhere near the library." *Would I have wandered around the house, or even back to the ballroom, dazed, with the letter in my hand, so that someone just took it from me?*

Another of those half-flashes of memory came to her. A desk in the room lined with books. Placing a pen tidily in its stand, rising to her feet, knowing she had been away from the ballroom too long and causing talk. She lifted her fan off the top of the desk, holding it in both hands as she walked away.

Dear God, I just left the letter there. I walked away, forgot what I was doing. What the devil was I doing?

"Not everyone was working or dancing," Franny said unexpectedly. "The guests' servants had very little to do."

Azalea blinked. "The guests' servants..." Many ladies took their dressers or personal maids with them to formal events such as balls, to aid with the changing of shoes, and last-minute hair and dress adjustments, to keep charge of shawls, combs, and extra hairpins, and to make any repairs on gowns that were snagged or trodden on. Azalea had never bothered to do so, although her mother did. So did Augusta. "Where were the guests' servants for the ball? In the servants' hall?"

"Yes, mostly, unless they were called or chose to help us. Most didn't, just enjoyed an evening with their feet up."

"Hmm." Still, maids were of no interest to her. She paused in the act of rubbing her chin for inspiration. She and Athena had once giggled at their brother Monkton's affectation in having his valet present at a ball they had all attended several years ago. If Monkton did it... "Franny, did any of the gentlemen guests bring their valets?"

"One or two. Mrs. Gently says it's so they can cadge a free meal and save their employers the cost."

Azalea gazed at the maid, almost afraid to breathe. For the second time, she had the feeling she was about to learn something crucial. "Do you know whose valets were there during the ball? Mr. Gunning's, perhaps?"

But Franny shook her head. "Don't recall that name. Mr. Hartstone's valet was there—apparently his master is a very pernickety gentleman. And Lord Darchett's, as usual."

Lord Darchett's valet...

What was it Darchett had said to her and Eric that day in the park? *What is another scold from one's valet? I would let him go if only I could afford to pay him...*

➤➤➤◄◄◄

TRENCH AND TIZSA both gazed expectantly at Darchett, who seemed to have been struck by some not entirely pleasant thought.

"You forgot about one of your mother's servants?" Trench prompted.

But Tizsa, not for the first time, was ahead of him. "He stayed the night. He brought his own servant with him."

"I always do," Darchett said defensively. "Useful chap, Jessop, and besides, he likes going to other people's houses and getting fed, if he can. It's no secret I'm strapped for cash. None of us eat well, the servants least of all. Can't have that fact talked about, of course, so I make it an affectation. Actually, your brother-in-law, Lord Monkton, gave me the idea of taking my valet everywhere."

"Your valet," Trench blurted.

"Yes, Jessop," Darchett confirmed.

"Tall, thin fellow?" Tizsa guessed. "Spry on his feet, with a top hat?"

"Yes...I gave him my old hat a couple of months ago, in lieu of payment. He wanted it..."

"Did you perhaps take him to the theatre with you last Wednesday?" Tizsa asked.

"Yes. Not in the box, of course. I suppose he lounges about in the pit, for I've no real need of him in such a place. Look, what is it you think he has done?"

"Is he here in the club?" Trench asked. He realized his fingers were clenched so tightly around his glass that he was about to break it, and hastily loosened his grip.

"No," Darchett said. "No point. He can't eat here, and there's nowhere for him to lounge around."

"So, when you go to your clubs," Tizsa said carefully, "such as on the night of the Braithwaites' soiree in Grosvenor Square, he is, basically, at leisure to do as he wishes?"

Darchett's eyes were darting from Trench to Tizsa and back. "I suppose so... Look, what exactly is it you think Jessop has done?"

"Did he, by any chance, have any bruise or similar mark on his face when you got home on Friday night?" Tizsa asked.

"Why yes. He said he tripped and fell against something in the box room."

Trench dragged his gaze back to Tizsa's and smiled with rare savagery. "Got him."

→»»«««←

WHEN FRANNY HAD gone, easily sworn to secrecy, Azalea paced the room, her thoughts swirling and planning impossible punishments. She paused only when Morris helped change her out of her gown into her night rail and robe and brought her dinner. She picked at the meal alone, without tasting it, before jumping up and continuing her pacing from the window to the door, into the bedroom for a quick circuit and back again. She barely registered where her footsteps led. She could not be still, and neither could her mind.

She kept peering out of the window for Eric's return, desperate to talk things over with him. But though she peered up and down the street each time, she saw no sign of him. In her heart, she knew he might not come in until very late, in which case she thought she would burst.

She even contemplated sending a note round to White's, asking him to return, but that could give him a terrible fright, make him think she was being attacked again.

At last, just as she was reemerging from the bedchamber for the umpteenth time, she heard the sound of his voice on the stairs and ran to the sitting room door, before backing off with the self-reminder that she was supposed to be ill.

Hurry up! She screamed silently at the door. And at least the footsteps she heard in the passage were rapidly approaching. *Don't dare go into your room!* If he did, she would just have to charge down there and hope no servants were passing.

But no, the hasty steps were still coming, and the door almost flew open.

"Zalea, we've got him!" he exclaimed, striding in at the same time as she flew toward him.

"I know who it is, Eric!" she cried before she fell into his arms, and they both laughed. He swung her up, still careful of her wounded arm.

"Darchett's valet," she said urgently. "I'm sure of it. He goes everywhere with Darchett, he's tall and thin, and he was at the Roystons, where I apparently wrote that thrice-damned letter. He could easily have purloined it, for the house servants were all too busy to pay attention to him. And I was clearly so dazed, I could even have walked right past him."

Eric was grinning. "We've come to the same conclusion. We can account for his presence everywhere we know the blackmailer to have been, including last night when he was with Darchett at his mother's house in Charles Street. He could easily have taken Darchett's key, slipped out, and returned just ahead of Griz and me."

His smile began to fade as he searched her face. "Tizsa wants to change your dressing. Can he come up now?"

"Of course! I thought he must have gone home."

"No, he's desperate to tell Grizelda, but he is a man of strong duty. Wait a moment…"

Releasing her, he went out again and, in a moment, she heard him shouting over the banister to a servant to ask Tizsa to step up to her ladyship's sitting room. That, too, would add to the story that she was ill. If they still needed to keep the pretense going now that they knew who the blackmailer was.

Of course, they still had to catch him.

Dragan came in briskly, carrying a decanter and three glasses, which made Azalea laugh.

He grinned. "Celebrating. I suppose Trench has told you the gist of what we learned from Darchett? Come, let's see to your arm so that you can be comfortable again."

Obediently, Azalea shrugged off one sleeve of her robe and sat down, resting her bandaged arm on the table. While Dragan unwrapped the wound, Morris appeared with fresh water, and Eric poured brandy into the glasses.

"She wrote the letter at the Roystons' ball," Eric said when Morris had departed once more with permission to retire for the night. "Jessop could easily have walked away with it."

"That makes sense. It all makes perfect sense," Dragan agreed. He inspected the wound carefully and reached for the water. "It's still looking good, but we need to keep taking care of it." For a few moments, he concentrated on gently washing and drying the neatly stitched wound.

"I remember walking out of the Royston's library without the letter," Azalea admitted, trying not to sound too foolish. "I felt...disoriented. It seemed important to prevent talk by returning to the ballroom. Only, I obviously forgot about the letter altogether. The only thing I can't remember remotely is the letter itself, why I was writing it in the first place in someone else's house at such a time. That makes no sense whatsoever. Not to me."

"Not to anyone," Eric agreed, taking the final seat at the table, while Dragan wound bandages round the fresh dressing and helped Azalea put her arm back into the loose nightrail and robe.

"There is one other slight problem," Dragan said at last, sitting back and picking up his glass. As one, they all clinked glasses, and Azalea enjoyed the satisfying burn.

"What?" she asked.

"We have no evidence," Dragan said.

Azalea stared at him, her glow of euphoria fading.

Dragan shrugged. "It makes sense to *us*, and I'm convinced we have the right culprit in Jessop, right down to the bruise Darchett saw on his face the evening Trench punched him. But that is not proof."

"What would be?" Azalea asked, although she knew.

"Your letter in his possession."

"How are we going to get that?" Azalea asked doubtfully.

"Well," Eric said. "As it happens, we have come up with an idea about that..."

≫≫≪≪

WHEN DRAGAN LEFT, Eric gazed into his empty glass, unblinking.

"Would you like more?" Azalea asked, rising to perform the duty.

He half-smiled, shaking his head, and caught her hand to stop her.

"Just thinking about tomorrow?" she guessed, feeling strangely nervous. She had always loved his hands. Strong and deft, and yet slender, elegant and sensitive to her every desire.

He looked up, meeting her gaze. "No, not yet. I was thinking about today and tonight."

He set his glass on the table and stood, still holding her hand. "Azalea, did you ever think I loved you only for your beauty?"

Her brow twitched at the oddity of the question. "I was glad if you noticed it. Why do you ask such an odd question?"

"It was something Tizsa said, made me wonder. We have been very close, you and I. And sometimes far apart. It is the way, I think, in marriage. But I never imagined you would believe I looked no further than the outer shell, lovely as it is."

Since his free hand brushed lightly over her cheek and chin, her skin began to tingle. But still, he waited for an answer.

"I know the way I look attracted you," she said honestly. "As the way you look attracted me. It still does, and I see nothing wrong with that. But you are so much more..." Strong and protective, gentle, funny, clever, charmingly undignified in his love of their children. A private man who hid his powerful passions beneath a veneer of urbanity. *Do I do that, too?*

"As are you," he said, his fingers lingering at her throat. "We have had eight years of marriage to learn about each other, to love more and more deeply, through the good times and the less good. Do you really imagine that I count all of that for nothing because of this one week?"

Her fingers clung hard to his. "It has been a good week in many ways," she managed. "I have loved being close to you again."

"And I to you. So why, since we spoke to the vile Ned, do you throw up this new barrier?"

"I don't mean to," she whispered, lowering her head to his chest where, for some reason, it seemed easier to speak. "I hate to think of myself wandering about the Roystons' house, dazed, unaware. I hate the *weakness*. I hate what I did and what I might have done. How I might lose you even yet, lose everything..."

He drew her hand up to his cheek and let his own fall to stroke her hair. "You never will, Zalea. Dear God, there is no weakness. You stood up to an armed bully, protected a girl who could not protect herself, have fought every step of the way to discover and defeat this other bully, this blackmailer. I know you, Azalea, so I will be amazed if there is anything to forgive. But you should also know, I always will."

She lifted her damp cheek from his coat to gaze up at him. "Always?" she repeated.

"Always." His head dipped. "I love you, remember?"

Her mouth opened to speak, to sob. She wasn't sure which, but it was covered with his own, and kissing was better, for it spoke without words.

In time, when the elation of pure happiness had flowed into growing desire, he released all but her hand, and they walked together around the sitting room, turning off the lamps, and then they moved as one into the bedchamber.

He eased off her robe and handed her into bed, covering her carefully to avoid her damaged arm, which throbbed in rhythm with her heart. She barely noticed the pain as she watched him undress and climb under the covers with her.

He leaned over, and she parted her lips for his kiss. Excitement spread downward, sweet and urgent.

But his mouth left hers, and he whispered an oddly desperate "Good night" before he turned out the bedside lamp and lay back on the pillow, shoulder to shoulder with her.

Stunned disappointment paralyzed her, and for several moments she lay still, listening to his breathing. Listening as he tried to calm his rapid breathing. She smiled into the darkness, understanding his reticence. Because of her injury, he would not risk hurting her.

She turned onto her side, then deliberately laid her cheek on his naked chest, listening with growing delight to the thundering of his heart. She moved one leg over his thighs and felt the hard proof of his arousal.

She spread kisses across his chest and lower, following the fine line of hair down toward his stomach.

"Zalea!" His hand clamped over her neck, drawing her gently but inexorably upward.

That was fine, too. She kissed his mouth until he caught her face between his hands and detached her.

"I don't want to hurt you," he whispered in something very like anguish.

"The only hurt will be if you don't love me, now."

He stared up at her, and she was afraid to breathe. And then, thank God, he smiled, and it was not a gentle smile, but a voracious one. Still, he rolled her onto her back with a care and tenderness he never lost, all through the long, sweet loving, even at the hectic, joyful conclusion.

"I love you," she whispered into his ear.

She thought he wouldn't hear for his thunderous breath, but she saw him smile into her hair before he heaved his head up once more and kissed her mouth.

"Never forget it," he commanded hoarsely. "Nor that I love you, always and forever."

CHAPTER TWENTY-ONE

AZALEA FROZE WITH her coffee cup halfway to her mouth. "The new governess is coming today!"

"That cannot be bad," Eric observed, propped up on the pillows beside her. Without a word of instruction, Morris had left a tray with coffee for two in the sitting room. One could never keep anything from servants. "I'm sure everything is prepared for her."

"Yes, but there is so much *else* to do today…"

"That can all be arranged without you. You are ill, remember? Your part comes later on."

"She will think she is employed in a madhouse," Azalea said ruefully.

"Then she had best get used to it." He drained his cup and set it down. "I must go and dress and set things in motion. Tizsa will be here shortly to see to your wound."

"I know. I meant to be dressed by now." She smiled with a hint of shyness and a good deal of remembered pleasure. "I just felt too comfortable."

He paused with his long, muscular legs out of the covers and leaned over to kiss her. "So did I." He rose with gratifying reluctance and covered his nakedness with the robe he had found in the sitting room before strolling off along the passage to his own room.

While they were in the country, she thought, ringing for Morris, they should have a connecting door made between their chambers.

While Morris helped her to dress, the maid said, "The servants are worried about you, my lady. It goes against the grain not to reassure them."

"I imagine it does," Azalea said sympathetically. "For me, also, but it is only for one more day, and we would not ask it if it weren't necessary."

Morris partially fastened her gown, leaving her injured left arm free. "I suppose it has something to do with that."

"Yes," Azalea said bluntly. Another thought struck her. "Perhaps they were reassured by his lordship's presence here last night."

"On the contrary. They believe he feared for your life and would not leave you."

"Oh dear," Azalea said shakily, unsure whether to laugh or be grateful. "Well, I shall have to hide up here for today and again receive no visitors. Except for Miss Farrow, the new governess, who will be here at any moment. You had better bring her to me here."

While Morris was pinning her hair, a knock on the door heralded Dragan's arrival.

"I'll bring fresh water," Morris said resignedly and departed.

"Good morning," Dragan greeted her. "Any changes? Are you still feeling well?"

"Yes, I and my wound both feel fine." Eric had been so gentle last night she was confident the stitches remained in place.

He unwound the bandage and grunted approval. "It seems to be healing cleanly."

"You are a good physician."

"I'm a former army surgeon with too much experience of gunshot wounds. Cleanliness wasn't always possible on the battlefield. But I am confident you will be fine."

"Then you won't forbid me from my duties this evening?"

"Not if Trench does not."

"I think he is glad that I'll be out of the house," she confided.

A smile flickered across his face, but he did not answer, merely took the water from Morris with a murmur of thanks and set about his familiar care of the wound.

"Where is Griz?" she asked.

"Fending off your family, in case they have heard rumors of your imminent demise."

"That will be helpful! And where is your next call this morning?"

"Scotland Yard," said Dragan.

AN HOUR LATER, Inspector Harris scowled across his desk.

Dragan didn't blame him. The first time they had met, the policeman had been interrogating him over the murder of a housemaid. The last time they had met had been at the trial of her murderer, whom Dragan and Grizelda, not Harris, had discovered.

"I hesitate to ask," Harris said, "but what can I do for you?"

Dragan took the invitation from his pocket and passed it across the desk. "Come to a party this evening at the home of Lord Trench. Sadly, Mrs. Harris is not included, for it is a male-only party."

"I don't go to those," Harris said shortly, not touching the card. "And I am not acquainted with Lord Trench."

"He's Lady Grizelda's brother-in-law. And you need not fear. He does not hold *those* kinds of parties either. It will simply be a gathering of gentlemen, with wine and cards and an excellent supper."

Harris lifted the card and read it before raising his gaze once more to Dragan's. "He wishes me to arrest someone for cheating at cards? I'm afraid that is not within my role at the Metropolitan Police."

"Oh, I think we can promise you a bit more fun than that. Let me tell you a story, Inspector…"

AT ABOUT THE same time, Griz had managed to collect both her parents and her brother Forsythe in the library of Kelburn House.

"What is the fuss, Grizelda?" the duchess demanded, bustling into the room. "I am on my way out to call on Azalea—"

"Don't," Griz said at once.

"Don't what?" her mother demanded.

"Go to Azalea's. She isn't receiving."

"I'm her mother," the duchess said flatly. "And I hear she is extremely unwell. Of course I shall go to her."

"She isn't unwell," Griz stated. "Well, she has a slight injury to her arm, but Dragan says she is in no danger, and he does know about these things."

"Then why," asked His Grace, who generally got straight to the heart of most matters, "is Azalea not receiving callers? It sounds most unlike her."

"She has her reasons, but it isn't sickness."

"What reasons?" Forsythe asked carelessly. He didn't much care, Griz thought, being able to spot a storm in a teacup when he found one.

"It doesn't matter," Griz told him, "but she needs us not to visit and not to dismiss anyone who asks about her health. Just say you are keeping in close touch with Eric or something."

Her mother frowned at her. "Grizelda, you are up to something. Have you dragged your sister into your nonsense?"

"No," Grizelda objected, stung. "She dragged me into hers. Look, it should only be until tomorrow, so there is no need to worry. Azalea is fine, and *she* will call on *you* tomorrow if you do as she asks today."

⟫⟪

HALFWAY THROUGH THE morning, Morris admitted the children and Miss Farrow, the new governess. Azalea was amazed to see Michael perform a neat little bow and Lizzie a wobbly curtsey before their wide smiles broke into laughter, and they launched themselves at her as usual.

"Well!" Azalea exclaimed, hugging them with one arm. "That was well done! I am impressed!"

"I feel it is never too early to practice the basic courtesies," Miss Farrow declared. "And they are naturally polite children."

"I hope so! You must tell us if they are ever anything else." Azalea held out her hand to the governess. "Welcome, Miss Farrow. We're all delighted you could join us."

"I am sorry to hear you are unwell," Miss Farrow said, taking the chair Azalea indicated.

"No, she's not," Michael scoffed. "She just has a sore arm."

"Actually, that is true," Azalea admitted. "Children, go and find Elsie for a few minutes while Miss Farrow and I discuss her duties and yours. You can come and play later on."

They went a little reluctantly, leaving Azalea to gaze thoughtfully at their new governess. She needed the woman's cooperation for today, even if it scared her off, and she left in high dudgeon tomorrow.

"There are reasons," Azalea said carefully, "why I wish to be thought unwell. Very unwell even. Obviously, I don't want the children worried, so the truth has to serve for them. I cannot imagine you discussing my health with the servants, so you will not be asked to lie."

"I am glad," Miss Farrow said calmly. "It is difficult to teach children the value of truth when one does not follow the same principle."

Azalea winced. "I shall not quarrel with you there. In the future, you will be able to take the children out with you at your own discretion, but for today, I would like them to stay at home."

Miss Farrow's expression gave little away. "Very well."

"And this evening," Azalea pursued. "I ask you to stay with them when they go to bed. My husband will be holding a small party, and I don't want them getting up and wandering about. It is important they stay in their rooms. With either you or Elsie in attendance until I tell you otherwise."

Azalea could almost see Miss Farrow wondering what sort of party this would be, but again the governess said only, "Very well." And then, as if she couldn't help it, "Will people not find it strange that your husband holds a party while you are so indisposed?"

"It is a distraction from his grief and anxiety," Azalea said sardonically. "Look, I know this must all seem very odd, and I assure we are not always quite so...bizarre in our behavior, but I ask your cooperation for today and this evening. After that, all should be well."

As she spoke, she could not help remembering that she had thought much the same thing about the evening she had been shot. This plan was not bound to work either.

HAVING SET IN motion the necessary arrangements, Trench decided there was time to deal with his other major problem, so that he would have nothing to worry about tomorrow except the journey to Trenchard.

Accordingly, he took a hackney into the city and strolled into Fenner's office. A clerk greeted him obsequiously and informed him Mr. Fenner was with another gentleman and that if his lordship cared to wait...

"Oh, no, that's fine," Trench said amiably. "I'll just step in and say hello."

The threat to open discussions in front of other people would, hopefully, catch Fenner's attention. And, in fact, Trench was more than happy to make the business public. So he brushed aside the alarmed and twittering clerks and opened the door to Fenner's inner sanctum with only the briefest of knocks.

"Good morning, Fenner," he said amiably and nodded to the man already seated on the visitor's side of the desk, who looked vaguely familiar. "Have you a moment to spare?"

"Certainly, my lord," Fenner said calmly, rising to his feet. "I'm surprised my people didn't say...but perhaps you are acquainted with Sir Nicholas Swan?"

"Actually, yes," Trench said. "I believe we were at school together."

Swan, a dark, saturnine fellow who looked even more forbidding as an adult than he had as a youth, rose to shake hands.

"Sir Nicholas is interested in investing in our next project."

"I shall be glad of association with Sir Nicholas," Trench said politely. "But I'm afraid the current project will take longer than anticipated. In fact, perhaps Sir Nicholas could take over your share of that? Considering you will need your current capital to make right the...errors in both buildings."

The twitch of his lips, a flicker of the eyes, were the only signs of unease Fenner betrayed. "I'm not sure I follow your lordship. Perhaps we could discuss this later when—"

"I am busy later," Trench interrupted. "But happy to spell out the details if you have forgotten. There are discrepancies between the designs we agreed to and what is being built. In St. Giles, instead of our designs, a slum is being built without running water or proper sewers. In Belgravia," he continued, raising one hand when Fenner would have interrupted him, "the foundations are far too shallow. Now I can resign publicly—very publicly—from this venture. Or you can make it right. Either way, the cost will be yours."

"Mine?" Fenner exclaimed. "If the builder has cut corners—"

"He has," Trench said calmly. "At your instructions. While you and he split the money, you have thus saved."

"Lord Trench, I cannot allow you to make such baseless allegations! You have no proof with which to—"

"Yes, I have," Trench said, perching on one corner of the desk. "I have a trail of accounts." Dragan Tizsa was brilliant that way. "They prove my accusations beyond all doubt. Now, here is what will happen. Using the builder *I* choose, you will pay to take everything down and rebuild according to the original design. After that, our association is at an end. If you do exactly as I say, we won't have you prosecuted. Good day, Mr. Fenner."

Eric eased off the desk and strolled out of the office. At the front door, he was slightly surprised to find Sir Nicholas Swan beside him.

"That was close," Swan observed. "You seem to be more the sort of man I want to do business with."

Trench smiled. "I'll write to you."

Swan handed over his card. "Thanks," he said and strode away.

Amused by the abruptness, Trench turned his feet toward home.

FOR AZALEA, THE day largely consisted of more endless hours of waiting. She could not even gaze out of the window much, in case she was seen and word got around that she looked perfectly healthy. Nor could she concentrate on a novel or more improving literature. She spent most of the day looking forward to her children's visit after lessons in the afternoon. And trying to remember exactly what she had done the night of the Roystons' ball, between Franny leaving her in the library and returning to the ballroom.

She concentrated on her blurry memories of the library, of laying down the pen and picking up her fan and walking across the room. What had she been thinking? Who did she see in her journey to the ballroom? She tried to remember the letter itself. But it was all like a fevered dream, disconnected and maddeningly elusive.

And as a reward, she allowed herself to dwell on last night in Eric's arms, his words of love and his delicious caresses. And the comfort of his reassurance, which God knew she was in need of, as she finally came close to the letter that had caused all the bother. Had she been trying to trick someone with words of love? Or had she fallen suddenly and violently in love at the ball and then forgotten all about such shameful emotion along with the dreadful events in the garden? Perhaps that explained why she had abandoned the letter. Only, why had she not destroyed it?

Her mental struggles were suddenly interrupted by a rush of footsteps and rustling clothes in the passage outside the sitting room door, which flew open with barely a knock to reveal Morris.

"Sorry, my lady, we couldn't stop her," the maid hissed as she all but fell into the room. "Lady Trench is here."

"Oh, bother," Azalea exclaimed before she could help herself, which meant she might well have been overheard by her mother-in-law, who sailed into the room almost on the maid's heels.

As always, the Dowager Lady Trench was dressed in black and grey, looking so splendid and haughty that Azalea was not entirely surprised her staff had backed down before her ladyship's entitled insistence.

Azalea rose to her feet. "Your ladyship. Thank you, Morris. You may go."

As Morris effaced herself, unusually subdued, Lady Trench looked Azalea up and down with undisguised contempt. "You look perfectly well to me."

"Thank you," Azalea said in the absence of anything else coming to mind. "So do you."

"But I do not spread it around that I am at death's door!"

"I don't believe I told anyone that. I merely said I was not receiving."

That appeared to fly straight over her ladyship's head. She never thought the normal rules of civility applied to her, at least not where her daughter-in-law was concerned. Her lip curled. "What is it all about this time? Extracting yet more attention from my son?"

"Actually," Azalea replied unwisely, "the reasons have nothing to do with him."

The dowager's eyes narrowed. "Do you really need such lessons in duty? Your task is to supply my son with heirs! Not mope around waiting to entertain lovers!"

Azalea couldn't help it. At that moment, the idea of hiding a lover behind the curtain or under the bed while her mother-in-law visited unexpectedly was so exquisitely funny that she laughed.

Which was hardly guaranteed to placate Lady Trench. Two spots of color appeared on her pale cheeks, and her cold eyes spat. "I'm glad you find it amusing that you fail in your duty, your only duty! One son in eight years is nothing to be proud of!"

That wiped the smile from Azalea's face. "On the contrary, I am extremely proud of my son. And my daughter."

"Then make my son proud of you, too," she snapped, a low blow that Azalea could not but feel. "How dare you cavort about the town making a spectacle of yourself, a by-word for scandal, when you could and should be at home, making yourself agreeable to your husband and giving him the heirs he married you for!"

Azalea's hands clenched in her skirts. "With respect, my lady, the making of heirs is not a matter for Eric's mother."

Lady Trent blinked rapidly, as if she could not quite believe that Azalea had had the temerity to answer her back. "I should not have to—" she began, but at that moment, the door opened once more, and Augusta walked in.

Oh, for the love of...! Torn between laughter and tears, she could not quite believe that the two people she had most wanted to avoid were the ones who had breached the household defenses.

"Azalea, what in the world is going on? Are you well?" Augusta demanded before she even caught sight of the other visitor. "Oh, Lady Trench, how do you do?"

"Lady Monkton," the dowager said graciously. "You, too, have been made anxious by this nonsense about my daughter-in-law's health."

"Well, it is unusual to find her not receiving for two days in a row," Augusta said, and Azalea knew that once Augusta had heard Lady Trench was inside, she would have insisted, too.

Beyond her two callers, Azalea saw Morris hovering just inside the door. "Remind them downstairs that I am not receiving," she instructed. "And that my boudoir is not a drawing room."

"Very good, my lady." Morris curtseyed woodenly and departed, her face aflame with both shame for allowing her mistress to be inconvenienced against her orders and fury with those weaker willed who had allowed the callers to penetrate so far into the private household.

Her visitors, meanwhile, seemed not to hear her orders, let alone feel the sting of them personally. How was she to be rid of them before the children were released from their lessons?

"My daughter Theresa was delivered of a third son last month," Lady Trench was telling Augusta.

"How wonderful. I trust they are both doing well?" Augusta said politely.

"I'm glad to say that they are."

"You must send Theresa my regards."

"Thank you, I shall. And how is your nursery, Lady Monkton?"

"We have two sons and two daughters," Augusta replied proudly. "And though I have not yet announced it to the world, we expect a new arrival before Christmas."

This was news to Azalea, and she was momentarily softened enough to congratulate Augusta on the imminent event. But before she could utter a word, Lady Trench had turned on her.

"You see? You have a fine example in both your sisters-in-law," she said regally. "Who not only present their lords regularly with sons but also behave publicly with perfect decorum. If you will not be guided by me, Azalea, you could do worse than follow the example of dear Lady Monkton."

As she had always done over the years, Azalea took a deep breath to prevent resorting to temper and prepared a civil response they would all know she didn't mean. But it was Augusta who filled the silence first.

"On the other hand, dear Lady Trench, it should probably be noted that Azalea, as the daughter of a duke, needs guidance from no one."

Azalea blinked. Had Augusta just defended her? Lady Trench seemed to think so, for her mouth dropped open. And it was, in fact, the perfect set-down, for the dowager was the daughter of a minor landowner in Yorkshire. There were ways, Azalea realized, to put the old tyrant in her place without rudeness.

Perhaps fortunately, Miss Farrow chose that moment to bring the children in. Remembering their manners, they performed their new party-pieces of bowing and curtseying to the company, although they then ran to their mother before turning to grin at the visitors.

"Good afternoon, Grandmama," Michael said cheerfully. "Good afternoon, Aunt Augusta!"

"Good afternoon, young man," Lady Trench said graciously. "And when do you go to school?"

"Not for ages," Azalea replied firmly. "He is barely seven years old."

The dowager sniffed. "You may give me a kiss," she informed him, and Michael duly went and kissed the proffered cheek. Lizzie was not invited and showed no inclination to follow suit.

"Allow me to introduce our new governess, Miss Farrow," Azalea said. "Miss Farrow, my mother-in-law, the Dowager Viscountess Trench, and my sister-in-law, Lady Monkton."

Miss Farrow curtseyed and received brief nods in return.

"I must take my leave," Lady Trench announced, pulling on her gloves. "Since you are well, I may go about my business without anxiety."

"I'm sorry you were anxious," Azalea said civilly. "And I thank you for your concern. Morris should be waiting to show you downstairs."

The dowager grunted and sailed across the room with Azalea at her heels to be sure she went. Miss Farrow still stood respectfully to one side of the door, drawing no attention to herself. Lady Trench paused and, perhaps feeling the need to reassert her authority over her son's household, fixed the governess with her steely gaze.

"And what are your qualifications to care for my grandchildren?" she asked haughtily.

As though Azalea had merely swept her off the street on impulse. Miss Farrow cast her a startled, almost hunted glance.

"Knowledge, experience, and character," Azalea said pleasantly, opening the door to find Morris waiting patiently in the passage. "And the approval of Eric and me. Goodbye, my lady. Be assured we shall call on you before we leave for Trenchard."

Lady Trench neither glared nor drooped, but for the first time, Azalea felt she had actually got the better of an encounter with her, that her mother-in-law could indeed be managed with firmness, without sacrificing civility and respect. A respect, it must be said, that Lady Trench had never shown Azalea outside of Eric's company.

As Morris conducted her ladyship to the staircase, Azalea closed the door thoughtfully and turned to her other uninvited guest, who had taken a chair and was listening amiably to the children's chatter. She even smiled once or twice.

And Azalea always paid her debts. She sat next to Augusta. "Thank you," she murmured, "for what you said to her."

To her surprise, Augusta colored slightly. "It felt good," she admitted. "The old termagant was downright nasty to me during my first London Season. She despised me as a jumped-up clergyman's daughter. She wanted Theresa to marry Monkton, you know."

"No," Azalea said slowly, "I didn't know." Because she had never troubled to find out about Augusta's life or what had made her the way she was.

Azalea had been content to tease her and, to her sudden shame, to laugh at her or dismiss her among her siblings. Augusta, by her marriage to the duke's heir, took precedence over all of them and yet had always felt the sting of inferiority, which she dealt with in her own way.

"Apart from Monkton," Azalea said, "we are a parcel of over-privileged, badly-behaved, overgrown children. You, too, are a gentleman's daughter. Monkton chose you for who you are. No one has the right or the reason to imagine you are not good enough."

Augusta's gaze flew to hers in some surprise. "And yet you do."

"No, Augusta," Azalea said. "I just don't like being scolded."

Augusta blinked rapidly until the faintest smile curved her lips in response to Azalea's.

Azalea nudged her, as if they were children. "I'm afraid you were accepted as one of us long since. Shall we have tea up here? And then, Augusta, I must ask you not to tell anyone I am perfectly well. At least, not before tomorrow, but I'll let you know."

Augusta frowned in a very familiar fashion, "Azalea, are you up to something?"

CHAPTER TWENTY-TWO

B Y THE TIME Eric came home, Azalea was already dressed to depart. As she entered the sitting room, she gave him a twirl in her uncharacteristically staid cloak and bonnet.

His lips twitched. "I didn't know you possessed such garments."

"I don't. I borrowed them from Miss Farrow. On the understanding that if she ever needs to borrow anything of mine, she need only ask. It seems a perfect disguise if I am mistaken for her. She is very discreet, is Miss Farrow. I like her. In fact," she added, sitting down on the sofa and catching Eric's hand to draw him with her, "I seem to like everyone today, even Augusta."

He sat beside her, warm, large, and frowning. "Augusta has been here?"

"Well, the servants found it difficult to refuse her when they had already admitted your mother."

He groaned. "Damn it, their orders were clear."

"Yes, but Given has been here since her day. He is used to obeying her."

"Well, if he can't obey *me*, he must find different employment," Eric said grimly. "What did my mother want?"

"Oh, she had heard I was mysteriously ill and came to inquire. And when she discovered me so hale and hearty—"

"You mean you didn't show her your arm?"

"I did not. She was offended enough. After a quick lecture on duty, she departed."

Eric blinked. "Duty? With regard to what?"

"Oh, everything. Mostly, the behavior and the number of children expected of a Viscountess Trench."

Eric scowled. "That's a bit rich!"

Azalea shrugged. "It doesn't matter. Is the hackney here yet?"

"No," Eric said without even a glance at the window. "Azalea, has my mother ever spoken to you like that before?"

Azalea hesitated. But they had promised honesty and openness. "Yes." She waved it humorously aside. "She thinks I'm a flighty flippertygibbet with no care for my social standing or yours."

"Since when?" he demanded wrathfully.

"Since we met," Azalea replied.

"But she has never said anything of the sort—" He broke off. "Actually, she did, once, when I first told her I was going to propose to you. I cut her off, and she has said nothing similar since. To me. Azalea, why didn't you tell me?"

"Well, she's not obliged to like me," Azalea pointed out. "And in any case, I never wanted to be the cause of trouble between you."

"Saying things like that to you, it's she who is causing trouble. I'll have a very clear word with her."

"Actually, I don't think there's any need," Azalea said, resting her head on his shoulder to the detriment of Miss Farrow's bonnet. "I have discovered a method of dealing with her that neither disrespects her nor lets her walk over me."

He reached around the bonnet to drop a kiss on her lips. "You are wonderful, you know."

"Of course I know. Is everything ready?"

"Yes, you are expected. And I think…" He stood up and walked to the window, "that is Dragan's hackney. It's time you were gone."

He came back to her, drawing her to her feet and straightening her bonnet. "You should be admitted without trouble, but if there is any difficulty at all, you must leave. The police can go instead."

"I would rather it was me."

"I know."

She touched his cheek, and he kissed her hand. "Come, mysterious lady resembling the new governess, your chariot awaits."

They went downstairs together. She kept her cloak fastened and her head bent so that the bonnet protected her identity, and she walked out the front door and down the steps with no more than a curt nod from her husband.

And climbed straight into the waiting hackney beside Dragan.

"All well?" he asked as the carriage jolted into motion.

"Perfectly. Morris will take my dinner to my room on a tray, as usual, and bring it back to the kitchen untouched while *he* is there. Is everything else arranged?"

"I think so. You just have to come and eat with us, and then the fun, as Griz puts it, begins."

⤜⤜⤛⤛

LORD FORSYTHE NIVEN, Azalea's youngest brother, was the first guest to arrive for the card party.

"Am I early?" he asked cheerfully, strolling into the salon.

"Not only that, I didn't invite you," Trench pointed out, although he softened the blow with a glass of brandy.

Forsythe only grinned. "Oversight," he assured his host.

"No, it was a conscious decision not to fill my house with relatives and scare off my prey."

"This is something to do with Griz, isn't it? That's why they sent me. In fact, if I hadn't agreed to come, you'd have got Horace and His Grace, and probably Landon and Monkton into the bargain. I assured them I would be less out of place at a gaming party, so here I am. You're glad of me now, aren't you?"

Trench sighed. "Delighted, dear boy. But I want nothing said to spread any suspicion via other guests or servants. Bear in mind, you are all cheering me up in my anxiety over Azalea's health."

"Oh, I'm mum," Forsythe assured him, making a fastening gesture over his lips. "Here are more guests for you! 'Evening, Naseby! Hammond."

After them came Lord Darchett, and Will Brunton, one of Trench's oldest friends. As he greeted them, Eric met Darchett's gaze with an infinitesimal twitch of one eyebrow.

Darchett nodded once, and Trench knew his quarry was here, on his way to being ensconced in the servants' hall with one of his cook's best meals.

He breathed again.

A few moments later came a large man, tugging at his collar and looking out of place, who Trench recognized at once, even though they had never met.

"Ah, you must be Mr. Harris," Trench said amiably, going to meet him with his hand held out. "I'm Trench."

"Pleased to meet you," Harris said, fortunately in accents that would pass muster as gentlemanly.

"Tizsa has been delayed," Trench informed him, "but he should be here later on. Let me introduce you to these other reprobates."

⋙⋘

ANOTHER HACKNEY CARRIAGE dropped Azalea, Griz, and Dragan at Darchett House in Grafton Square. Since there was no carriage waiting at the door for his lordship, they had to assume he had already left as planned with his valet.

Even so, Dragan stepped in front of the ladies to knock at the door and wait. The door opened rapidly, and a porter inquired their business.

"Mrs. Day, if you please," Dragan said.

The porter eyed them all without enthusiasm. "Wait there," he said severely. "I'll see if she's available." And he shut the door on them.

"Well," Azalea observed. "This never happens to me in real life."

"You should spend more time with us," Dragan murmured.

A moment later, the door opened again, and they saw a motherly woman hurrying across the hall to them. "Come in," she said pleasantly. "I'm so sorry, Gregor didn't know I was expecting you. Follow me."

She led them out of the porter's sight toward the baize door that separated the main house from the servants' quarters.

"I hope you don't mind," she said nervously. "I thought I should take you up via the servants' stairs. That way, Gregor will assume I'm taking you to my sitting room."

"Is Gregor a friend of Jessop's?" Griz asked.

"I don't know about friend," Mrs. Day replied, leading them up a narrow staircase. "I suspect Gregor is more of an informant. Jessop likes to know everything that goes on in the house, every detail of his lordship's business, which I've mentioned to his lordship and to her ladyship, isn't right. But his lordship wouldn't hear a word against the man until now. Don't worry," she added. "We should meet no one on the way. With his lordship out for the evening, everyone is enjoying an extra cup of tea in the servants' hall."

"We're sorry to disturb what should have been a quiet evening for you," Azalea offered.

"It will be worth it if you find something that finally makes his lordship dismiss that man. Especially with his lordship about to bring a sweet young bride into the house."

"Why do you think his lordship has put up with such a valet?" Dragan asked.

"I think he can't dismiss him because he owes him too much salary," Mrs. Day replied. "In fact, he owes several of us, but that is between you and me." She turned, wheezing on the top landing in the attic corridor. "His lordship said I should trust you and show you to Jessop's room. I wasn't to tell anyone else, which I wouldn't in my position. I've no idea what you expect to find there."

She plowed along to the left and opened the second door. "Here is his bedchamber. Let me know if I can help."

"Actually," Dragan said, "if you wouldn't mind watching us so that you can bear witness to whatever we find. If anything."

Mrs. Day seemed more than happy to perform such a service. "Gladly." She looked about her. "He's a tidy body, though. I'll say that for him."

"Start with the obvious places," Griz instructed. "The desk, drawers, wardrobe, under the pillow and the mattress, and we'll progress to floorboards."

Dragan dropped their small, empty carpetbag in the middle of the floor and walked to the bed, where he picked up the pillow, squeezed it, and threw it down again. Then, he began feeling under the mattress.

Griz opened the crooked, roll-top desk.

So Azalea began opening drawers in the tallboy and raking through clothes. In the third drawer, she felt something wedged at the back and hastily dragged it out. A little packet containing banknotes, together with the letter she had first sent him.

"Eureka," she said, holding it up.

Dragan dropped the mattress back and held up something similar. "Snap."

"What is it?" Mrs. Day asked, intrigued, then her mouth fell open. "Oh my! Where on earth could he have got such a sum? Is that what you came to find?"

"Partly," Dragan said, dropping his packet of money into the carpetbag with Azalea's find. He moved to the narrow wardrobe. "And it certainly proves we're in the right place."

"He has a lot of correspondence," Griz observed, rifling the desk drawers. "Full of gossip."

Azalea carried on looking in the bottom drawers of the tallboy. She found a purse of coins in one. "Is this Jessop's?" she asked Mrs. Day.

"I've never seen it before," the housekeeper replied. "He usually uses a much smaller coin purse, but I suppose it could be his savings."

"Take it anyway," Dragan advised. "He's probably been blackmailing other people for years. If we're wrong, we can always give it back."

Azalea dropped it into the carpetbag, too, and carried on rifling among the towels.

"Zalea," Griz said.

Something in her voice sent chills down Azalea's spine. She rose slowly from her kneeling position and walked toward Griz, who was holding a folded letter in her hands. At least, she held two pieces of a letter. A piece in the middle had been torn out.

"It's your writing," Griz said hoarsely. "And it's the only one of yours. Dragan was right, and there was only ever one letter. I won't read it, but Zalea, look."

She thrust the top part of the letter into Azalea's hand, her finger trembling as she pointed to the first line under the address, which she had written simply as Royston House, and the date, May 23, 1851.

Oh yes, this was the missing letter. And she was trembling.

"*Look*," Griz insisted, tapping her finger where she wanted Azalea to read, where Azalea was too frightened to look.

Eric will forgive me. Eric will forgive me, she kept repeating in her head for courage. *God knows I no longer care a fig for whoever this is. Only, please let it not be Gunning...*

She swallowed and forced herself to focus on the letter once more, to read the line above Grizelda's pointing finger.

My dearest Eric,

BY NINE O'CLOCK, Trench's party was in full swing. Wine and brandy were flowing freely, as was good-humored banter and laughter. Excessive gambling was not encouraged, so the games set up in the salon were for small stakes, avoiding the possibility of serious losses.

Inspector Harris, who no doubt supported a family on a salary most of the men present spent on fripperies, held his own. But when Trench stood up from his game and strolled into the other salon, where a cold supper had been laid out for constant grazing, he was aware of Harris standing up from his table. While Trench looked out of the window in both directions for any sign of Azalea's return, Harris helped himself to two sandwiches and an elegant, savory pastry, all of which vanished with remarkable rapidity.

They were, currently, the only two men in the room. A burst of laughing protest drifted in from the other salon.

Trench wandered toward the supper table and selected something at random. He could barely taste it anyway.

"I should say," Harris began, "I will deliver an accounting of what I lose and return the rest to you at the end of the evening."

At least Tizsa had remembered to pass on the purse Trench had given him. "No need. You are doing me a considerable favor."

"I am carrying out my duty which is investigating crimes and bringing perpetrators to justice."

"My apologies," Trench said tolerantly. "I have had little to do with the police. I just don't want you to lose out to a parcel of wastrels like us."

"You must be very convinced of this fellow's guilt if you let your wife go and search his rooms."

"I am. And besides, I don't want her here while Jessop is around the house. Just in case he decides to investigate how close to death she really is. We can count on a few of my friends and servants to help when the time comes to arrest him, but I do hope you have your own men in position?"

"By now there should be one burly constable at your back door and one at the area steps. He won't get out of here. Unless we choose to let him."

"You don't believe my wife will find the evidence, do you?"

Harris chose not to answer that. "Mr. Tizsa has gone with her, I understand."

"And Lady Grizelda."

"Of course," Harris said sardonically. "And they will just be admitted to this lord's house and allowed to poke around?"

"Darchett privately instructed his housekeeper, who is, he tells me, a trustworthy soul."

"But then, he presumably thought his valet a trustworthy soul."

"You are a great comfort to me, Mr. Harris."

A faint smile flickered across the austere face. "That is my duty, sir. Should you not return to your guests?"

Trench cast another glance at the window, then turned away. "After you, Mr. Harris."

My dear Eric,

Eric. Of course, who else would she write such a letter to? The words danced before her eyes, and as she read them, she remembered writing them. That terrible guilt landed on her once more like a deluge, flooding her, crushing her.

Grizelda's arm was at her waist, lowering her into the chair, holding her. Dragan knelt at her feet, gazing up at her with something like alarm. Guilt at taking the life of the dreadful footman, at ruining Eric's life and that of her children by that act, for she would go to prison, she would hang. She *should* hang because she had taken a life.

Only she hadn't.

She clutched Grizelda's shoulder. "I knew he would be told the

LETTERS TO A LOVER

rest. That *I* could tell him the rest, even from prison—about Ned and what I'd done to him—but it seemed most important of all that… I had to tell him I loved him. It just poured out because we had been so distant for so long, I had to be sure he would know."

She released Griz, blinking, gazing from her to Dragan as she re-membered, clearly for the first time, what had happened next.

"As I signed it, I heard a movement behind me. I thought it was Franny. I put down the pen and turned to her. Only, it wasn't Franny. It was a tall, superior manservant. He bowed to me very politely, said he was there to escort me back to the ballroom. I thought Franny must have sent him. And that Lord Royston might be angry I was in his library without permission." She frowned. "And then I thought, if I do everything I'm supposed to, if I behave normally, perhaps I will have one more night with Eric, one more chance to see my children."

She rubbed her forehead. "I was not thinking straight. As I picked up my fan, I think I was already forgetting why I was there, why I was writing to Eric in the first place. I left the letter on the desk. A thought flitted though my head that I would come back for it before I left. The manservant held the door for me, bowed me out of the room, and walked with me as far as the stairs, where I told him he could go."

Her breath caught. "He did go, back toward the library. I went on to the ballroom, feeling most peculiar. I went through the motions, smiling, dancing, wanting only to go home, though I soon forgot why."

She paused, suddenly remembering her dance with Gunning and the words that misled him. He had asked if he could call on her, and receiving no response but a smile, had suggested, *"Alone?"*

And she had laughed, knowing that she would always be alone now, that by the time Gunning called, she would be in a police cell, without Eric or the children, or anyone she loved. *"Probably,"* she had replied.

And Gunning had taken that as his invitation, as her promise that she would see him alone.

Then there was the mysterious David Grant. She remembered dancing with him, too. He had been shy, admiring, tongue-tied as Dragan had once suggested but had been worried she would faint. He had kept asking if he should fetch someone until she had left the dance floor and the ball. When she had met him again outside the Exhibition, he had probably only wanted to ask after her health.

She shook her head impatiently. "I left without going near the library again. The letter never entered my head. I went home alone and climbed the stairs to bed. When I finally closed my eyes, I felt the darkness pulling at me, and I went willingly, gratefully."

She caught Dragan's serious gaze. "Is that normal? Was I insane? *Am* I insane?"

"I don't believe there is a normal for the mind," Dragan said thoughtfully. "I think yours was protecting you until you were more able to deal with what had happened."

"I'm able now." She stared down at the letter, then folded it and put it not in the carpetbag but in the bodice of her gown. Somewhere, there was relief and triumph, but mostly she wanted to cry. Fiercely, she fought back the tears. "Let's go home and have this monster arrested."

CHAPTER TWENTY-THREE

G RIZ PULLED HER up while Dragan closed the carpet back and led the way out.

"Thank you, Mrs. Day," Azalea said, offering her hand to the housekeeper. "You have been a huge help to us, as well as to Lord Darchett."

Mrs. Day took them back down via the servants' stairs and walked with them to the front door.

"Ramshackle bunch of friends for you, Mrs. D.," the porter commented as they returned to the waiting hackney.

Mrs. Day laughed.

"If only they knew," Dragan murmured as the carriage set off, "that her ramshackle guests were a duke's daughters."

"Do you think she heard me?" Azalea asked anxiously. "I just couldn't stop the flow of words."

"They needed to be said, and no, I don't think so. You spoke in little more than a whisper."

Azalea nodded, gazing blindly out of the window as they were drawn through the fashionable streets and squares toward Mount Street. It would not take long.

"I felt so alone," Azalea blurted.

"You're not alone," Griz said gruffly, finding her hand and squeezing it. "You never were, and you never will be."

Azalea squeezed back. "I know." She frowned. "I think Augusta feels alone sometimes. We should be kinder to her."

This seemed to flabbergast Griz, who sat in silence for the rest of the short journey.

A large policeman in his tall hat was walking up and down the length of Trench House. He stopped at the area steps as Dragan handed the ladies down and paid the driver.

"My lady?" the policeman hazarded, low-voiced.

Azalea nodded.

"Everything's quiet, my lady, and the inspector's inside." He glanced at Griz, apparently recognizing her, and smiled shyly. "Ma'am. Sir."

"Good evening, constable," Griz murmured while Dragan took Azalea's latch key from her and opened the door. He put his finger to his lips when the porter saw him, then stood back to let the ladies enter.

As they'd previously discussed, they walked smartly across the hall without removing outerwear and ran lightly upstairs. On the landing, they parted, Dragan throwing Griz his hat and striding off toward the salons, while Azalea and Griz ran upstairs to her sitting room with the evidence of Jessop's guilt.

⇾⇾⊰⇽⇽

WALKING INTO THE salon, Dragan immediately captured all Trench's attention. The younger man wore evening dress but otherwise looked much as he always did, careless, darkly handsome, and curiously untamed. But not grim, not anxious. Was there a hint of triumph in that casual stride?

For his part, Dragan must have beheld a picture of very English upper-class dissipation.

The room smelled of alcohol and cigar smoke. Voices and laughter were too loud for sober men. The guests lounged mostly around two tables, some with coats off or ties askew, throwing cards and coins onto the tables with abandon, between mouthfuls of wine and spirits from the glasses at their elbows. A few others wandered through from the room beyond, happily munching and spraying crumbs on the floor. Two men were arguing in a friendly sort of way, but both talking at once so neither they nor anyone listening could have a clue what was being said.

"Tizsa," Trench said when he had reached him.

"We've got it."

And so, he could breathe. "Thank God. Are they back?"

"Upstairs," Dragan replied as Inspector Harris joined them.

"Got what?" the policeman demanded. "What is it you think is evidence?"

"Two packets of banknotes amounting to over a thousand pounds," Dragan replied calmly. He glanced at Trench. "And a letter written by Lady Trench and stolen from her. Plus, with the money, there is a note written by her, clearly to a blackmailer. Lord Darchett's housekeeper witnessed where we found those things."

"You never cease to surprise me, Mr. Tizsa," Harris said, almost smiling.

"Dragan!" Lord Forsythe called from the more rollicking table of gamers. "Come and join us!"

Dragan lifted one hand in acknowledgment but made no move toward him. Trench's gaze was locked with that of Lord Darchett, who rose and came toward them, a bit like a condemned man.

"Well?" he said warily.

"It's as we thought," Trench replied.

"Dear God." Darchett closed his eyes. "I am so sorry." His eyes opened again. "What now?"

"Better send for him," Trench said with undisguised satisfaction. He strolled to the door of the salon, where he addressed the footman in the passage. "Henry, Lord Darchett wants his valet. Be so good as to bring him up here."

"Once you have him safe in your custody," Dragan told Harris, "my wife will bring you the evidence."

"Must we do it in here?" Darchett said nervously. "I detest scandal and, more to the point, so does my future father-in-law."

"Your future father-in-law," Trench said dryly, "has enough scandal of his own to worry about. He will be doubly glad of a noble son-in-law, believe me. Besides, it is more enclosed here." And he wouldn't be surprised if Azalea didn't watch from the passage—which was another worry.

All the same, he crooked a finger at Forsythe, who was heading toward the other salon but changed direction at once.

"Aha," Forsythe said, grinning with anticipation. "Is something going to happen?"

"Yes, but discreetly," Trench said. "I have a task for you, Forsythe. See what you can do to keep the others distracted or, preferably, in the supper salon."

A moment later, he could see a group of the younger men heading purposefully toward supper, though Forsythe doubled back and began jabbering at those left at the gaming table.

Jessop walked so quietly into the room that it took Trench a moment to register it. A tall, thin, well-dressed manservant who, with a different posture, could easily pass as a gentleman, and Trench expected he had, at the theatre for one example. He bore a faint mark, still, just below his left eye, where Trench had thumped him in Grosvenor Square.

Apparently the perfect valet, he glided up to Darchett and bowed, murmuring, "My lord?" Perhaps he read something wrong in his master's face, for his brow flickered, and he glanced hastily around the company, coming to rest on Trench.

"This is Jessop," Darchett said quietly.

And Harris's blunt, heavy hand came down on the valet's shoulder. "Jessop, I am arresting you on suspicion of attempted murder and blackmail."

Jessop's face fell ludicrously in pure astonishment. And then, without loss of confidence, he laughed. "Don't be silly. I am his lordship's valet."

"Nevertheless," Harris said, clearly unimpressed, "you are under arrest."

"Will you not speak up for me, my lord?" Jessop said warningly to Darchett. And unbelievably, the man's eyes were still threatening. He still thought he pulled everyone's strings.

"Not this time, Jessop," Darchett managed.

"But they are lying. He—" He jerked his head at Trench before hastily correcting himself, "*Someone* is mistaken. There can be no proof against an innocent man."

"But there is against a guilty one," Harris said flatly. In one movement, he caught Jessop's arm and all but threw him at the constable just entering the room. "Hold him while we fetch his carriage."

As Harris strode from the room, presumably to send his other constable for a conveyance, some of the men with Forsythe were glancing toward the huddle near the door, but not with a great deal of interest. Dragan followed Harris out, perhaps to fetch the evidence or send for Grizelda.

"Your wife is a whore," Jessop said quietly to Trench. "*I got proof of that.*"

Trench surged forward, fists raised to strike the vile creature who had already injured his wife in so many ways and who now *dared...*

At once, Jessop stumbled backward, even while the constable was cuffing him across the head.

"Here! Watch your mouth," the policeman commanded. But he had shifted his grip, both to fend off Trench and smack his prisoner. And with a jolt like lightning, Trench realized this was exactly what Jessop had planned. To rile them, set everyone off-balance and force the policeman to change his grip.

Trench dropped his fist. But taking advantage of the constable's loosened grasp, Jessop tore free and charged toward the door. The constable, Trench, and Forsythe sprang close on his heels.

Trench was damned if he'd lose the bastard at this stage, and he didn't truly expect him to get far.

But in the passage, to Trench's sudden horror, Azalea and Griz stopped dead as Jessop erupted from the salon. Azalea shouldn't have been there at all, and Griz had been meant to wait for his summons.

At the other end of the passage, Harris stopped, instructing another constable, and started furiously toward his prisoner, Tizsa at his side.

Jessop didn't hesitate. He bolted straight toward the women.

"Let him go!" Trench shouted in something very close to panic, and to his unspeakable relief, Azalea and Griz split apart, one against either wall as Jessop sprinted toward them. Griz held a carpetbag between her and the wall—presumably the evidence they had promised Harris.

If Jessop *touched* Azalea, touched either of them...

But the valet was intent only on escape. He didn't even look at the women. He had already picked them as the weakest link in his siege, his easiest way out.

Which was his mistake because at the last minute, just as he passed, Azalea put out one elegantly shod foot, and Jessop tripped his length on the floor.

Trench, appalled to see him so close to Azalea, hurled himself on top of Jessop, knocking what was left of his wind out of him. By the time Trench had yanked his arms behind his back, both constables and Harris were there, too.

Panting for breath—from fear, not from exertion—Trench looked up over the policemen's heads and met Azalea's gaze.

She wasn't frightened, his wonderful wife. Her beautiful eyes were glowing, and she was smiling with triumph.

Beneath him, Jessop began to scream.

"I wrote it to *you*, Eric," she called joyfully over the din. "I wrote it to you!"

Until he heard the words, he hadn't known how much the damned letter had troubled him. He loved her far too much to reject her over one love letter, or even, God help him, one affair. So long as she loved him still. But now, he couldn't deny how much it would have hurt. The strength of the relief flooding him at that moment gave him the first clue.

He stumbled off Jessop, who was now being put in steel handcuffs and seized Azalea in his arms.

She was laughing and crying at once and clutching him as if she would never let go. He never wanted her to.

➤➤➤◄◄◄

"HE COLLECTED INFORMATION," Griz said. "About everyone, *from* everyone." She sat very close to Dragan on a drawing room sofa, one way Azalea knew the evening's events had upset her more than she would admit.

The guests had finally gone, led off to new and no doubt greater pastures of debauchery by the very useful Forsythe. Some of them, clearly, had seen the brief but spectacular scuffle in the passage before Jessop was marched off by the two large constables. No one mentioned that Harris, their fellow-guest, had gone, too. But most knew Jessop as Darchett's valet. He was a familiar figure around the young peers, and there was bound to be gossip of some kind. Darchett himself had looked somewhat despondent before Forsythe had taken him in hand.

"I'll give you one more piece of advice," Eric had said quietly to Darchett as they parted. "When you are married, have nothing to do with your father-in-law's schemes. Hire a reputable man of business if your family does not retain one."

"And my lord?" Azalea had added as Darchett had bowed over her hand. "I know you and your bride will be much happier without Jessop. Mrs. Day thinks so, too."

Darchett had perked up at the thought of his bride, and Forsythe, with a friendly arm around his shoulder, had dragged him off.

Now, in the blessed peace of the drawing room, Azalea was serving tea, and Eric was pouring hefty glasses of brandy for himself and Dragan. Eric set Dragan's glass on the table between the two sofas and took his place by Azalea. He put his arm loosely around her.

She was surprised, for he was not normally demonstrative in public, but with gladness, she leaned into his warmth.

Griz sipped her tea. "I think Jessop saw Azalea writing in the Roystons' library the night of the ball, and when he had escorted her to the stairs, he went back and took her letter."

"It must have been a disappointment to him," observed Eric, who had now read the letter in question. Azalea laid her head on his shoulder.

"Yes," Griz agreed. "Words of love from a wife to a husband might have made for a little mockery in certain circles, but it was hardly the stuff of blackmail, so he did nothing with it at first."

Dragan sipped his brandy thoughtfully. "Only then he must have overheard Gunning telling Darchett about his rejection by Azalea. I suspect he also picked up from other sources that Azalea had forgotten a good deal of that night, including meeting David Grant. Jessop hasn't been paid for months. He must have wanted to leave but was trapped for lack of funds. He had no hope of getting the money he was owed, at least until Darchett married Miss Fenner. And so he took a chance to see if you would bite."

"I bit," Azalea said ruefully. "I did not even remember writing the letter, let alone who I had written it to. I played into his hands—just as you said—by not telling Eric about it at once."

"Yes, but then it all went wrong for him," Dragan said. "He got the thousand pounds in Grosvenor Square, but he also very nearly got caught by Trench. He knew he couldn't exploit you anymore if your husband was already aware of such a letter. Worse, he must have realized that you were in possession of blackmailing letters in his handwriting, which he hadn't even troubled to disguise."

"He despised me that much," Azalea observed. "But he didn't despise Eric."

Dragan shrugged. "I suspect he is one of those men who think very little of women's worth or intelligence, except in terms of the men they are related to."

"More fool him," Eric said with contempt.

"But wasn't he taking an even greater risk by killing me?" Azalea demanded. "He would have hanged for that."

"He must have thought it a necessary risk," Eric said, his arm tightening. "You saw him in the Roystons' library. It was only a matter of time until you remembered that and, now that I knew everything, identified him to the law. I'm just surprised he didn't destroy your letter and hide the money better."

"I don't think it's in his nature to destroy information," Dragan said. "And he saw no reason yet to hide anything. He must have thought Azalea was as good as dead, and that he would never be identified."

"And I have to say, Zalea," Griz said with glee, "that it was supremely poetic justice that you tripped him up—so elegantly, too—and were responsible for his final capture."

"I have never been so frightened in my life," Eric declared, dropping a kiss on top of her head.

Griz finished her tea and set down the cup. "We should go, Dragan."

"I'll send for the carriage," Eric said.

"Don't be silly," Griz said. "It's a lovely evening for a walk."

"So it is," Eric said, almost in surprise. "Even in London."

"About Trenchard," Dragan said. "I would be happier if you put off your journey for another few days until I can take the stitches out of Azalea's arm." He drained his glass and rose, drawing Griz to her feet. "But it is up to you. Presumably, you have a physician in the country who can see to the stitches."

"We'll leave it a few more days," Eric said, "and see where we are." He disentangled himself from Azalea and stood, as did she. He held out his hand to Dragan. "Thank you. For everything."

"There is nothing to thank me for," Dragan said, though he shook hands at once.

Eric then hugged Griz and kissed her cheek. "We'll call tomorrow if you're free."

"You'd better call on Their Graces first," Griz said. "Or you'll have the entire family descending upon you."

So they parted with smiles and affection, and when they had gone, Eric and Azalea wandered into the garden room and through the French windows into the small, walled garden at the back of the house.

Hand in hand, they gazed up at the stars, and Azalea imagined the weight of the world slipping from her shoulders and rising up into the sky to be dispersed like so many fading clouds.

"Will you be able to persuade Dragan to take payment for what they've done?" she asked.

"Some. I'll pay him for the business information about Fenner. And the Roystons paid him for finding Ned. For the rest, I'll find some way to pay."

"They are a little precarious, are they not?"

He shrugged. "In terms of money, perhaps so. But I foresee a growing demand for Tizsa's unique services. In more personal terms, they are extraordinarily well-suited."

Azalea nodded agreement and gathered the silence about her. But she knew he would ask. She wanted him to.

"Was there ever anyone you thought you might have written love letters to?" Eric asked at last.

She had already thought about it honestly. "No. That's why it confused me. But I had forgotten so much...and when Dragan explained how my mind might refuse to remember things it didn't like, I imagined it doing the same about other things. I didn't want to have had an affair with anyone. I couldn't imagine loving anyone but you. But I didn't *know,* and that tore me apart. I have been...frail. Since Lizzie."

His arm came around her. "You were never that frail."

She dragged her gaze down to his face. "Did you never doubt me?"

"I think I doubted myself and my ability to make you happy. The way we have been...I could hardly have blamed you for seeking romance."

She slipped her good arm around his neck. "I have all the romance I need. I always had. Dance with me, Eric."

And he waltzed with her under the stars until it grew chilly, and they made their way back inside and upstairs to bed and a little more romance.

EPILOGUE

THEY HAD BEEN two weeks at Trenchard when Eric walked out into the garden to find his wife smiling at nothing in particular. She sat at the rustic little table under the chestnut tree while the children sat on the lawn close, doing their lessons outdoors with Miss Farrow.

In her sun hat and light summer dress, with stray locks of hair escaping across her forehead and one cheek, Azalea looked extraordinarily beautiful, almost ethereal, in her own private world.

"A penny for them," he murmured, taking the chair next to hers.

She blinked as though she had indeed been miles away and laughed with curious breathlessness. "For my thoughts? Oh, they are going to cost you considerably more than a penny. Or at least the cause of them is."

"What cause?" he asked.

Before his eyes, her other-worldly quality seemed to melt away. She was a physical, very desirable woman and arousal stirred. Especially when she picked up his hand, playing with it as she gazed up at him and then, slowly, spread his fingers across her abdomen.

His breath caught. "Zalea? Really?"

Her eyes laughed at him. "You needn't sound so astonished. Considering how often we have loved in recent weeks, it would be more surprising if there were *no* physical consequences."

"Oh, there are always physical consequences to that," he said fervently. He stroked her belly in wonder. "You are not afraid?" he asked because he had to. "Of the melancholy returning?"

"No," she said frankly. "And even if it does, we shall deal with it together. I cannot imagine ever being less than deliriously happy with my life."

He leaned forward and kissed her lips lingeringly. "Neither can I," he said contentedly. "Neither can I."

About Mary Lancaster

Mary Lancaster lives in Scotland with her husband, three mostly grown-up kids and a small, crazy dog.

Her first literary love was historical fiction, a genre which she relishes mixing up with romance and adventure in her own writing. Her most recent books are light, fun Regency romances written for Dragonblade Publishing: *The Imperial Season* series set at the Congress of Vienna; and the popular *Blackhaven Brides* series, which is set in a fashionable English spa town frequented by the great and the bad of Regency society.

Connect with Mary on-line – she loves to hear from readers:

Email Mary:
Mary@MaryLancaster.com

Website:
www.MaryLancaster.com

Newsletter sign-up:
http://eepurl.com/b4Xoif

Facebook:
facebook.com/mary.lancaster.1656

Facebook Author Page:
facebook.com/MaryLancasterNovelist

Twitter:
@MaryLancNovels

Amazon Author Page:
amazon.com/Mary-Lancaster/e/B00DJ5IACI

Bookbub:
bookbub.com/profile/mary-lancaster

Made in the USA
Middletown, DE
02 June 2021

40865760R00146